MW00422822

PRAISE FOR
HAVEN

"Not since Robert Marasco's *Burnt Offerings* has a house felt like such a dizzying abyss to its hapless inhabitants. *Haven* is no safe haven. Every evening under its roof is a nightmare, and every flip of the page leads its readers deeper into uneasy dreams." **—Clay McLeod Chapman, author of *What Kind of Mother* and *Ghost Eaters***

"*The Shining* meets *Funny Games* in an unsettling, unnerving and chilling depiction of a seemingly normal family slowly turning on each other during a seemingly perfect holiday." **—Neil Sharpson, author of *Knock Knock, Open Wide,* and *When the Sparrow Falls***

"From beginning to end, *Haven* is a fascinating look at a family unraveling, and the phenomenal writing and subtle characterization brings to mind the best of Shirley Jackson." **—D. W. Gillespie, author of *One by One* and *The Toy Thief***

"In Mia Dalia's debut novel, *Haven*, prepare for the unexpected. This slow burning fuse of a novel leads to an explosive and shocking conclusion. A fascinating exploration of the myths of what it means to be an All-American family. Buckle up." **—Christopher Barzak, Shirley Jackson Award winning author of *Monstrous Alterations***

HAVEN

HAVEN

MIA DALIA

CamCat Publishing, LLC
Fort Collins, Colorado 80524
camcatpublishing.com

Hardcover ISBN 9780744311341
Paperback ISBN 9780744311754
Large-Print Paperback ISBN 9780744311778
eBook ISBN 9780744311761
Audiobook ISBN 9780744311433

Library of Congress Control Number: 2024931341

Book and cover design by Maryann Appel
Interior artwork by Md Saidur Rahman, Memories, Seamartini

5 3 1 2 4

TO CHELSEA,

UNTIL THE END OF THE WORLD.

"The past is never dead. It's not even past."
—William Faulkner

PROLOGUE

Once upon a time . . .

But no, of course not. Too many stories have begun that way, and this was no fairy tale, even though it might have been easier to think of it as one. A fairy tale with ogres and princesses. How lovely.

How wrong.

A life so meticulously structured around the present can become easily overwhelmed by the past rushing in. All it takes is one careless glance back. Those are dangerous. Just ask Orpheus.

All this free time can be dangerous too, making one nostalgic, retrospective. Looking back, looking forward, the pages of the book of time turn.

JEFF

DRIVE, DRIVE, DRIVE until the road is done with you. Until it spits out the final destination at you like some kind of begrudging reward. Until you're through. That's the deal.

The summer morning is unseasonably autumnal, as crisp as a freshly starched shirt. The leaves are looking festive, though it is much too early for them to change colors. Maybe they are gearing up for the months to come, putting on a dress rehearsal. In theory, at least, the leaves are meant to make up for the miserable New England winter that inevitably follows their departure.

Jeff Baker tries to enjoy nature, and when that fails, he focuses on the road itself—the way it disappears beneath the wheels of their five-year-old forest-green Subaru. It's soothing in a way, the certainty of the motion, the steady progress forward. North.

There used to be a time when Jeff loved driving; a time that by now is but a vague, faded memory. His first car was a beat-up '87 Mustang, produced decades after that pony was at its prime, and the two of them were inseparable. The AC never worked, so the windows were rolled down for as long as the weather permitted, the wind blowing through his hair like freedom, like youth itself.

It seems that ever since then, his vehicle selections have been increasingly less exciting, more sedate, staid. Practical. Now here he is, behind the wheel of a car that positively announces to the world that a liberal-minded, environmentally conscious family is inside it. A cliché if there was ever one.

Jeff knows that it suits the man he is today: a husband, a father, someone with a stalled but reasonably lucrative middle management job; a man with a softening gut and receding hairline, wading knee-deep into the still, murky waters of middle age.

He sighs, adjusts the rearview mirror, and tries valiantly to ignore the kicking at the back of his seat. When that doesn't work, he snaps, abruptly and frustratedly.

"JJ, how many times have I told you not to do that?"

Jeff can feel his son's insolent shrug without turning around to see it. It's one of JJ's signature moves—the kid is the personification of a sullen, surly teen. Although they share a name and Jeff loves the kid, he recognizes nothing of himself in Jeff Jr.

His son is lazy, aimless, slovenly in a way that physically upsets fastidious Jeff. What's worse is that the kid doesn't seem to be clever or interesting or even funny. He gets by in school with barely passing grades, participates in no sports or extracurriculars, and spends most of his free time glued to one screen or another. The video games he plays seem too violent to Jeff, but he can't figure out a way to ban them outright, because: (a) he doesn't want to be that dad, and (b) he doesn't necessarily believe in the connection between on-screen and real-life violence. After all, violence has been around long before video games were even invented.

Still, it's difficult to think of a bigger waste of time than these stupid games. At least the kid wears headphones to play them. The constant *rat-tat-tat* of guns in the background would have driven Jeff crazy by now. Jessie is sitting next to her brother, occupying, it seems, only half of her seat. Wherein her brother's girth is forever expanding, Jessie appears to be shrinking. It makes her brittle, Jeff thinks, in appearance and temperament. So much like her mother.

The two kids are only a couple of years apart, but you'd never guess they were related. Never guess they came from the same house, the same people. There is a lot of nature vs. nurture baggage there that Jeff doesn't care to unpack.

His daughter is unfathomable to him; the way she talks in text message abbreviations, the eager manner in which she subscribes to the latest trends without ever taking a moment to examine them for herself, how appearance-conscious she is.

This isn't a great time to be a kid. There's a steady bombardment of social media disseminating shallow values, unchecked materialism, and flat-out lies.

He doesn't even know what wave of feminism everyone's supposed to be riding now. Jenna might, but he loathes to ask. She wouldn't just answer, there'd be a lecture. Jeff despises being lectured and tends to avoid long-winded debates. He likes simple things, short, clear-cut explanations, yes-or-no answers whenever applicable.

Jenna is doing her nails next to him; *screech-screech* goes the thin emery board—a sound Jeff can feel in his vertebrae. He hates it, hates the way he has to just sit next to her and inhale the dead nail particles she's sending into the air, but asking her to stop would be as futile as expecting JJ to stop kicking the freaking seat.

Jeff likes to think of himself as a man who picks his battles. And there have been some. Over the years, that number has dwindled. Lately, he doesn't know if it's just something he tells himself to cover the fact that he has, slowly and inexorably, become a pushover.

Jenna is thin like their daughter, all gym-tight muscles and yoga-flexible tendons. She has been dying her hair the same shade of blond for so long that sometimes Jeff is surprised to see her natural light brown color in the old photos. She looks good, younger than her years, certainly younger than Jeff.

If he doesn't tell her that enough, it's only because they don't talk that much anymore in general. Or maybe it's because her undeniable physical attractiveness appears to have lost the sunny warmth, easy charm, and shy sexiness of the Jenna he fell in love with so long ago. It's almost like his wife has Stepforded herself, trading in all the delightful aspects of her character, all of her fun quirky self for a perfect surface appeal.

Is that what two decades of marriage do? Or living in a society obsessed with youth and beauty? Or being a mother? Or—a more somberly horrifying thought—is that what living with Jeff for twenty years does?

Jeff wants to hit the rewind button and watch their lives again, in slow motion, noting every salient plot point, every crucial twist and turn, to understand how they got here. But it doesn't work that way, does it?

From one of his more interesting but ultimately useless college courses, Jeff remembers a quote: "Life can only be understood backward, but it must be lived forward." It's one of those sayings that sounds smart unless you really think about it, because once you do, you'll see that the former part of it is ultimately useless, while the latter is simply unavoidable.

Jeff had a good time in college. He did well in high school too: just smart enough, just fun enough, just inoffensive enough to ensure certain easy popularity that enabled smooth sailing amid the various social cliques and characters. After graduating, out in the real world, his stock began to slowly but definitively tank. He could never quite figure out why; perhaps, something about the absence of predetermined social structure, or increased expectations.

Either way, by the time Jenna came along, he grabbed onto her like a life preserver and held on steadily and faithfully ever since.

He had never done well on his own when he was young, found solitude oppressive. Depressing, even. Now, of course, he'd kill for some, but it is much too late. Even his man cave occupies only a corner of the basement at home, sharing the rest of the space with laundry and storage and the moody boiler, and thus is perpetually loud and nowhere near private.

He likely isn't going to get much peace and quiet for the next month either, but he agreed to go anyway.

After all, one simply doesn't say no to a free vacation.

And sure, as he pointed out to Jenna while they were making plans, it wasn't entirely free: there was the cost of gas, tolls, food, etc., but the main expense, the house, was taken care of, and so here they are now, driving, driving north.

"Are we there yet?" JJ pipes up from the back seat, too loudly because of the headphones he rarely takes off.

It was funny the first few times—no, not really—but now it grates on Jeff. He forces a smile. "Almost," he replies with false cheer.

The truth is, everything around here looks exactly the same to him: the same tall trees, the same tiny weather-beaten towns, the same road signs. If not for the chatty GPS, he would be hopelessly lost. He wants to thank his digital navigator every time she points out a turn amid a number of interchangeable ones; she seems to be the only helpful person around.

Though, of course, she isn't even a person.

Jenna is listening to an audiobook. Without even asking, Jeff knows it's one of those domestic thrillers she loves that really ought to be shelved under women's fiction.

Something about scrappy heroines untangling their husbands' dark secrets. He tried a couple out of curiosity some time ago at Jenna's prompting and found them unoriginal, uninteresting, and blandly indistinguishable from one another. When Jenna asked for his honest opinion, he gave it to her, like a fool. They never spoke of books again.

He shouldn't have said anything; he certainly shouldn't have added that it was still a step up from her normal self-help fare.

Jeff returned to his historical tomes, fictional and otherwise, spicing it up occasionally with a science fiction novel. Though lately, the sci-fi has been garbage; he hates all the space operas, all the sociopolitical messages overriding the plots. To him, the genre has always been progressive, subversive, and thought-provoking. He doesn't know why it needs to try so hard now.

He tried giving some of his old books to his son, only to find them unread, languishing amid the piles of trash obscuring the floor of JJ's room. Watching movies together proved equally futile. Jeff cannot force himself to sit through the mindless violent crap his kid enjoys. And if he has to see another freaking superhero movie . . .

Jeff doesn't know what his daughter is listening to, but it's likely the latest in pop music. Of all his family, Jessie is the most mysterious one to him. Almost a complete stranger, with his wife's features and his surname. He loves her just as he loves JJ, but the kids remain baffling.

They are supposed to be a team. That was presumably the grand idea about the obnoxious cutesiness of giving their kids J names.

"We'll all be a J. Baker," Jenna told him at the time, back when he still found her enthusiasm, if not all of her ideas, adorable, and here they were. A family with interchangeable initials. Like they were the sort to embroider them on sheets and towels.

Like it mattered.

Jeff is the only one listening to the radio. Never politics—after the last election, he had stopped following them entirely. Now that there is another one coming up, it's difficult to care or remain hopeful. A new decade is looming ahead.

The 2020s have an apocalyptic feel to Jeff. He sticks with music. The station he played while driving out of the city had faded into static miles ago, and now he's stuck with some local DJ inexpertly mixing '80s and '90s hits, plying the nostalgia factor.

And hey, it's working. Jeff remembers these songs. Remembers singing along to them, driving to them, drinking to them, making out to them. Sometimes he even sings along, but quietly. If his voice gets louder, he gets a kick in his seat, which may be unintentional but feels like an unspoken criticism.

He wishes he didn't save up his vacation days so diligently. He wishes they weren't set to expire due to the new company policy so that splurging them all on a month-long vacation was his best option. He wishes Jenna didn't have to inherit access to this supposedly amazing lake house within driving distance that's simply too good to pass up.

The house was never mentioned to him before, but then again, neither was Jenna's aunt, Gussie. Or maybe she was, and Jeff forgot? Would he forget a name like Gussie?

From what he gathers, the childless, eccentric aunt left the house to her entire extended family to delight in on a timeshare basis, and Jenna finagled a month just for them.

They haven't had a vacation in a while, and never one this long. Jeff faked excitement at the idea the way he felt he was supposed to, but his actual reaction was closer to the eye rolling the kids gave when Jenna made the announcement. At the time, he thought it was going to be trying and likely tedious. He still thinks so, but he went along with every step of the plan, and now they are almost there and it's much too late to change a thing.

Maybe it will be relaxing, he tells himself without much conviction. Maybe the house will be larger than their small town house or have better soundproofing. Maybe he'll finally be able to finish the Nero biography he started months ago.

The voice of experience pipes through, laughing at the tentative hopefulness of Jeff's maybes. Jeff sighs and focuses on driving. "Sunglasses at Night" plays on the radio, and he sings along under his breath. "Don't switch a blade on a guy in shades, oh no . . ."

A kick in the back of his seat follows as swiftly as a slap.

JENNA

IT'S SUCH A beautiful drive. Such a scenic one. Jenna wishes the kids would unglue themselves from their phones and enjoy it. Some days she feels like she can't remember the last time she established meaningful eye contact with either of them. She knows they are just teenagers being teenagers, but then she remembers herself at that age, and she wasn't like that. Or was she?

Memory is tricky. Jenna once read in a self-help book that it rewrites itself ever so slightly every time we reach for it. What a concept. It unsettles her, makes her feel like she's been lying to herself, like parts of her life have been a lie. But no, she knows better.

She can trace every path that led her here, to this car, sitting next to a balding, somewhat overweight version of a man she married twenty years ago with two distracted teens behind her. For the most part, Jenna is pleased with her choices.

Or at least she tells herself often enough so that it comes to constitute the foundation upon which her life is built.

When Jenna reaches back into her memory box, it provides her with a picture of a shy brown-haired girl who was pretty good at a variety of things and great at none. She had nice but unexciting friends and nice but unexciting boyfriends. An English degree from a middling small college because she couldn't think of something she was passionate about. A decent and supportive family with entirely too many people in it to genuinely know and adore anyone individually, though it lent itself easily to a sort of warm, if much too general, connection to all of them.

Her father was one of nine. The Doyles are a proper brood of towheaded New Englanders, with open, honest faces, ruddy cheeks, and large, trustworthy hands. All boys and one girl, the elusive Aunt Gussie.

Augusta at birth, but that never took.

The boys of the clan all went on to have solid, if unremarkable, middle-class lives as CPAs, bank workers, and project managers, but Aunt Gussie was the adventurous one.

At some point in her adventures, she managed to displease the family to such an extent that they spent the remaining decades of their respective lives pretending she never existed at all.

Though her family was generally chatty and forthcoming, Jenna was never able to find out what grand transgression Aunt Gussie was guilty of. She was barely, if ever, mentioned. The ultimate persona non grata, a taboo.

The woman spent most of her later life in Europe, so Jenna had no direct recollections of her. They'd never met.

In the few early family photos that featured Gussie, she looked fierce and determined, sharp jutting chin pointing directly at the camera, something like a smirk playing on her lips. A character, for sure.

Jenna wishes she got to know her aunt, but it is too late for that now. She did find it distasteful the way her family pounced on Gussie's inheritance. She had never seen them display such naked greed until then.

How the woman managed to accumulate her wealth no one really knew—unless they knew and weren't saying—but each of her brothers got a precise amount of thirty dollars and each of their children a princely sum of ten grand and a share in a vacation house upstate.

Jenna had seen the photos her cousins took of their time there; it looked idyllic. A place sprawling enough to qualify as an estate, it even had its own name like the houses in books, Haven, though everyone always referred to it simply as Gussie's.

Vacationing there was known as "going up to Gussie's." It was like suddenly, after decades of exile, her aunt had become a proper family fixture once again. Apparently, the proverbial absence did create fondness in certain cases.

Jenna had meant to go for a while, but it seemed like something was always getting in the way. She sensed her husband's reluctance and her kids' ambivalence, but eventually, she simply made a choice to ignore it.

It was her time to attend to her needs, and everyone else was just going to have to put up and shut up. She didn't read all those self-help books for nothing.

Jenna was proud to establish her agency, proud to be in control. She made all the plans, worked out the timing with her family, checked out the area for family-friendly activities, all that.

If only the heroine in the book she's listening to had similar self-possession, but no, the simpering imbecile is kowtowing to her brute of a husband and practically asking to be murdered in some elaborate and mysterious way.

Jenna has the book all figured out, and she's barely halfway through, but she continues to listen because she likes the plucky voice of the audio narrator, and she enjoys the feeling of superiority the story gives her.

They are all the same, these thrillers she borrows at the library through the app she figured out all by herself, thank you. The women in the books are either victims, which makes Jenna feel great about herself, or they are heroes fighting back, which gives Jenna a vicarious thrill of relatability.

She too, she thinks, is a protagonist of her own story. Sure, her story isn't all that interesting and certainly not book-worthy, but maybe one day. She'll be ready.

At that thought, she pats her husband's doughy thigh and elicits an uncertain small smile from him. It pleases her how easy it is to make Jeff happy. It's such a wonderful quality in a spouse.

Her hands look good, she nods approvingly to herself—she did a good job on her nails. For the longest time she kept them mommy-short; now they are in longer, sexy predator mode.

She wonders if Jeff notices. She hopes he does.

Jenna remembers the young man she married, because he was decent and nice and—if she's completely honest with herself—the first one to ask.

At that time in her life, she was a tiny fish in a giant pond of the city's publishing industry, watching her friends marry and move away. Burned out on passion but still craving companionship, Jenna eventually came to recognize and appreciate decency and niceness as attractive qualities in a partner.

Jeff didn't so much sweep her off her feet as steadied her by the elbow. She told herself it was enough.

The thing is, it's still, mostly, enough. Jeff is still nice and decent. And not imaginative enough to have ever cheated. The thought elicits a small, confused pride.

Sure, they often talk at cross-purposes, and sure, their sex life has dwindled to special occasions, but they are still a solid team. They are raising nice, decent kids.

Or at least, she thinks they are. It's difficult to tell. Her kids are a mystery. At least Jessie looks like her. Who is JJ supposed to look like, exactly?

Both of them have the strangest relationships with food. Jessie is always dieting, washing down apples with coffee, and snacking on hold-the-peanut-butter celery stalks.

JJ eats like a zombie freshly released into a crowded mall. No food is safe around him. Her son's size bewilders Jenna, though she'd never let it show. JJ is too old to pass for something cutesy like husky, and the kid smells too. Like stale sweat, unwashed hair, and dirty socks. Jenna wishes Jeff would talk to him about it.

Jessie, on the other hand, spends way too much time watching online tutorials and following instructions carefully for just-so hair and just-right makeup. It makes her look simultaneously too old and too young for her years, like those toddlers dressed up to compete in pageants.

The last time Jenna attempted to have a heart-to-heart with her daughter, it crashed and burned on the topic of safe sex. Jenna comforts herself with the knowledge of having done her best; she isn't ready to be a grandma.

Some of her cousins seem to have perfectly happy well-adjusted children, and she quietly resents them for it. It isn't like she didn't have the time.

Jenna stopped working—slightly reluctant but mostly, overwhelmingly, relieved—after Jessie was born, and since then, never found the right time to go back.

Once the kids reached the age when they didn't need full-time mothering, it was nearly impossible to reenter the workforce. Too many blank years on her resume. The business had changed too much. Etc., etc.

She turned her energy to housekeeping and working out instead, with pride and dedication any career woman might appreciate. And it shows, she's certain of it.

Their house is the cleanest, most organized one she's been in; and she is in the best shape of her life, looking fitter and more attractive than any of the women her age she knows.

Jeff may not appreciate it, but those women do. She knows they do. Women are like that, no matter what they say, competitive to a fault.

It gives Jenna a thrill to be compared and found superior. It's what drives her to push herself at the gym, walking, running, pedaling. It's what motivates her sweaty uncomfortable yoga sessions. Jenna is being her best self. The rest can just fall in line around her.

She notices JJ kicking the back of his father's seat and contemplates saying something, but then again, that ought to be on Jeff.

For the longest time, her husband, never much of a disciplinarian, was content playing the good cop. When that appeared to zap too much energy, he became a content listen-to-your-mother second fiddle. Now he seems to have just given up altogether. He'll say something but never with any feeling behind it. No wonder the kids don't listen.

She reminds herself that he's busy, that he's working, but it annoys her still. To shoulder the majority of parenting means to also shoulder the responsibility for the majority of parenting mistakes. Jenna hates being wrong.

She was wrong to suggest music lessons for either of her tone-deaf offspring. Wrong to push JJ into sports. Wrong to ever discuss weight and fitness with Jessie.

But she isn't wrong about this vacation. It'll be the thing that'll finally brings them closer, she just knows it. The thing they'll remember years from now with fond recollections.

Their return to family values, to nature, to each other.

Jenna had even, optimistically, packed her good underwear, unearthed from the bottom of the drawer.

Not like she particularly desires Jeff's heavy, unimaginative lovemaking, but she misses being the center of his attention. Frankly, anyone's attention, but she is much too fastidious for an affair, so Jeff will just have to do.

With the lights off, her husband can still pass for a tentative, considerate young man whom she once taught about her body, about the precise spot on her neck to kiss, and the exact time to pull her hair just so. She wishes he'd use Rogaine or a gym, but he's still tall and still smells the same, like sandalwood and pine, and sometimes it's enough.

With time-worn affection, Jenna watches him mouth words to the song on the radio.

"Twenty years and you haven't killed each other. Congrats." That's what it said on the card Jenna's favorite cousin gave to her on their last anniversary.

Going by the books she's been into lately, it is indeed quite an achievement.

The heroine in the audiobook gasps in shock, uncovering a clue about her duplicitous husband that Jenna figured out an hour ago. Lying in fiction seems to come as a surprise each and every time. Jenna rolls her eyes and chuckles to herself. Now the fool is in for it.

JJ

OUTSIDE, THERE'S SUNSHINE and trees; in his headphones, there's war and mayhem. JJ likes the contrast.

He waits a decent interval, then kicks the back of the car seat in front of him again. He tries to do it just infrequently enough to claim it as an unthinking motion rather than a deliberate act; he knows all about plausible deniability. And anyway, fuck Jeff. And fuck this stupid vacation.

JJ was just as happy at home, meaning not that happy at all, but still . . . He doesn't care for a change of scenery. Doesn't relish the idea of being stuck with his family for a month in some freaking house in the middle of nowhere, like they are on some inane reality TV show.

At home, he at least has places he can go: the game store, the comic book shop, the arcade on the offhours.

JJ makes up names for the reality TV show he feels he's stuck in. He can't decide between Trapped with the Fam and Family Trap. Either way, this vacation feels phony. Like his parents are pretending to be the sort of parents who do these sorts of things, and he and Jessie have to fall in line and pretend to be the sort of kids who enjoy it. Just goes to show how little Jeff and Jenna know them.

He feels like calling his parents by their names gives him a certain agency, denotes a certain maturity of character, but he hasn't done it out loud yet.

JJ's preferred method of rebellion is a quiet, resentment-flavored simmer.

He shifts in his seat and elbows his growling stomach. Hungry again. It's frustrating how often he is hungry.

He didn't use to be this way. JJ was a skinny kid before; all this weight, he tells himself, is the same puberty nonsense as his squeaky voice and bad skin. Because if it isn't, then it's all his fault, and he doesn't like that at all.

He does like the way his weight separates him from the rest of his stupid family. Jeff isn't skinny but he's nothing like JJ; he's just got a dad bod. JJ is properly fat. The more he eats, the hungrier he is.

While he doesn't love his new body, the heaviness of it all, the swooshy sloshy way it moves, there's something liberating about being fat. He doesn't have to waste time working out the way his mom does, doesn't have to watch everything he eats, count calories, or, worse yet, throw up like Jessie.

JJ doesn't think his parents know this about Jessie, but the two of them share a bathroom and it's impossible not to notice.

Jessie uses an air freshener afterward, like he's dumb, like he can't hear her. Then she drags out the digital scale she keeps in the bathroom and weighs herself. She's as skinny as the girls on TV, but she never seems to be satisfied. JJ can't tell if what he feels for her is sympathy or pity or something else altogether, but he keeps her secret.

In school, JJ went from being an unnoticeable entity to "pizza face" to "fatso." None of it is all that imaginative. He used to get pushed around, but not so much since he stopped showering on a regular basis. The nicknames have expanded to "stinkbomb" and "turd," but JJ's blubber protects him from it all like a squishy carapace.

He works hard at pretending indifference. When he plays his first-person shooter video games, he imagines the generic digital faces on the screen are those of his classmates. He's very good at shooting and wonders if the skill would carry into real life, but his parents are staunchly anti-gun, so he has no way of finding out.

Once JJ actually walked into a gun range to ask, but they turned him away, saying he had to be at least seventeen and with a parent present. Fucking rules.

JJ pauses his game and searches around in his backpack until he finds a half-eaten Snickers bar. The processed goodness of chocolate and caramel-covered peanuts is like a small high. He almost moans audibly with the sheer pleasure of it. Then he notices Jessie eyeing him with pure disgust and looks away.

Jessie probably thinks she'll put on weight just by looking at a candy bar. Her stupid twig-like body makes him think of walking sticks of the order Phasmatodea. Something he saw in a documentary once. It's weird but nature shows balance him out. He can play at war for hours but then fall asleep to the soothing voice of David Attenborough talking about animals.

JJ doesn't like being in nature, but he enjoys watching it on TV. Most things, in his opinion, are better on a screen than they are in real life.

If they were a TV show family, they'd be fun and quirky and kind and happy in each other's company, and all their problems would be solved neatly by the end of a thirty-minute episode.

As things stand, JJ wishes his parents would hurry up and get divorced already. They don't seem to get along or like each other all that much. JJ's old best friend had divorced parents and recommended it highly, said they were always competing for his attention and affection, going so far as bribing him; plus, he ended up with two allowances and double the amount of Christmas gifts. It sounds good to JJ, but no, these two are stubbornly sticking it out. Even dragging them on this dumb vacation like it's meant to make up for all the time they spend snapping at or ignoring one another.

JJ used to fantasize that he was adopted. It made perfect sense to him; it explained everything. The way he had nothing in common with his family and looked nothing like them. But then, his parents had to go and dash his dreams by showing him his birth certificate. And sure enough, in black-and-white official ink, there he was, their flesh and blood, their son.

Jeffrey Baker Junior. What a stupid name. Why'd they want two of those? JJ was not much of an improvement, kind of like a clown name, but he was used to it. At least it set him apart.

JJ kicks the seat again. Watches his father tense up but not turn around.

The drive feels endless. The road is a corridor of trees. The more JJ looks at it, the heavier his eyelids get. He unpauses the game, gets to the end of the level, then saves it and shuts it off. Through the now silent headphones he's wearing, he can hear Jeff singing badly to a song on the radio. Jenna's emery board *shrik-shrik* across her talons. Jessie's phone is blowing up with cutesy cartoonish noises as she's scrawling through her Insta feed, probably dreaming of being on there.

That's the soundtrack of his family, the ugly noise of their lives.

JJ boots up the game and leaves it on demo mode; heavy metal techno combination punctuated rhythmically by firing arms thrums in his ears, lulling him to sleep.

JESSIE

THE TREES ON either side of the road look blandly uniform in a way that makes Jessie want to use some effects on them. Even in sepia, they'd look more interesting, she thinks. Something different, at least. She finds uncurated nature flat and uninspiring. Nothing like the wild explosive life happening in real time on her phone.

She flips between her Insta feed and TikTok, obsessively checking her number of followers. Ugh. It's not enough. It's never enough. Just when she thinks she's getting some traction, she compares herself to others and despairs.

If she were thinner, if she were prettier, if her family had more money . . . There are so many ifs. Online fame is an if-based business. And Jessie wants to be famous.

She's thought of being other things, of going to college, getting a degree, a job, but it all feels daunting and somehow unreal. What is her best-case scenario there? To end up like her parents? Yikes. No thank you.

Objectively speaking, Mom is hot. Jessie knows it because she's heard the uncomfortable MILF comments at school. Her mom's probably hotter than she is. Jessie is well aware those comments are sexist and wrong, and yet a part of her wishes those boys would talk about her that way.

Mom works out like a fiend and eats such a healthy diet. Ugh! Annoying. She doesn't even seem to crave junk. Jessie wishes she had that kind of discipline, but every now and again she slips up. Of course, she purges right afterward, but while the calories may disappear, the guilt remains.

The girls on her phone, the ones with the most followers, look impossible. Their stats are impossible too.

They never went to college, they don't have real jobs, and nobody cares. They have millions of people paying attention to them. They probably have millions of dollars from all that attention.

Jessie has read all the articles about it that she could find, all the interviews. The endorsement fees alone are astronomical.

But besides the money, Jessie fantasizes about what it must be like to be that important. That significant.

Have her depressingly ordinary parents ever felt that way in their entire lives?

She doesn't get them. They are not interesting enough to even try to get. Their rules are dumb. They never have meaningful conversations the way families on TV do. Once her mom even butchered a birds-and-bees talk. Hilariously. As if Jessie would ever be so clueless as to get knocked up. Yuck.

Body functions are pretty gross. Jessie's an old hand at vomiting, but the rest of it sounds absolutely disgusting. Childbirth? No thank you. Sex . . . she isn't so sure.

Not like she's even having that much sex. Not like she particularly wants to. She craves attention, sure, but she wants to be adored with eyes, not hands.

Something about the sweaty leering boys in school turns her off. She tried fantasizing about Mr. Polk, her hot young history teacher, but it gets her nowhere. She's had sex, of course. She's sixteen, after all. She doesn't want to be known as a virgin, a snow queen, a prude. And yes, Mom, she used a condom. Every time.

The sex was stab-like uncomfortable at first and later just . . . perfunctory. Nothing special. Nothing like she thought it would be from hearing about it everywhere all the time. The Earth didn't move or anything. Sometimes she wonders if the people who talk about sex being so amazing are lying. To her, to themselves, to each other. If the greatness of sex is just some myth perpetuated generationally because no one wants to be the outlier who says, "But really, what's so great about it?"

Jessie likes that idea because otherwise, it's her. Being weird. Being different.

Still, listening to everyone talk about sex is helpful in its own way. She's watched some porn with her friends, giggling at it but also mentally taking notes. She learned to fake orgasms from it. And from practice, she learned that the fumbling boys didn't care one way or another. They were too busy basking in the sticky afterglow of their exertions.

The only time she felt anything resembling the wow everyone's talking about was during a Spin the Bottle game, six months earlier, when her spin landed on Ainsley Grant. Ainsley is a natural blond, vaguely British, and heartbreakingly pretty, with a name like a movie star.

They were both drunk at the time because no one plays that game sober, and also no one ever says no. Not really. The protestations are all part of the game, because then everyone starts to shout and make fun and cheer you on, and amid that cacophony, on the cheap linoleum floor of the Andersons' basement, Jessie had the best kiss of her life.

Ainsley, always the wild card, pretended to be amused by Jessie's reluctance, so she leaned over and pulled her in by the collar of her T-shirt. Their lips met, and Jessie forgot herself. She forgot the time—

much too late and she'd have to lie to her parents about it. She forgot the place—Jim Anderson's parents were never home. She forgot the crowd—as many as the basement could hold and then a few more. It was the most magically liberating moment. Nothing but pure sensation.

Afterward—after Ainsley playfully pushed her away and laughed, after everyone made their stupid comments and moved on as the party continued—Jessie found that she felt the absence of Ainsley's mouth on hers, that it registered as a loss. She had only seen the word "bereft" in a book and had never used it, but that's how she felt. Bereft.

The feeling confused her, and she asked for another drink. Then another.

Later, throwing up outside the Andersons' shed before heading home on unsteady legs, she saw Ainsley hooking up with Jim. She didn't pull away from him, Jessie noticed before averting her eyes.

Tears stung her eyes, but vomiting often had that effect.

The kiss was never mentioned again, but Jessie thought about it all the time. And no tongue-aggressive, saliva-heavy, sloppy makeout session that followed had ever held a candle to it.

Jessie is woke. She follows all the current trends and brands with all the right values. She stands for all the right things. She has gay friends. Well, at least gay boy friends. She has queer acquaintances, people she knows enough to say hi to.

Jessie believes herself to be the most progressive, open-minded member of her entire family. But something inside her shuts down when she tries to think about that kiss, about Ainsley, about what it might mean for her. She doesn't want to be different, no matter how normal it may be. Jessie wants to be like everyone—well, most everyone else. Life just seems easier that way.

It's like, what would her friends say? And her followers? Her parents?

Jessie hates that she has to even consider the latter. Jeff and Jenna are hip enough as their generation goes. They don't stockpile guns or wear red baseball hats; they don't casually slur and dismiss it as generational gaffes. They don't go to church. But she's never seen them hang out with anyone who might stand under the LGBTQ+ umbrella and has no idea how they feel about that.

Anyway, soon it won't matter one way or another. Just two short years and she'll be free of them. This gives her two years to get internet famous . . . or she'll end up stuck in some crappy cheap college her parents can afford, studying for a useless degree and emerging with a ton of debt into an impossible job market. That's no way to make money. No way to be.

Jessie wonders how this Aunt Gussie, whoever she was, made her money. She obviously had plenty. Gifting this house to the family as a vacation home was proof. And that was before the internet, too.

Jessie imagines her as an impossibly glamorous character having international affairs and hobnobbing with the who's who of the time. Maybe she had rich lovers. Or was secretly a movie star or something. Not that many ways for a woman to make her own money back in the day.

Mom knows nothing about it, of course. She's a tragically incurious person by nature. But Jessie intends to find out. She'll snoop around the house, spend an entire month doing it if she has to. But she'll figure this Aunt Gussie character out.

Now if only they would just hurry up and get there already. Her phone doesn't have much charge left, and she's tired of fighting with JJ for the plug. Plus, she's hungry, and her disgusting, not-so-little brother keeps eating next to her. A freaking Snickers bar. She can't remember the last time she allowed herself such a luxury.

Oh well. She pets her concave stomach. It's worth it. Jessie presses her nails into the palms of her hand and counts to ten. She doesn't know why, but it helps.

Then she turns her attention back to her phone screen.

AVA

GUSSIE. SHE HAD always hated the diminutive. The forced cutesiness of it, the way it seemed to reduce her to someone smaller, quainter, pliable.

Augusta was a good, strong name. An imperial name. Gussie was just . . . ugly.

In time, she had come to hate her last name too, by association alone. Wanting no connection to her family, she changed them both, and forever since relished the freedom it brought.

Only once in all the years to come did she tell anyone of the name she was born with. Nina agreed—Gussie was ugly. But Gust, the way she exhaled it, the breezy elegance of it, her accent harshening the consonants into something exotic, Gust she loved.

"The wind that blows clean through me," Nina would whisper, cigarette smoke trailing her words. "My Gust."

To everyone else she was Ava St. James. But then, almost no one else had ever really mattered.

She had found that out early on, adopted the credo to survive, made it her buoy to cling to when the vagaries of life battled her like the waves, threatening to pull her under.

Nina mattered. But that came later.

In her twilight years, when her mind fed upon reminiscences of golden days with desperate, voracious hunger, Nina was almost all Ava thought of. She occupied her mind exclusively, fully. Like a welcomed ghost.

Ninotchka. Ni-notch-ka. Her native language so strange, so foreign; even their diminutives were longer than the original. But what a beautiful sound. Like raindrops cascading on water.

They met in Paris. But of course, one could hardly last in the ballet business. Then Ava followed Nina and her ruined toes back to Moscow. Both of them were much too cosmopolitan for the place, so they left once more. Traveling. Eventually settling up north.

Ah, Scandinavia. The place spoke to both of them. Neat, almost toylike architectural arrangements, a deep abiding sense of history, reserved, polite, mind-your-own-business people. Mild enjoyable summers and striking white winters Nina had so loved since childhood.

They alternated between Sweden and Norway, teaching themselves the strange new languages, admiring the precision of it, the myriad of peculiar differences and surprising similarities to what they spoke before. How cleverly interchangeable they were, the Swedish and the Norwegian languages. Conveniently understood in either place due to shared history.

The last house they lived in together was in Bergen, on the picturesque Norwegian coast. Surrounded by countless fjords and the famous Seven Mountains. It was as peaceful and as beautiful of a place as either of them had ever seen or imagined. Home in every sense of the word.

When Nina left her—all those damned cigarettes—the place became a house haunted, leaving Ava to wander its rooms, tracing and retracing the memories they held, looking for crumbs-on-the-trail emanations of her lost love: lingering perfume, decorative touches, the art projects dabbled in and abandoned in various stages of completion.

After a while, it was difficult to tell who was haunting who. They were intertwined too tightly for too long for one of them to suddenly relearn to function as a single unit.

Ava's mind began retreating into itself, taking her further back, watching and rewatching her life as if it were a movie.

Her hair went gray in the absence of someone to dye it her original night-black, and her bones grew weary with the years. Her eyes needed glasses, and her hearing wasn't quite what it used to be, but her memory was as sharp as ever.

She remembered everything. And eventually, with nothing else to do, she decided to write it down. Nina used to say that everyone is the hero of their own story. Ava loved the way it made lives sound like books. Like fiction. Exciting, thrilling, adventurous. Why not tell her own story?

JEFF

"YOU HAVE ARRIVED at your destination," Jeff's phone announces cheerfully, breaking through an old Police song.

He forgot to turn off the navigation, even after the house came into view. It's sitting on top of a hill, because, of course, it would be. Jeff tries to think of what he's heard about the place. It comes up frequently in Jenna's family get-togethers, but then again, he tends to tune out of those just as frequently.

It's barely a family, more of a clan or a brood. Jeff is an only child and is perfectly happy about it. He has two cousins, both of whom live out of state; he hasn't seen them in years.

His wife's family . . . well, he'd actually lost count of them a long time ago; learned to offer a smile and a nod instead of trying to recall anyone's names. There are just so many of them. Too many. Jeff used to joke that the Doyles were a grand breeding experiment to take over New England, back when Jenna still found his jokes funny. But then again, apparently the Irish are particular about reproductive humor, so he stopped. Drinking jokes had to go, too, although Jenna's people drink like the proverbial fish. Jeff figures he'd drink like that too if he had to deal with all of them on a frequent basis. There's always so much drama. Divorces, affairs, suicide attempts—so much for their staunch Catholicism.

And then, of course, there's the mysterious Aunt Gussie. By far and away his favorite of Jenna's relatives. She's never chewed his ear off, and she left his wife some dough. A winner all around.

Jeff can't remember seeing the photos of the house. Jenna is always shoving her phone in his face to show him this or that from her social media, and he nods without really looking.

But he does recall her describing the place as estate-like and he fails to see that now.

The house is large, sure, but clumsily so, as if executed by several different architects who never spoke with each other. It does have a certain imposing quality, but that might just be its hilltop positioning.

The driveway is long and curved. Jeff hears the small rocks pebbling the sides of the Subaru and winces, wishing Aunt Gussie had sprung to have it paved. The car takes enough abuse already from being parked in the city, Jeff doesn't want to add to it.

There's a small man of indeterminate age standing in front of the house waving at them.

"Who's that?" Jeff asks his wife.

"Oh, that's Angus."

And who the crap is Angus? Jeff wonders. The butler? He has seen enough *Batman* movies to like the idea, but he wishes he'd known in advance.

Jeff parks in a spot he deems appropriately shady and gets out of the car. He stretches and his limbs scream in protest, unfolding with the ominous cracking of someone depressingly aged.

Jenna gets out too, looking annoyingly fresh. He should have let her drive more, but she's a terrible driver—too sharp on the turns, too quick on the brakes. Her own car, an older Honda, bears the scars of it all, and Jeff is reluctant to let the Subaru suffer the same indignities.

Jessie gets out too, waving her phone around like she's lost reception. Shit, Jeff thinks, without reception this is going to be one long holiday. Surely there's bound to be a tower somewhere. It's upstate, not Timbuktu.

JJ remains in the car, so Jeff raps his knuckles on the rear window, then louder. The kid reluctantly pulls his oversized headphones down and climbs out.

Looks around with a distinct lack of enthusiasm.

The small man—Angus, Jeff reminds himself—approaches them, smiling.

"The Bakers, I presume. It's a pleasure to meet you. I've had the house all set up. Three bedrooms opened and aired out on the second floor, plus, you'll have full use of the parlor, kitchen, library, etc. I understand it is your first time here. Would you care for a tour?"

The man has some sort of an accent. A light burr. Scottish, maybe? Jeff is crap with accents.

His idea of the Scots seems to be shaped by the movies, from *Highlander* to *Braveheart*. Large, long-haired, kilted macho men.

Angus can't be much taller than five and a half feet. Whatever hair he might have is mostly hidden by a flat hat Jeff normally associates with old-timey cabbies. The man appears to have a slight but sturdy build, and he's wearing a plaid button-down with neatly rolled-up sleeves, and sensible khakis.

They introduce themselves and get a brief firm handshake each.

Jeff doesn't wait for the small man to offer them help with their bags—it might topple him; he grabs his and Jenna's and tells the kids to bring theirs.

Angus ushers them inside. The large heavy door with an old-fashioned metal knocker appears well-oiled; none of those creepy haunted house creaks.

The entire place, in fact, appears to be in good repair. At least from what Jeff can see. The furnishings and decorations belong to a different era, but Angus assures them the plumbing and electric are fully up to date.

It is the largest private residence that Jeff has ever been in, and he doesn't care for it. Doesn't like how small it makes him feel.

The kids appear vastly indifferent until it comes to choosing bedrooms, at which point they squabble until Jessie gets the larger one with an en suite.

"Well, fine," JJ mumbles snidely. "Take it, you need it more."

Jeff wonders whatever the heck that's all about, then forgets it.

Jeff hopes that eventually his kids get to a place where they can appreciate each other as siblings as opposed to the barely hidden hostile standoff they've got going on now, but he isn't holding his breath.

JJ shoves past him, tosses a beat-up oversized backpack on the floor of his new room, and plops down on the neatly made bed. He looks, Jeff observes, like a beached whale. Then, guiltily, he banishes the unkind thought.

Jessie's luggage is color-coordinated, a backpack, a tote, and a small suitcase. That she manages to bring all of it up by herself is almost impressive.

Jeff would have helped, but Jenna is a notorious overpacker, and he is struggling with the weight of her bags. Now he kind of wishes that Angus offered to help and hopes the guy doesn't expect a tip.

The last stop on the tour is the kitchen. Impressive, retro style but with clearly modernized appliances, it's vast, about the size of Jeff's first studio apartment.

"I'm something of a baker myself," Angus says, and Jeff rolls his eyes inwardly. He's heard that same stupid pun for ages. "Made you these as a welcome."

He gestures to a basket of muffins. Jeff's stomach growls its gratitude in response.

Ah, the man's good for something, after all. The muffins look huge and delicious and as photogenic as something from one of Jenna's beloved baking shows.

He reaches for one, takes a bite, and almost moans in delight.

Better eat more than one, Jeff thinks. Once JJ gets wind of the muffins, they'll be as good as gone.

Jenna picks a small section from the top of one of the muffins and chews it slowly. Probably contemplating how many calories she's going to have to work off afterward.

They both thank the man.

"Well, I'll be off, let you settle in."

"Oh, you don't . . . you don't live here?" Jeff blurts out, carb-high and fuzzy-brained.

"Oh goodness, no. I've a cottage in the village below. I just take care of the place for the family. Left my number on the fridge for you. Anything you need, just call. Some other numbers there too—local things. Take-out menus too."

"Is there Wi-Fi?"

"Oh sure, it's everywhere these days, isn't it? Just a bit spotty at times."

Jeff doesn't think of Angus as someone who uses the internet much. There's something distinctly dated about the man, beyond his indeterminable middle-ageness. Some bygone old-world quaintness.

"Well," Angus says again, rubbing his hands together. "Off I go. The keys are on the table by the front door. Enjoy your stay."

And then, he's gone.

Jeff eats another muffin, while Jenna picks at one. Jeff wants to tell her to just eat the entire thing and enjoy it, but he knows better.

"Should we have tipped him, you think?" he asks.

"Maybe we can leave something at the end?" She shrugs.

"Did you know he was going to be here?"

"Yeah, Jeff, I told you." There's a tone creeping into her voice that he doesn't care for. Annoyance. Petulance. "You never listen, I swear."

He tries to recall the conversation, but nothing comes to mind.

"Did you tell me he made muffins this good?" Jeff tries to joke. "Had I known, I would have come sooner."

Jenna sighs, brushes the crumbs off her fingertips and says she's heading upstairs to rest.

Jeff doesn't know why everyone needs so much rest—he's the one who did all the driving. Well, doesn't matter. More alone time for him.

He takes the muffin basket into the living room—the one Angus calls the parlor. It's all leather chesterfields and quaintly embroidered footstools and small side tables of dark wood. There's a large ornate fireplace and an imposing portrait above it of an older woman, with a face he'd call more handsome than attractive. Something too somber about her sharp features as if her face had been carved from a rock, but the combination is interesting, compelling. There's an undeniable wry intelligence in the eyes, in the way they seem to follow Jeff around the room. A slight quirk to the corner of her mouth, not quite a smile, not quite a frown. It's like . . . she's summing him up.

Jeff isn't much of an art fan, but he thinks it's a good portrait. He doesn't love it hanging there, watching him, but he can appreciate the quality of the work, how alive the woman looks.

That must be the famous Aunt Gussie, he figures, toasting the woman with a fresh muffin. Wishing he had a proper drink. And shouldn't there be one? Isn't there always a bar cart in places like these?

Jeff looks around and finds nothing. A dry Doyle house—what a joke. He'd have to make do with soda or whatever Angus left for them.

He gazes up. Gussie looks amused. Or so Jeff thinks. It's difficult to tell in the low light streaming through the tall windows.

Jeff plops himself onto one of the chesterfields, his feet up. The baked goods are lulling him into a pleasant stupor. The place is quiet. It's unusual to have a quiet house when all the family is present.

Jeff smiles contently. He can get used to this. Maybe this vacation won't be a total shit show after all.

JENNA

SHE ISN'T SURE what she expected, but not this. Not exactly this, anyway. It looked different in the pictures. She supposed deep down she was hoping for more of a *Downton Abbey* situation.

Haven is not quite as stately or as elegant. It has more of an . . . ominous quality.

Unless the place proves to be spectacularly photogenic, she's blaming her cousins.

They do tend to lie and exaggerate. What her uncles affectionately refer to as fibbing. They say it's an Irish trait, but Jenna isn't so sure. It might just be the Doyles.

Angus is something of a disappointment also. But that's all on Jenna. She heard the name of Haven's caretaker, it sounded Scottish, and her mind completed the rest in the style of *Outlander*, a TV show she's been quietly obsessed with for years.

Nothing's ever how one imagines it would be, she thinks. Not the good things, at least.

The inconsiderate way her kids are stomping around, her tire-gutted husband shoving muffin after muffin into his hungry maw—that's all very much on brand.

She catches herself, all that negative thinking. Where is it coming from? All the self-help books are always talking of positivity and gratitude. Of course she is grateful for her family. It's only that such emotions are easier to access in the abstract. In real life, the details tend to get in the way, snagging at love like splinters. Jenna sighs. Maybe she's just hungry.

After Angus's departure, she looks around and begins to see the quiet appeal of the place. It isn't pretty, but it has character. She recognizes it as a perfect setting for any of her beloved domestic thrillers. A perfect place for murder.

The thought gives her a shudder. Or maybe it's the house itself. Too thoroughly shaded by the surrounding trees, it seems reluctant to let in August's warmth.

Jenna gives herself a tour, wishing her husband would join her but unwilling to ask. He's already found a couch to melt into and she lets him be—he did do all that driving. Not like she didn't offer, but Jeff seems to have some weird control issues when it comes to the Subaru. Or is it her driving? No, can't be. Jenna's a fine driver. And, unlike Jeff, she can and will stop for directions to avoid getting lost.

The house doesn't seem to have a clear, well-thought-out design to it; some of the rooms branch out from the main corridor, some flow into each other. It's confusing enough to require a navigation system of its own. Jenna imagines it: the Haven's GPS that speaks with Angus's voice. The thought amuses her.

From the windows of their preselected master bedroom, she can just about see the lake through the trees. It lies below, glistening invitingly. She hopes the water is warm.

Spending too much time in this house, she imagines, can make one forget that it's summer outside.

The master bedroom is excellently appointed. Jenna admires the four-poster bed with a comfortable queen mattress and soft-feeling sheets. She runs a hand over the quilt laid on top of it, noting the absence of creases. Nicely done, Angus.

There's a cedar trunk at the foot of the bed with extra blankets, and up against the far wall stands a large wardrobe of dark wood, looking like an entrance to Narnia.

Jenna remembers reading the kids those stories back in the day. She had loved them as a child, and they seemed to also, but neither of them retained that appreciation of books into their teenage years. The screens took over and won.

Jenna wonders if Haven didn't have Wi-Fi, would their love of reading come back? Would her sullen teenagers actually enjoy it if given no other choice of entertainment?

Wandering from room to room, she tries to imagine what her Aunt Gussie might have thought building this place. Was she happy here? Happy enough to forgive her family for the mysterious banishment?

Jenna isn't sure she could be so forgiving. She's always been taught that family is everything, and she's got enough Catholic values remaining for the turn-the-other-cheek approach, but she isn't sure how it would translate in a real-life situation.

Real life is too messy, much like families. In regard to either, Jenna has never had to deal with anything drastic enough to truly test her character.

More power to Gussie.

Jenna heads back to the kitchen. It is the room she feels most at home in, the one most unlike the rest of the house. Specifically, the one most similar to something she'd have in her own house given the money and space.

People don't think of someone Jenna's size as much of a cook. They are wrong. Jenna doesn't eat much, but she is very particular about the things she does permit into her body. Her choices are precise and curated and more often than not have to be crafted from scratch to ensure just the right measure of calories and nutrition.

Frankly, it takes up an inordinate amount of time, but every time she looks in the mirror, she thinks it's worth it.

Cooking for her family on the other hand is a consistently thankless task. Jeff will eat anything with the same amount of enthusiasm and appetite. JJ has a similar, albeit terrifyingly bottomless, approach. And Jessie, at best, will push her food around the plate and pick at the vegetables.

Jenna has tried talking nutrition with her daughter; it went only slightly better than the sex talk.

Somehow, at the ripe old age of sixteen, her brittle, delicate teenager has become a self-contained person wanting nothing from her, needing nothing from her. Except, of course, financial support.

Jenna hates how useless her kids make her feel. Sometimes that hatred burns so brightly that it obliterates the upbeat pop music in her ears as she exercises, until all she hears is the angry swooshing of her own blood.

It's likely an overreaction, but motherhood has been her life for so long now that she isn't sure what is left to her outside of it. She has poured all her hopes, dreams, and energy into them, and it's impossible not to take the rejection personally.

How dare they, she thinks. After all she's done for them. Not a single person in her family would be able to survive childbirth, soft and selfish as they are. How dare they.

The sight of a fully stocked fridge pleases her. She had sent Angus the list in advance, and he did well. She makes a mental note to thank him when next they meet. He may not look like a dashing Highland warrior, but the man knows how to grocery shop. A skill her own husband hasn't mastered in twenty years.

Jenna is pleasantly surprised at the selection; can the local stores really be that well-versed in natural foods? The places they drove through looked so small and sleepy, like something time forgot, but it seems the long arms of progress reach far and wide after all.

Out of habit, she starts planning their meals. It's quite late in the day for something heavy, so she begins chopping vegetables for a light repast. The rhythmic sound of the knife meeting the cutting board is the only thing that breaks up the silence around her. Haven, indeed.

JJ

THE ROOM IS serviceably bland. Nothing special. He doesn't care. So long as it's got a Wi-Fi connection and a bed.

JJ doesn't bother unpacking. What's the point? Eventually, he'll just have to pack it all back in. It's the same with making the bed, another pointless morning ritual his parents insist on that's nothing but a waste of time. The bed he reluctantly climbs out of every morning is the same bed he eagerly falls into every night. He and he alone. Who cares if the sheets on it are tightly stretched corner to corner or a wrinkled mess during the in-between time?

JJ likes this bed. It's the same size as the one he has at home, a double, and at least as comfortable if not more. He musses up the sheets some to make them feel more lived in. There is a small table next to the bed, on the side that isn't pushed up against the wall. On it, a plain lamp and an old-fashioned alarm clock.

As if he'd need one of those. He's got another month of sleeping in before the torture of school begins once more.

And why isn't the clock digital? How's he supposed to tell time at night?

There are other old-fashioned things around the room. A wooden desk and chair. A tall, narrow wardrobe. A rocking chair in the corner by the window.

Curious, JJ gets up to try it out. The chair gives a panicked squeak as he lowers his body into it. Each rocking motion elicits a further screech of protestation, or maybe a cry for help.

Screw that, JJ thinks, heaving himself out. The chair looks solid, but it must have been built for some dainty old lady. He doesn't need another reminder of his size, and he halfheartedly kicks the leg of it.

The view from the window is nice, he notices. Looks like there's a lake nearby. He doesn't remember his parents mentioning the lake, which isn't the same as saying they never did.

JJ is a good swimmer. All his blubber, so unwieldy on land, makes him as graceful as an aquatic mammal in water.

Jeff once suggested he try out for the school's swim team. JJ just looked at the man, like, how clueless can he be?

As is, he goes swimming in a baggy T-shirt and an oversized pair of swim trunks. Not the most hydrodynamic getup, but it works for him. Never in the pool, be it school, private, or public, only at the beach, only somewhere he can get by mostly unnoticed.

The water is the only place where JJ feels light. The exhilarating gravity-defying sensation of weightlessness relaxes and soothes him.

He's very happy about the lake being here. It's the first decent thing about this ridiculous vacation.

JJ wonders if it's a last hurrah sort of thing, this month. One of his friends' now divorced parents did the same thing. Put on a shiny happy togetherness show before splitting up.

He plops back on the bed and unzips his bag. There aren't many clothes; the bottom of the backpack is mostly snacks. He wasn't sure if there'd be any in the house or if there would be a shop nearby.

He has his own money. Both his and Jessie's allowances are chore-based, but he supplements his by selling things online through a Marketplace account set up in his father's name. Mostly things he finds around the house and doesn't think anyone will miss. Books, some random collectibles, Jessie's clothes. She has so many, she never notices. Sometimes he finds things on the street worth selling. Once even a brand-name watch. It helps to always walk with your head down.

None of it brings in a lot, but he likes his craftiness, the independence it brings. None of the strangers who meet him to pick things up ever think twice about his age. If they look like they might, he just says he's doing it for his dad who is busy.

It keeps JJ in snacks and video games. Which is all that matters.

Now, he stashes the snacks under the bed where, unlike back home, it is surprisingly clean. Not a single dust bunny. He takes off his socks, wads them up, and throws them under too, for camouflage. His feet stink and he fantasizes briefly about lowering them into the refreshing lake water, then sliding all the way in like a seal and swimming away.

The room doesn't have a TV. Of course it doesn't. JJ's got his Fire tablet, but it's only a seven-inch screen, not enough for the proper splendor of a David Attenborough nature show. He puts one on all the same, pulls his headphones on, and feels the relaxation flowing through him.

He stays that way until his stomach demands more calories than a Snickers bar can provide and then, reluctantly, shuffles downstairs to the kitchen. He hopes there's food. Lots and lots of it. Enough to eat himself thoughtless.

JESSIE

HER LUGGAGE TAKES a while to unpack. She then puts the backpack and the tote inside the now-empty suitcase, zips it up, and stows it at the bottom of the freestanding wardrobe. The thing is huge; it reminds Jessie of those silly stories Mom used to read to them when they were kids.

Jessie selects K-Pop on her phone, adjusts the volume, and putters around the room until everything is just so. The place is too old-fashioned and wooden for her liking, but it'll do. The en suite bathroom is perfect. Her brother is a little shit most of the time, but she's very thankful he didn't fight her too hard on this.

She checks the toilet—it's spotless. She places a can of extra-strength air freshener on the tank lid. Just to be safe.

Vomiting is gross, she knows it. She wishes there was another way. There isn't.

From under the bed, Jessie slides out a digital scale she brought with her, hidden at the bottom of the suitcase like a dirty secret. Undresses, exhales deeply, and weighs herself. The number she notices with a self-satisfied smile is the same as last time. And she's feeling only slightly faint.

Perhaps, she can eat something. Something light. If her mom's cooking, it's a solid possibility.

The rare few times her dad's in charge, it's greasy takeout, unfailingly. Chinese or pizza. Jessie starves. Or gives in and suffers the indignities of regurgitated cheese and MSG.

There's a lake somewhere here, her mom told her. Jessie can't recall if she's ever swam in a lake. She isn't as good of a swimmer as her brother, but she knows she looks good in a bathing suit, so she enjoys going to the beach.

She brought three swimsuits with her. Credible knockoffs of the brand a popular InstaStar is pimping. Jessie dreams of affording the real deal. Or sometimes, vividly and excitedly, about having a brand of her own.

As is she doesn't have enough followers; she checked this morning, and the number is still pitifully low. Doesn't have enough money either. Her parents' allowance is an embarrassment. They said if she wants more, she could get a job, but unless she wants to work in a local strip mall—and she really doesn't, wouldn't be caught dead there—she would need a car. And she can't buy a car because she doesn't have enough money, and her parents won't buy her one because they suck. Ugh. It's like that *Catch-22* thing from the book she was made to read for English. She didn't read the entire thing—yawn—but got the basic idea. Enough for a passing grade essay, anyway.

When she makes it, when she's famous and loaded, she'll remember her parents' stinginess and act accordingly. She likes the notion, the bittersweetness of spite tastes much like vomit's aftertaste.

Jessie thought she brought three swimsuits, but she can't find one, the teeny tiny number with a sequined logo. That was the most expensive one she owned, too. She should look again.

She changes into a skimpy romper in cute yellow and heads downstairs.

The house is large enough and convoluted enough to get lost in. She doesn't like it. Makes her think of houses from scary movies.

Jessie hates being frightened, but everyone seems to love it, especially boys. Like they get a thrill out of watching her jump. Like it's not enough that she has to sit there, enduring their greasy, groping fingers, pretending to but not really eating the popcorn, the fake butteriness of which almost makes her swoon with want. Like her discomfort has to be highlighted by fear in order for them to have a good time with her.

Those movies always give her nightmares too.

Once, in her nightmare, she was trapped in a haunted house with Ainsley Grant, and they were both running away from something they couldn't see, only hear. It was terrifying but exciting at the same time. The most time they spent together, the two of them, and it wasn't even real. Dreams are meaningless anyway. Jessie has a dream dictionary book someone gave her as a birthday gift once, and it's always wrong.

She passes the living room. Or what did that man with a funny accent call it? Ah, yes, the parlor.

Her father has made himself at home on one of the leather couches. Jessie abhors leather on principle. No one should use the skin of innocent animals for furniture. And yes, she does have a nice leather belt, but it's a thin thing, virtually harmless.

A basket of muffins is resting on her father's soft gut, and Jessie's feet carry her to it before she can course correct.

"Hey, kiddo," he says, crumbs in his stubble. "Want one?"

"No, thanks," she replies automatically. Then forces herself to look away. "Who's that?"

"That is our munificent benefactor, Aunt Gussie."

"Oh." Aunt Gussie isn't at all how Jessie pictured her. She isn't an old crone or an old biddy or any of those old women clichés. She's actually kind of . . . good-looking. In a weird, aged way.

She looks like she has secrets. Like she has stories. She looks fascinating.

"What do you think?"

"She isn't how I imagined," Jessie admits. "She's nothing like this weird house. I mean, you know . . ."

"No, I get it. She looks like someone who'd sooner have a pied-à-terre in Montmartre, Paris."

Jessie doesn't know what or where that is, but it sounds right. She nods.

"Sure you don't want one?" her father asks again. "That Angus can really bake."

"Angus? I thought his name was Ansel."

"Angus. Ansel. The man knows his way around a muffin."

That sounds weirdly dirty, Jessie thinks, or maybe the muffins are making her woozy. "I'm going to the kitchen to find some real food."

If her father gives her a look, she doesn't see it. So long as he doesn't voice his opinions on her diet, she doesn't care.

Her mother is in a chopping frenzy. The knife is going up and down like she's a contestant on one of those stupid cooking shows she loves.

Jessie steals a few cut-up veggies and eats them raw. Her stomach sighs in gratitude.

She doesn't offer help, and Jenna doesn't ask. They have long accepted certain aspects of each other.

Jessie eats another piece of carrot and contemplates the portrait in the parlor.

All of her uncles or granduncles or whatever they are supposed to be are such a crude bunch of politically incorrect drunks and cranky old men. But Aunt Gussie looks classy. If she were on social media, Jessie would follow her. She wishes they could meet. Talk.

They say a picture is worth a thousand words, but she finds it frustratingly silent. Secrets firmly locked behind their owner's eyes. It isn't fair. Finally, someone interesting in this family and they're dead. Ugh.

Carelessly, Jessie reaches for a thin crust of bread, slathers it with brie her mother has set out, and crams it into her mouth. For a moment it tastes like pure happiness. Then it's gone, a memory, soon to be a waste. Jessie can already taste the sourness of it on the way out.

Nothing perfect lasts, she thinks. Nothing.

AVA

EARLY YEARS

Augusta Doyle was born to a large Irish family. The world was in the throes of a great upheaval—another war had just begun, threatening to tear the world apart. The wounds of the first one were still all too fresh, and yet blood was being spilled once more.

Her parents were strict, hard people. Perhaps the Great Depression, perhaps life itself had beaten into them a certain harshness that veered toward meanness. Her father had never been in a war, saved by age and flat feet, but to hear him talk about it later made it obvious that he thought himself a hero for staying home and producing soldiers for the next one. Son after son after son. But then one day, the Doyles had a daughter. Augusta was the youngest of nine. And the only girl. Forever the baby. Forever a standout.

Her brothers were a broadfaced, towheaded bunch so similar looking and so evenly spaced out in age, it was almost as if they were designed that way.

Augusta, whom everyone would call Gussie despite her protestations, was slight, sharp-featured, and dark-haired. Jokes were made about how different her appearance was, though never in polite company and never spoken by sober lips.

If she was only unlike the rest of her family in appearances, she'd be okay with it, but with the years, other differences became glaringly apparent.

The willfulness of her, the indomitable spiritedness. The qualities Doyles might have relished in boys but could not abide in a girl.

She was smart too. Whip-smart. Reading from an early age, voraciously discovering a world beyond the boundaries of their small New England town, and dreaming of it vividly, ambitiously.

From an early age, Augusta questioned everything. It's how she learned that there's nothing so quick to irritate the dull-witted as to challenge the baselessness of their rules and assumptions.

Researching, then proudly mentioning to her family that Doyle is a surname that means dark stranger, a Viking name, used originally to distinguish the darker-haired Danes from the lighter-haired Norwegians, and that she is therefore the only one among them to live up to it, earned her a slap.

Her parents seldom raised a hand to her. Mostly, she thought, due to the fact that they were too busy beating discipline into her brothers. So the slap stung doubly. She never forgot it.

But then she couldn't help herself either. All that lovely knowledge she had acquired by devouring books from the local library tended to spill over.

And no one but Mrs. Dow, the librarian, was ever interested in what she had to say. Their conversations were the highlights of Augusta's life.

The library was on the other side of town, but fortunately, the town was small enough to make the distance walkable.

Her parents wouldn't get her a bike, though the Doyle boys had several that they shared and were forever breaking and fixing up.

Augusta had an old rucksack she inherited from her brother Conor, its straps so worn they threatened to give out every time she loaded it with books from her fresh haul.

"You're going to run out of books to read at the rate you're going," Mrs. Dow teased her.

When she was a child, such a thing was easy to imagine. When all the books in the world amounted to what their small library's shelves could hold.

Once she had asked Mrs. Dow about it, this running-out-of-books scenario. The question elicited a laugh, but a kind one, nothing like the sneering cackles of her brothers.

"Oh dear, you will never"–Mrs. Dow's eyes sparkled behind her large tortoise shell glasses–"ever run out of books to read. This I promise you."

And she was right, of course.

In all the years since, Augusta, and later Ava, had from time to time run out of money, patience, chances, affection, friends, but never, ever books.

They were the one constant, the one reliable thing in life. The abundance of them. The abundance of worlds within them.

School didn't challenge her, so she became restless. She read ahead, asked too many questions. Her teachers, she sensed, did not appreciate this, so eventually, opting for an easier path, one that would not cause the involvement and subsequent ire of her parents, she became pliantly quiet. Did her work. Kept her eyes down, her hand down. Curiosity, it seemed to her, was not a universally appreciated quality. She decided she'd save it for the right company.

One by one her brothers would leave home, striking out on their own to make a life for themselves. They never went far, though, and they never went wild. Their jobs and their lives were steady, stolid, unexciting. One after another they became a version of their father, marrying women eerily resemblant of their mother.

They all drank. Every family get-together had inevitably devolved into a drunken shouting match. Sometimes they fought. Bare-knuckled, outside in any weather, breaths steaming. Alcohol fueling their tempers, and later on, their slurred apologies.

Augusta observed them from a distance, feeling more and more like a stranger in her childhood home, amid her family. She had been reading a new-to-her genre, science fiction. One Mrs. Dow promised had its merits beyond what the lurid technicolor covers had promised.

And so, she let herself fantasize that she was an alien sent to Earth to observe a typical human family. An alien carefully disguised as a person on the outside. The thought comforted her, contextualized her feeling different, separate.

The future, as desperately as Augusta had been wanting to leave her family home, daunted her. No matter how much she read, how much she dreamed, there was something unformed about the years ahead, something unimaginable.

Augusta was never good at making friends, or rather she was, but only for a short while, before realizing they were either not interested enough or interesting enough.

The other girls her age talked about getting married and having babies; both thoughts made her shudder with undisguised disgust.

It was almost as if she could see them then, their life's progressions, as clear as a cinematic time lapse. Their eyes losing shine, becoming dull with duties, their arms heavy with screaming kids, their worlds shrinking down to the size of their houses.

How tragic, she thought. That would never be my life. Still, she couldn't clearly imagine any alternatives.

She talked about it to the only person she could, and Mrs. Dow was shockingly candid in a way that's always thrilling for a kid.

"You're not wrong there." She smiled a sad smile. "The world does shrink."

Mrs. Dow was married–unhappily, it seemed. She shrugged off the question of happiness, saying she was content enough. But then she told Augusta of the dreams she once had: city life, career in publishing. "Imagine that, dear, not merely reading books for a living, but choosing the ones everyone else ought to read," she said wistfully, and for a moment, Augusta thought she could hear the wind whistle through the great divide between the librarian's dreams and her reality.

"What happened?" she asked. "Why didn't you?"

A heavy shrug, eyes lowered. "Got pregnant. Got married. Stayed put. And afterward, it was just too late."

Later in life, Ava came to realize how easy it was to dismiss something as too late to do. And then, remembering Mrs. Dow, she vowed to never use that excuse, no matter how convenient it might be.

But the conversations with Mrs. Dow did help Augusta shape her own dreams. They now came with a map. A compass. A way ahead. A road awaiting.

All she had to do was graduate and get into a good school far enough away.

Her parents wouldn't hear of it. None of the Doyles, they said, went to any fancy school, and none of them was worse for wear.

They said they didn't have the money for it, and Augusta countered by promising to get a scholarship.

They said it was unseemly for a girl to be that far away from her family, and she grinned inwardly.

They said she ought to just get married. That got her hackles up.

Augusta studied their sunbeaten, florid, broad faces and tried to ascribe the word to the feeling they evoked in her. She didn't think it was love.

She didn't know what they saw when they looked at her. A dark stranger? Someone to contend with? An unruly, disobedient child who dared not to want the same things they did?

Either way, they tightened their reins after that. Making the house a prison, strolling it like proud wardens, supervising her every move.

They wouldn't let her leave, it seemed. They'd hold her down, tie her up, if they had to. The thought suffocated her. Their world, the one they had dwelled in for so long, gave no rights, no voice to daughters, to women.

It didn't matter what year it was; the social progress steadily marched right past the Doyles' house. They wanted her married, and they wanted her staying put.

She'd have to improvise. Run away. But penniless? They wouldn't let her get a job, deliberately preventing her from being able to save up.

Eventually, though, it simply got too tiresome to fight against a current that strong. And she started thinking, what if? What if she did get married? Only to get out from under Father Doyle's meaty thumbs. Only for a few years. Only to divorce later, get some money from it, and leave.

If only she could find someone unobjectionable enough. Someone tolerable. Someone decent.

Basically, someone unlike her family.

So far, everyone they'd introduced her to was a version of one Doyle or other. And then she met James.

ꕥ ꕥ ꕥ

Ava St. James shook her head rereading her words. It wasn't enough. So much was omitted. The third-person perspective, which she thought initially would provide just enough distance for objectivity, now seemed too remote. She felt limited by her words. The basic facts were there, but they lacked texture and color and feeling. They didn't show what it felt like growing up a Doyle daughter: the claustrophobic atmosphere of her childhood home, the endless slights and sharp, cutting cruelties of her family.

In modern-day parlance, it would have been considered abuse. After all, it comes in so many shapes, forms, and sizes. And it stays in a myriad of scars invisible to the naked eye.

Should she tell all? Ava had always prided herself on discretion. It was an art polished to perfection by years of necessity and later carried on as an acquired virtue too indistinguishable from one's essential character.

In life as in love, there's always that conflict between wanting to be known and fearfully holding back from revealing yourself.

Without Nina by her side, was it even worth it? Who would care? Her family was as manifold as it was indifferent. All but one, and he already knew most of this.

Still, there was nothing else to do but reminisce, was there? Old age, the subtlest thief of all, had been slowly robbing her of all that mattered.

Ava sighed and picked her pen back up.

3

JEFF

"THIS IS NICE." His cheerfulness is somewhat performative, but he is being sincere. It's difficult to remember the last time they all sat down to eat as a family.

Four different people with different schedules and different appetites. Jenna used to joke it was like herding cats.

Sure, he would have preferred more red meat and less veg, but at least they got the kids to put the phones down, if only for the moment.

The conversation is terse, punctuated by the clanking of silverware on china that Jeff finds grating. It sounds like a symphony of repressed hostility. Or maybe he's exaggerating—he's always been sensitive to sharp sounds.

Yet he feels like he ought to play the patriarch, the man at the head of the table, a TV sitcom character.

"So, anyone got any special plans for this vacation?" he asks.

Jessie sighs and rolls her eyes. It's meant as a joke, but he knows she also means it. Just like he knows she's likely to leave most of the food on her plate after artfully pushing it around for a while. She seems to be picking up the worst of her mother's eating habits.

Shouldn't children, in theory, be the distillation of the best in their parents?

JJ, on the other hand, is shoveling food in like a tractor combine. Jeff studies his son for a moment; the messy hair that's long enough to cover his ears and get in his eyes.

JJ notices the attention and looks up. "I'm gonna swim," he says. "Nothing else here to do."

"Well, that's just not true at all," Jenna chimes in. "I've found all sorts of fun things to do in the area. There are museums and hiking trails and a waterfall only a short drive away. There's a farm that makes its own cider and pies."

"Oh yeah?" Jessie says with vague interest. "Any shopping?"

"Maybe."

"Well, then maybe that's what we can do?"

"Jessie, you can go shopping anywhere. This is our opportunity as a family to do something different, something unique." Jenna seems to be getting exasperated. "Right, Jeff?" she reaches for backup.

"Right," he supplies automatically.

He's thinking how he doesn't want to do any of it; how it all sounds like too much driving and too much walking for insufficient reward. Except maybe for the farm. He could do with a cider and a pie. Then again, he knows he's likely going to be dragged to or guilted into these things anyway, so it's best to just agree. And who knows, maybe family activities will do them good.

"So what's with the house?" JJ says suddenly.

"How do you mean?"

JJ pushes his unruly mop from his eyes. "This place, why is it like this?"

"Like what?"

"So . . . large?"

Jeff has been noticing that kids these days tend to talk in questions, making even simple statements sound uncertain and tentative. He wonders what that means for their development.

"Well, we don't know what was going through the architects' minds when they built it, but I'm sure they had a plan."

"It was probably Aunt Gussie's plan," Jessie says. She's been slowly and methodically masticating the steamed broccoli on her plate.

"That's right," Jenna says.

"She looks like someone who had lots of ideas?" Jessie makes her statement into a question.

"I guess so." Jenna shrugs. "I mean, I really didn't know her."

"It sounds like no one really knew her," Jeff says. "The woman of mystery."

"But she was rich, right, Mom?"

"Yes, Jessie, I think she might have been."

"Well, there's no way I'd build a house this ugly in the middle of nowhere if I were rich."

Jeff smiles. Continues the kindly wise patriarch charade. "You know what they say, beauty's in the eye of the beholder."

"Yeah, but ugly is for everyone to see."

Touché, kiddo, Jeff thinks. He doesn't have it in him to defend the house in all of its design and structural peculiarities. He long ago stopped caring enough to weigh in on issues that do not affect him. All he knows is that the house is larger and more accommodating than any of the hotels they've ever stayed in. And it's free.

Jeff recently missed out on a small promotion and is still stewing over it. Or maybe he's just stewing over missing out on the small raise the promotion came with.

He isn't a particularly ambitious man. Comfortably recognizing his worth and setting up expectations accordingly is how he's gotten through most of his adult life, but losing out to that asshat Richie eats at him. What sort of an adult goes by Richie anyway? An obnoxious, oleaginous scum like his coworker, that's the sort. The man who, well into his thirties, is still stylizing himself like the frat bro he once was—perfectly coiffed hair, strategic stubble, popped polo shirt colors, and leather loafers worn sockless. The man knows how to kiss ass, though, gotta give him credit there, knows how to play the game.

At this rate, eventually, he'll be Jeff's boss, a shudder-inducing thought. Jeff hasn't told Jenna about any of this, doesn't see the point. He might have if he knew her reaction would be sympathy, but he knows it'll be disappointment.

None of them are living their dreams—who is?—so why add one more reminder?

Jeff is content to stew quietly. No, stoically, he corrects himself. Like a man.

Not that he had much of an example of manliness as a kid. His father, a tall, taciturn man he barely recalls, known mostly as the unsmiling presence in the few early family photos, took off when Jeff was eight. His mother didn't remarry until Jeff was in college.

In the intervening years, there was a steely resoluteness about her, like she'd had enough, like she was determined to do it all herself, no men telling her what to do. She worked long late hours, and they wanted for nothing. Jeff had never wondered if she was lonely, because it seemed to him, she was simply too busy for loneliness.

Jeff minded himself, a stereotypical latchkey kid, never feeling particularly neglected, never feeling particularly rebellious. It was, to him, by all accounts a perfectly nice childhood.

Her marriage announcement came as a surprise. He hadn't even known she was seeing someone. The man, Stuart, turned out to be the opposite of his father: a warm, gregarious presence in his mother's life. An accountant with his own small firm. A maker of model planes.

They got along well whenever Jeff came to visit. Enough to make Jeff wonder what his life might have been like had Stuart come along earlier, but what use was thinking that?

The past was set in stone, as was the character it shaped.

Jeff told himself he'd never be like his father; he'd never leave his family. And sure enough, here he was all these years later, a man who stayed put.

"Is there dessert?" JJ asks.

Jessie exhales a derisive ugh his way.

"I ate my dessert earlier," Jeff smiles, patting his paunch. "Angus bakes muffins to die for."

"Angus? Who's Angus?"

"That guy, JJ, you know, the caretaker." The kids just do not pay attention.

"Oh, I thought his name was August?" JJ scratches his head.

"What sort of name is August?" Jessie scowls.

"It's a name."

"No, it is a name. A male version of Augusta," Jeff confirms. "But I'm pretty sure it's not the caretaker's name."

"Whatever." JJ shrugs. "So, are there any of those muffins left?"

"There might be one."

"Shotgun."

"That's only for car rides, you dweeb."

"You're a dweeb."

The conversation deteriorates into an exchange of mild insults between the kids, and Jeff finds it all rather enjoyable: to see his kids behave like kids for once, to know that young people still use words like dweeb.

And all too soon it's over.

"Wanna watch a movie?" Jeff says, eager to stretch out the moment.

"What kind of movie?" Jessie asks.

"A horror movie," JJ screams.

"Ugh, no, no way."

"A comedy?" Jenna suggests.

"Maaaaybe. They're all so stupid lately?"

It shouldn't be a question, but Jeff doesn't disagree. The comedies have gotten progressively unfunnier over the years.

"Maybe action or sci-fi?" he offers.

"Maybe *Game of Thrones?*"

"Definitely not *Game of Thrones.*"

"Boo."

Jeff laughs. "Let's just see what's available."

Eventually, they settle on an eighties classic too fun to object to. Frankly, Jeff's surprised there's even a TV room in the house. It seems at odds with the place somehow. But he's grateful for it.

He chooses not to notice that the kids have whipped their phones back out and are using them more and more as the movie progresses, small glowing screens distracting from the large one.

He chooses not to notice that Jenna sat on the opposite end of the couch from him, sticking him with her pointy, never-warm feet, not her head on his shoulder like back in the good old days.

He chooses to squint at the scene just enough to find a nostalgic idyllic appeal in it and then, contented, dozes off.

JENNA

LYING IN BED at night, awake, unable to fall asleep, while the person next to you is easily and effortlessly dreaming away has got to be the loneliest feeling in the world. Jenna hates it. Hates the thoughts that come to her at night. The way every tiny thing gets magnified. The way every noise amplifies into creeping significance.

They had a long drive and a surprisingly nice family evening. She ought to be tired. And she is, in a way, but it just will not translate into sleepiness.

Maybe if they had sex . . .

She idly contemplates initiating something, but it feels like too much effort for an uncertain reward, and Jeff seems too deeply asleep.

Jenna regards his prostrate form; the facedown position tends to make him snore. Over the years, she perfected the technique of shoving him just so to make him stop. Her husband doesn't have a preferred sleep position; he passes out whichever way his head hits the pillow first. A skill. A talent.

In the city, there's always enough ambient light streaming into their bedroom to see by. Out here, it's country dark. Jeff could, technically, be anybody and she wouldn't know. Just a heavy amorphous shape depressing the right side of the bed.

But then he turns and lets out that half-snort/half-snore thing he does, the one she used to find cute once upon a time, and he's Jeff once again.

And Jenna is still very much herself. It is way too early for the vacation to weave its transformative magic upon her. Or maybe that only happens in books.

Could she really eat, pray, and love her way through the next month and, come September, be reborn as a kinder, softer, happier version of herself?

Is it wrong to feel unsatisfied when she has so much?

Jenna closes her eyes and repeats her yoga instructor's mantras. Or are they the sayings on the tiny paper bits attached to Yogi teas? It all sounds the same in the dark—inane.

Aspirational, inspirational. You are the light. The world delights in you. That sort of thing.

She often wonders how much the others in her yoga classes and in her meditation group buy into all of it. On the surface, she's all about it, 100 percent gung-ho enthusiasm. But then classes end, participants disperse, and it's just her again, with her thoughts, her doubts.

For her family, she tries to be her sunniest self. But they don't make it easy. Somewhere between being a wife and a mother, she is losing being a woman, being a person.

Or maybe that's just the night talking.

Jenna tries to think of practical things: where they can go, what she can cook. Her mind turns to Aunt Gussie. What did she do around here for fun? Did she have fun?

It's difficult to think of one's own parents as bad people and only slightly easier to do so when it comes to extended families, and yet there's something categorically bad about the way the family treated Gussie.

It wasn't just their disapproval of her—in some respects, their values are old-fashioned enough for the Pope to condemn; disapproving is a Doyle's favorite pastime—it was the way they went about it. The shunning, the stonewalling, the silence. And then the hypocritical ease of using Gussie's money and house.

Sometimes Jenna can see why Jeff doesn't care for the Doyles. Of course, whenever he says something critical, she instinctively, knee-jerkingly rushes to their defense. "They are family," she says. "We are family," Jeff counters. "It's different," she states and shrugs helplessly, which usually ends the conversation.

Jeff barely has a family to speak of; he doesn't get it. It's easy for him.

Jenna was raised with a staunch "blood is thicker than water" mentality she can never just shrug off. Though Aunt Gussie must have had pure water in her veins.

Why the mystery, though? The Doyles are usually quite fond of parading around someone's shortcomings, if only to lambast them or make fun of them; in fact, that's pretty much the majority of their family get-togethers. The faults get more attention than accomplishments, every time.

And yet, every time come holidays, birthdays, or anniversaries, Jenna drags Jeff and the kids through it. The Doyle show, as Jeff puts it.

The Doyle show has been getting darker lately: adultery, divorces, even suicide attempts. Sometimes, it seems to her that whatever crazy glue held them together all these decades might be finally drying out and letting go. Or maybe they were always sinners, and it's only the tongues that are getting looser and waggier these days.

Either way, Jenna prides herself on having nothing to report, nothing to offer up for slaughter. She keeps her cards close to the vest or whatever the expression is, tries to stay out of the gossip grapevine. It's one of the reasons she waited this long to even use her vacation time at Gussie's—that strategic arm's length of distance.

If these walls could talk, she thinks, what tales would they spin? Which Doyle indiscretions would they speak of?

Jenna stops herself. Thoughts of her family have never been conducive to restful sleep. She knows she should get up and busy herself in some way. That's what all the insomnia experts say. Not that she's an insomniac.

But she feels lazy, heavy-limbed; the way her weighted blanket at home makes her feel. And she doesn't relish skulking around a large unknown house in the middle of the night.

What if there are ghosts? The Doyles, notoriously unadventurous in their convictions, almost uniformly believe in ghosts. Every other one of them, it seems, has had some encounter they couldn't explain or felt some presence. It's another thing her pragmatic husband enjoys making fun of.

Jenna has never seen or felt a ghost, but she likes to keep an open mind. If there was ever a place suitable for such an encounter, it's here. And so, she stays put.

Counting sheep. Just counting. Trying and failing to meditate to the choppy sounds of Jeff's snores. Eventually, sleep takes pity on her.

JJ

THERE ARE FEW things more peaceful than floating in the water. JJ hates walking the path to the lake—the way the brambles or whatever the crap they are tear at his ankles, the creepy familiarity with which the low branches brush up against his calves, especially the part where the tall trees meet each other above his head to obscure the sun so that he always, if only momentarily, feels lost—but once he gets into the water, all is forgiven.

It's quiet enough that he doesn't need his headphones, light enough so that he doesn't feel his heaviness. He swims. Sure, even races when his father insists. But ultimately, all he wants to do is float. He's been at it for a week now, and it hasn't gotten old yet.

Jessie and Jenna seldom go in the water, preferring to sunbathe on the shore. He doesn't get it. Considering how diligently they slather on sunscreen every two hours on the dot—how could the sun possibly get through? He thinks Jenna dislikes the lake, and Jessie, consciously or otherwise, is echoing the sentiment.

JJ doesn't see what there is to dislike. Sure, the lake floor is muddy and can suck at your feet in a weird quicksand-y way, but otherwise, it's perfectly nice. And the best part is that there's no one around. It's like this place is private or something. JJ didn't know people had private lakes, but maybe Aunt Gussie did.

It's even better than the beach. No one to gawk at him, to judge him. One day he forgets himself and removes his swim T-shirt, but then Jessie lets out something like a half-suppressed yet distinctly disgusted snort, and he ends up pulling it back on.

Sorry, Jessie, not everyone can be a freaking stick, he thinks bitterly. But then again, maybe not for long. JJ has noticed some of his stash going missing.

It isn't Jeff or Jenna, he knows. If those two found the stash, they'd probably end up confiscating it altogether and throwing a well-meaning, tedious lecture in for good measure.

No, this is some strategically clandestine pilfering; one or two candy bars at a time. Easily enough overlooked if he hadn't been keeping score.

JJ is waiting for the right moment to confront his sister. Trying to think of what advantage such confrontation might gain him.

For now, to make himself feel better about his dwindling stock, he stole a necklace of Jessie's. It didn't look particularly valuable, but it's the principle of the matter that counts.

He thinks about it with a self-satisfied smile when Jeff floats up to him.

"Whatcha daydreaming about, kiddo?"

"Nothing anymore." JJ shakes his head and dives under. When he resurfaces, Jeff is still there.

"Wanna race?"

"Nah, I'm pretty beat, kinda just wanna float."

"Swimming's a great exercise, you know."

Not very subtle. So that's what all this racing was about.

Jeff has been exercising him, the way the gym teacher does at school. Screw that. And screw Jeff for his sanctimony. He's not exactly skinny either.

"I mean, for me, you know. Gotta shape up this dad bod." Jeff playfully slaps at his paunch but it's too late. The damage has been done.

"So go race Mom."

"Your mother is convinced there's a lake monster living here."

JJ snorts. "She is not."

Jeff joins in with his weird honking laugh. "She might as well be for how much she's avoiding the water."

"Maybe she just doesn't like swimming?"

"Well, she isn't as good of a swimmer as us." Jeff winks. "And she can't float at all."

"Floating is the best," JJ declares.

It occurs to him that Jenna probably can't float because she's so freaking skinny—no natural buoyancy there.

He doesn't share the thought with his father, waiting for the man to get bored with the conversation and drift away, but Jeff seems determined. Like he's got this idea of how a dad on vacation is supposed to act. Cringe.

"So, are you having a good vacation so far?"

JJ shrugs. "S'all right."

"Ah, the enthusiasm. Be still, my heart. Anything you wanna be doing more of? Wanna drive out, find civilization, grab tacos, catch a movie?"

The answer to that would normally be a resounding yes, but JJ is feeling lazy. Something about the house makes him feel heavy. Heavier than normal. Like he's being weighed down. The feeling isn't uncomfortable, just the opposite, in fact, but it makes him want to do as little as possible and mostly just be by himself.

Jenna's really been laying into shared meals, and Jeff's been pushing movie or game nights afterward. JJ doesn't care for any of it. He misses the city, the way everyone tended to leave him alone.

He knows he smells better now, owing to spending so much time in water every day, but surely, deep down, his family is as disgusted by him as ever. They are just hiding it better for the sake of this precious vacation. Like these few weeks are going to make them into different people.

So, no, JJ doesn't want to go on a fun outing with Jeff, because he can just see it turning into some weird bonding experience he didn't sign up for. Just be your normal self, JJ tries to telegraph to his father. Just go read your book or something and gently ignore me.

Out loud JJ says, "Maybe some other time." A diplomatic answer if ever there was one.

"Well, lemme know if you change your mind."

"Sure."

JJ is levels and levels away from beating his latest game. His mind will not be changed, it'll be occupied trying to figure out the most efficient way to shoot his path to victory.

JJ would never want to be in a war. The real thing seems terrifying to him. Virtual simulations of it, on the other hand, he can't seem to get enough of.

He waits for Jeff to get the message and drift off. The sun beats down on them like it missed them. The house is always some shade of gloomy, the sunlight doesn't seem to penetrate the windows no matter how large they are. Must be all the trees around it. When JJ is inside, it's easy to forget it's August outside. Even near the house, even walking here, there are still only patches of summer warmth and brightness. Only here, in the lake, is he hit with its full force.

His pasty skin doesn't tan, though it does occasionally burn bright angry red when he forgets to use sunscreen.

JJ dunks down once more, stays under as long as he can, then heaves up bucking. Brushes his wet mop off his face.

Jeff is still there. Fu . . .

"Ah, there you are. I was forgetting what you look like under all that hair."

Not like you and not like Mom, JJ wants to say. Neither Doyle-blond nor even light brown, his shaggy mop has a curl to it unlike his parents' perfectly straight hair. He certainly isn't built like either of them.

JJ has seen pictures of his father as a young man—he was pretty good-looking. JJ wouldn't mind looking like that eventually, whenever puberty gets done with him. Hell, he'd settle for just being taller. Fat and short is too tragic of a combo.

"Oh yeah, so what do I look like?" JJ prods and hates himself for asking.

"Like a handsome kid. Like your dad."

Liar, liar, Jeff. Your pants would catch on fire if they weren't in the water. Then again, what did he expect his father to say?

"What'd you think of that movie last night?" Jeff changes the subject.

"I thought it sucked. Why can't we watch a scary movie or something good?"

"Because your sister and your mother would have nightmares for weeks and blame us."

"Might be worth it." JJ shrugs.

"Ha. Wait till you're married and a dad."

"No thanks."

Jeff laughs like JJ said something funny. Like having a wife and kids is one of life's inevitabilities on par with paying taxes and getting old.

"Well, if you won't race me, I'm getting out. Before I turn into Aquaman."

Lame dad jokes. JJ rolls his eyes but offers an obligatory chuckle. He recognizes Jeff is making an effort and feels compelled to reward it in some small way. Personally, he's content to stay in the water until he prunes, raisins, and disappears into one shrunken wrinkle.

JJ closes his eyes against the beating-down sun, spreads out his limbs like a starfish, and floats.

JESSIE

WHAT'S THE USE of starving yourself, of beautifying yourself, if no one is there to appreciate it? It's like one of those if-a-tree-falls-in-the-woods conundrums. Frustrating. Maddening.

Here she is, technically at a beach, in her best bikini. Or second best, since she never found the sequined one. To be fair, her closet is a mess. Too much clothing, not enough space. Whenever she mentions to her parents that she could use another, they suggest she downsize, so she no longer brings it up. When it comes to clothes her motto is "better to have and not need." She's got clothes for every occasion, even ones that exist only in her imagination.

Sometimes, she also buys things she'd seen Ainsley Grant wear, if only to have something in common, something shared. Jessie doesn't wear those clothes to school, doesn't want to take the risk of matching, but she brought them on this vacation since there's no one here to see her. But that's the problem, isn't it—there's no one here to see her. She feels invisible. The way social media makes her feel. Jessie hates that feeling. She wants eyes on her, a lot of them, and likes, and attention. It's pathetic just how much she wants it.

She can get that in the city. It's easy. Just put on something skimpy enough, walk around, and as sure as the sky's blue, someone's going to whistle or comment. Usually some gross older dude, but still, it's a notice.

Out here, no matter what she puts on, no matter how expertly she does her face and hair, the best she can hope for is a clumsy compliment from her parents, which is just . . . ugh.

They are probably just happy she isn't as gross as JJ. That she at least looks like them. Well, like her mom, anyway.

Jenna offered to work out together in the mornings, and Jessie tried, but it's freaking exhausting. No wonder her mom's in such awesome shape. Jessie felt like passing out before the thirty-minute workout was even over. No thank you, was her takeaway from the experience. She'd stick to her own methods.

Except that she thinks she might be failing. And weirdly enough, she isn't sure.

A few mornings in the past week, she woke up holding a candy bar wrapper, the sinfully delicious taste of chocolate and caramel lingering in her mouth, mixing with morning breath's sourness. She doesn't know what happened and can't figure out how or whom to ask.

But it's disgusting. She's disgusted with herself, with her lack of self-control. Sure, she forced herself to throw up first thing in the morning like she's preggers or something, but still . . .

How could it have happened even? She knows her mother doesn't keep things like that in the house. The only person who does is JJ, and he'd never share.

That means she snuck into his room, found his stash, and stole from him? And then ate it?

Except that she has no recollection of any of it. Zero, zilch. Nada. All she remembers is going to sleep and waking up.

Jessie's heard about sleepwalking but only abstractly, only on TV. It seems to her like one of those weird things that only happens to other people. Like ghostly encounters. The Doyles certainly never shut up about that.

But Jessie has never seen a ghost and has never sleepwalked.

She does research on her phone, cursing the spotty reception, and as it turns out, sleepwalking is more common than she thinks. And people indeed do all sorts of weird things while asleep, including eating.

Well, crap. Now what?

She isn't about to let all that perfect daytime control be discounted by nighttime slip-ups. Just going to have to figure something out. She'll tie herself to the bed if she has to.

Jessie has been going to bed hungry for a long time now; rising hungry too. It's all part of the deal. Size zero doesn't just happen. Well, maybe to some, but Jessie suspects they are lying.

Curiously, for the few moments before horror and shame set in and lead up to a vomiting session, these mornings are pure bliss. The first ones in a long time where she woke up sated. No growling stomach. Nothing. It's almost kind of nice . . . except that, of course, it's terrible.

She's surprised JJ hasn't said anything. Should she be grateful? There's not much about their relationship that would suggest discretion, but stranger things . . . Unless he just hadn't noticed. The kid might have a stash the size of Donald Duck's treasure trove of gold, so what's a few candy bars? Or wait, she thinks. Was that Uncle Scrooge McDuck?

It makes her sad that she can't remember. She used to love those goofy cartoons as a kid. She recalls the funny duck diving and swimming around in his money room full of gold, but which one was it?

Anyway, Jessie isn't ready to tie herself to the bed quite yet. She'll just police stricter what she eats throughout the day and hope the calories balance out.

At any rate, she still looks great in her swimsuit. She hopes all the freaking trees appreciate it since there's no one else around.

She doesn't really like swimming. Something seems unclean to her about lake water, the way it just sits there without moving like a river or an ocean might. Gross.

Her mom's the same way, so the two of them spend most of their time on the shore.

"Sunscreen time." Jenna is clockwork-punctual about this. "It's been two hours."

They re-lather with 70 percent SPF, getting each other's backs until they are slick and UV-protected.

Her mom waves her fingers in the air. "Don't want to get my book greasy," she explains. Each time.

Jessie's mom is always reading, and all her books look the same. The same distressed-looking woman half-turned away on the cover. The same kind of titles featuring words like Her, She, Mother, Daughter, Wife. Something vapid and dramatic. Jessie would bet all the plots are similar too.

What's so special about reading then? Jessie wonders.

At least, the contents of her feed are always changing. At least, those are real people. Real women.

Jessie is a feminist. She proudly describes herself as one and supports those who do the same. Anything from glittery girl-power manicures to inspirational *And Nevertheless, She Persisted* tote bags.

If she had to give a succinct definition of feminism, she'd probably fumble it, but no one ever asks. These days, it seems, it's enough to say you're something, and others will respect it. Or crap on it. Such are the joys of social media. But being a feminist is easier than other things, like being a vegan—that only lasted about two months. Sure, eating animals is wrong, but it's too hard to think about constantly avoiding doing so.

Jessie likes animals. A lot. She used to want one, a cat or a dog, but someone—she's never quite sure if it's her dad or her mom or JJ—is allegedly allergic, so that's that. Deep down, she suspects it's just something her parents said to avoid having to deal with a pet.

It isn't fair.

Ainsley has a dog. The cutest looking thing. Jessie has seen it on her Insta feed. They wear matching outfits. Which is cringe, but also adorable.

If Jessie had a dog too, they could have playdates. Did people do that for pets?

"What are you thinking about?" her mom asks.

Like I'd tell you, Jessie wants to reply. "Nothing much."

"Are you enjoying your vacation so far?"

"It's fine."

"Fine," her mother repeats and scoffs. "Not many people get to spend a month-long vacation in a private lake house, you know."

"It's private, all right," Jessie mumbles.

"Oh." Jenna screws up her pointy features into that understanding-mom-from-TV face. "Are you missing your friends? Do you wish there were some kids your age around?"

Jessie shrugs.

She's watching her brother float in the water like a pale aquatic mammal. Actually, the mammal would have to be albino or dead to be that color. JJ is printer-paper white everywhere but his face, where the whiteness is angrily punctuated by acne.

Her dad, on the other hand, seems to be getting a tan. The two of them float together for a while looking nothing alike, talking about who knows what. Male bonding? Something lame like that? They look content enough.

Jessie wonders how they can stand the water. It's too green, too murky for her liking, the creepiness of the mossy bottom beneath their toes.

"Look, I know spending time with your family can be a drag. Believe me, I know. But you got your entire life ahead of you to hang out with people your own age. One day, you'll look back on this with fondness, you'll see."

And one day you'll be old and saggy and no amount of working out will save you, Jessie thinks with unexpected venom. She covers it up with, "It's really fine, Mom. Just, you know, there's nothing to do."

"We can drive into town sometime?"

Jessie doesn't care to visit some stupid hick town. There'd be nothing to do there either.

"No, it's okay."

"I'd be happy to lend you one of my books?"

"Moooom."

"Look, I know, I know, but this one is really fun."

"Oh yeah? How so?"

"This woman thinks she married her Prince Charming and then, five years later, she finds out he's actually killed someone in his past. His ex-wife. And his ex-wife's sister has been looking for him to avenge . . ."

"Moooom."

"What?"

"That sounds just like the last book you tried to get me to read."

"It does not."

"It totally does." Jessie rolls her eyes. Her mom can be so clueless sometimes. "And anyway. You're going to spend like, what, six or seven or eight hours reading this book? And then you'll read another one? And it'll be just the same?"

"There are differences," her mom insists.

"But, like, it's always the husband, right? I mean, always."

"Not always."

"Name one where it wasn't."

Jenna pauses. "Sometimes it's the wife?" she says with a smirk.

"Ugh."

Jessie lies back down on her towel. She runs her hands over her sides, enjoying the way her hip bones stick out.

"You're so skinny, honey," her mom says, and she can't tell if that's concern or approval in her voice. She opts for the latter.

It's something. It's better than nothing.

She closes her eyes behind her oversized designer-knockoff shades and wishes there was someone around to talk to, someone other than family. The only person she knows of who lives nearby is that caretaker, whatever his name is.

Guys his age are usually creeps, but still, she'd talk to him. If only to find out more about the mysterious Aunt Gussie. Her mom doesn't seem to know crap. But somebody must.

Jessie has spent her entire life with the privilege of internet access and can't imagine a properly unGoogleable mystery.

She tried looking up Gussie Doyle, of course, but nothing relevant came up. Just a bunch of strangers who had nothing to do with the woman in the portrait. But she's determined to figure it out. After all, there's nothing else to do and no end in sight for this vacation.

AVA

~~~

MRS. ST. JAMES

He wasn't like any man she'd ever met. In fact, James Sullivan was by far the nicest man she'd ever encountered. The mildest too.

She had become accustomed to a certain brand of brute overt masculinity, the Doyle brand, and James was nothing like it. He was gentle, kind, quiet. There was a pronounced dreamy aspect about him. She saw it in his turn of phrase, in a faraway look in his eyes, that longing for a different, better world. Augusta recognized it like blood, like her own scent.

A kindred spirit. In a world so short on them.

He worked with Tommy, at the same factory, only her brother did the grunt work, and James managed the books. A sturdy, solid job and an Irish last name were enough for the Doyles.

Introductions were made, and courtship ensued.

It wasn't anything special—the movies, the walks, the restaurants—but it was enough. Shooting for the moon will leave you empty-handed and frustrated. Augusta's sights were set much, much lower, and on her checklist, James scored every mark.
~~~

There was no talk of love. But they spoke of books, and a shared passion was almost as good. Or so she told herself, too young to know better, and too desperate to get out from under her parents' oppressive thumb to care.

They were wed in a Catholic church. She wore a stiff white dress, and James looked boyishly handsome in his dark suit. Augusta remembered thinking how unfair it was that he got to wear something so comfortable, so versatile, so multiuse, and she was stuck in the lacy monstrosity she couldn't wait to relegate to the depths of her closet and never touch again.

She wondered what it would be like to wear a suit, admired the slickness of its lines, the purposefulness of its design. The ceremony itself was largely unremarkable. Their kiss tentative and chaste.

James was an orphan, but Augusta's family was more than enough for both of them at the after-party. True to fashion, the Doyles got drunk and rowdy. The rest didn't matter; the rest was forgotten.

The next clear memory was the honeymoon. A small bed-and-breakfast in Maine, right on the coast.

The ironed perfection of James' pajamas against the rumpled bedspread. The salty breeze coming through the open windows.

The tender way he kissed her forehead, almost like a loving parent might. The questions in his eyes: Did she want to? Was she ready?

She didn't know the answer to either. And so, he didn't press. It felt surprisingly natural at the time. After all, there were many ways to be intimate. Many different kinds of intimacy.

He was handsome, her James. Ocean-blue eyes and strawberry-blond hair. Handsome didn't quite cut it even, he was almost . . . pretty. Prettier than her, at any rate, she thought.

His body was lithe and fit, so unlike the crude, broad axe-hewn men in her family. In the morning, he'd do sit-ups and push-ups until sweat glistened on his hairless torso and caught the light like rain droplets.

She found it curious that she could admire him so without desiring him.

Something must be wrong with the way she was wired, she thought. But who could she ask?

And they were happy, weren't they? On their honeymoon and after. James's house was comfortable and plenty big for both of them. And he was funny, charming, and asked nothing of her. Only company, only friendship, it seemed.

She came along to his work events, wearing the fashionable dresses he bought her, feeling slightly out of place. Forever fending off the tactless inquiries about when they might begin having babies.

"When will you start a family?" they'd ask, with a prurient glisten in their eyes.

"We're already a family," she wished to answer, but, of course, didn't. Smile and prevaricate was the name of the game. James with his quick wit and sharp sense of humor could always joke things away, so Augusta just let it roll off her skin.

At home, they'd roll their eyes at those people, watch some comedy on TV, and laugh, until all was forgotten.

If she wasn't happy then, she decided it was close enough. She missed James when he went on his business trips. She hadn't realized that accountants had to make so many business trips.

He always brought her presents. Small silly things to make her smile. Things from the city that made her remember the world is larger than their small town.

He really was perfect. As a private joke, Augusta had begun to think of him as Saint James.

Meanwhile, she was left with too much time on her hands to figure out her life. What did she want to do? James promised to be supportive no matter what she decided.

Eventually, after much consideration, she chose to stick to her original plans and go to college.

Her family was appalled by her decision, fully expecting her to stay put and start popping out babies, like a proper Doyle. But then again, she was a Sullivan now. Blueprint-free and ready to be her own person.

She was accepted at a small school within driving distance, closer to the city. For her major, she chose Literature, though more so to have something to declare. Art History was looking more and more tempting.

It was strange to be among so many of her contemporaries, so many women. For the longest time, Augusta's life revolved around older men.

Even James was a good decade her senior. Though it never mattered outside of being an inside joke between them.

Now she was the older one among her classmates, though not by a lot. The married woman. How strange it seemed, this new world of knowledge and opinions and seemingly endless possibilities.

James approved, gladly, readily. Happy for her to have a passion to pursue, happy for their conversations to be taking on new depths and dimensions.

He started inviting her along on his city trips, now and again. Museums, theater, it was like having windows of her world unbricked one by one, revealing their stunning vistas.

"I knew I recognized a budding cosmopolitan when I met you," he'd joke.

They even talked about moving to the city eventually. Augusta had begun to dream in street cafes and subway stops.

In school, she had started to make friends, reluctantly and tentatively. People from places she'd never been. Her world was expanding one person at a time, though she was still too shy, too reticent to approach someone just to chat.

That was okay because Leilani talked to her first. Sun-kissed, that's how Augusta thought of the pretty Hawaiian girl before they had ever met properly, when she was only a lovely vision in the classroom. It was such a pretty name, though everyone was always abbreviating it to Lani.

They shared an art class.

As fascinated as Augusta was by art, she was terrible at it. Forever embarrassed by her sketches, especially in live drawing classes.

Leilani, on the other hand, was as natural of a talent as Augusta had ever seen.

Whenever she sat next to her, Augusta felt doubly ashamed by the inadequacy of the lines on her paper. Though, to her credit, the other girl never laughed. Never even looked, really, so lost was she in a world of her own when she drew.

Or maybe she did look, and Augusta just never noticed.

For one time, Leilani offered her help with a particularly tricky bit of shading. The next, a different, better pencil. And so, their friendship began. Outside of the classroom, Leilani was outgoing, almost boisterous. Funny, fun, and so very lively.

"Lani's fine, really," she said when Augusta asked her about the diminutive, having always been so touchy about her own. "In my language, it means Heaven."

"Haven?"

"Heaven." Leilani pointed up and winked. "Can't go wrong with that."

She missed her home, missed the sunshine and the ocean. Augusta could scarcely imagine ever belonging to a place that would evoke such strong emotions.

Lani was here because her parents got divorced, and she went to live with her mother. Visiting her father became a holiday treat, one she looked forward to for months in advance.

Augusta avoided talking about her family whenever possible, sheepishly confessing to being embarrassed about her art instead.

Lani shook it off. "Do you know why you can't draw people?"

"Why?"

"Because you're not comfortable with nudity."

"I am too. Sure I am."

"No, you're not." Lani laughed and threw a lollipop stick at her. "You're so perfectly puritanic in your sensibilities that I always forget you're married."

Augusta blushed having no answer. Was she a Puritan? She liked to think of herself as open-minded.

"Well, what do you suggest for this poor Puritan?" She smiled gamely.

Lani's suggestion was a private live drawing class. Augusta didn't quite realize what she had in mind, until her friend invited her over, locked the door, and took off her clothes.

"Draw," she said, handing Augusta paper and pencils.

Drawing was the furthest thing from her mind just then, but she took both obediently and sat down on the chair. Across the room, Leilani reclined on the bed with the lazy grace of an Ancient Roman.

Augusta tried to concentrate on what she was doing, but her pencil wouldn't obey. Her hands shook.

Her face, for how it felt, had to be on fire.

And there was that deafening jackhammering of her heart. Could Lani hear it?

Until now, Augusta's ideals of a female body came from museum statues. In flesh, it was so much . . . hot, hotter, and hotter, the room had to be boiling. Was she staring? Could she help it?

How does one separate that from merely studying the subject?

And if it was staring, the subject did not seem to object. At one point, she even winked.

"How's it going?"

"Terribly." Augusta frowned. "Can't seem to do the model justice."

"Let me see."

Lani leaned over, as comfortable in her nudity as Augusta had ever been clothed, and pulled at the drawing pad. Augusta pulled back, reflexively, and the brief ensuing playful tug-of-war landed Lani in her lap.

"Ha." She laughed. "I'm going to get charcoal marks on my butt."

Augusta was suddenly afraid to speak. Afraid to move. To do anything to chase away this moment.

She looked up, and Lani was so close, Lani was all she could see.

I'm staring now, Augusta thought, staring, sta . . .

Lani kissed her. A gentle pressure of a mouth, a slight insistence, a tentative flick of a tongue. And suddenly the unimaginable was undeniable. She would do anything, anything at all, to never leave this moment.

Lani pulled back and looked her in the eyes. Is this okay, she seemed to be asking.

A loud resounding yes, Augusta wanted to scream it, but in the end, couldn't even whisper it. Instead, she wrapped her arms around Lani, pulling her close into another kiss.

If she could stay like that forever, she would, she thought. And then, all thoughts left, and a sheer somatic pleasure flooded her body instead.

༄ ༄ ༄

Ava put the pen down, massaging her tired hand. The recollection had left her undone. Some of them still have that potency, after all these years.

Life, after all, offered up so few perfect moments and no trick for how to prolong or revisit them. No time machine. Only inadequate, fraught, forever failing memory.

When she looked down, she saw old lady hands—veiny, fragile, slightly bent with arthritis. But when she closed her eyes, she was young again, her hands as supple and strong as the rest of her body exploring another perfect body.

That was her, a lifetime ago. It seemed like only yesterday. Such a bittersweet comfort.

It had happened, and it would never happen again. They say that time is an illusion. If so, it is the cruelest trick of all.

By the time you are old enough to appreciate it all, you're too old to enjoy it.

But at least she had her memories, no matter how gossamer-thin their threads were worn. All those perfect moments. Back then with Lani.

And in the years to come.

Then decades of them with Nina.

She wished she could assemble them all into a cohesive narrative, then lose herself inside it. Being stuck here, on the outside looking in, had embittered her, hardened her.

There didn't seem to be a way to select her memories. To ensure that the good overpowered the bad. To keep the ugliness out of it, to not let it steer the plot.

When that happened, Ava felt like she'd lost pieces of herself, of her soul, but she couldn't stop it. The past rushed in at her unedited, uneditable, and broke her heart every time.

MRS. ST. JAMES (PART TWO)

Outside, in the world, there was talk of changing times. The swinging sixties. With a promise of handing over the reins to an even wilder, freer decade. And yet, for all that, secrets still had to be kept. So much of it was just talk. Sexual revolution. Defying the conventions. It all seemed impossibly far away. Ideas have the ability to outpace the society they spring from. Strange but true.

For now, to anyone looking, to anyone asking, Augusta and Lani were just friends. What they did behind closed doors was nobody's business but their own.

"You taste like the ocean."

"You've never tasted the ocean."

"I can imagine."

"Ha, impossible."

There was no such thing as impossible when you're young and in love.

Augusta lived for what they did behind closed doors.

It gave her life a singular focus, reducing all else in scope and meaning. There was no context for the feelings, the sensations, the connection the two of them shared. Well, for her anyway. For Lani, this wasn't new, though Augusta wished to hear nothing of her love's past romances.

Every time we meet someone new, we start anew, don't we, she'd rationalize. After all, her life had been jump-started by her marriage to James. And now this . . .

Was it always like that? Would it always be? A series of starts. A jerking procession of progress. She'd speculate about it, idling in bed, twisted limbs amid twisted sheets, forgetting the world, refusing to get up and seize the day, for how could it possibly compare with the delicious conquests of the night before?

Lani mellowed her out the way the sun's warmth might. In her presence, Augusta felt an unparalleled relaxation. Even with James, there had always been other things to do, futures to consider, but here, in a small, cheaply furnished room adorned with Leilani's art, there seemed to be nothing but the marvelous now. If James had noticed the change in her, he didn't say. Or rather he did in his own way, telling her he was happy she was happy and leaving it at that. They were forever skirting on the edge of each other's lives, tactfully, caringly, delicately.

What Lani and Augusta shared was so different, so interwoven, until you couldn't tell when one ended and the other began.

Nothing that perfect was ever meant to last. But still, the abruptness with which it ended, the swiftness of the proverbial rug pulled from under them, stole her breath away.

They were seen. The rumor mill churned. That was all it took.

All those months of careful tiptoeing around for nothing.

Expulsions followed.

It was all so quiet, so quick, such a hush-hush tsk-tsk sweep-it-under-the-rug job. And all those supposed progressives as wicked as Salem's accusers, with their pointy fingers and dyed-in-wool morals.

"It's a sign," Lani said the last time they saw each other. The next thing she knew, Lani was back in Hawaii. Postcards with impossible-looking waves followed for a few months then stopped.

It made sense. Someone like Lani wouldn't take too long to find happiness again. Wouldn't dwell in her sadness the way Augusta did.

Bereft is how she felt. And then, once the rumors reached the Doyles, mortified. James didn't seem like a substantial enough protection from her family. And so, to mitigate the damage, he provided the next best thing–distance. He found a job in the city and rented them an apartment downtown.

Only there, amid the noise and mad sleepless energy of the city, did Augusta's broken heart begin to heal.

They didn't talk about her aborted attempt at a college education. James had casually mentioned he was open to whatever she decided on, would support her if she chose to get back to her studies, try a different school, but something had shifted in her priorities. A subtle but permanent rift between the world imagined and real. Maybe the real world was the one she ought to concentrate on now, Augusta thought. Maybe she ought to get a job.

Eventually, she did. A lowly but pleasant enough desk position in a small publishing house. Her duties were small and simple, but she buoyed her spirits with stories of people starting at the bottom and working their way up.

They were busy people then, the Sullivans. Work, social obligations. Small, meaningless acquaintanceships that could, in the right light, pass for friendships.

The city offered so much so vividly, it tended to overwhelm her. She'd go to a park and even those were huge, imposing, like some impossible urban jungles thrown in to break up the monotony of stone and metal and glass.

There was a restlessness of spirit within her. One she was hardly aware of until James pointed it out to her.

"Oh, I'm all right," she'd say, smiling, waving him off. "I'm all right," she'd say, waiting to believe that.

For her next birthday, James took her to a club that changed her life once again.

❧❧❧

Ava put down the pen once more, noting the change of light outside. She took off her glasses. The text before her turned into an unreadable blur, words lost all shape and meaning. Must be a metaphor there somewhere, she thought.

Sometimes a blurry world is easier to take. The way it softens around the edges can almost pass for kindness.

Now *there's* an underrated quality. Young people seldom mention it as something they desire in a partner. Or in life. Had she given it much thought in her early years? Later, she'd come to value it above rubies.

Even when money stopped being an object of concern, when virtues became commodities one could buy and sell, she still craved it. The sudden warmth of unsolicited kindness—the rarest gift of all. Save for love.

James, Saint James, had always been unfailingly kind.

4

JEFF

THE SUREST, TRUEST way to judge people is by the contents of their bookshelves. Jeff had always believed it to be an unequivocal fact. These days, with the proliferation of e-reading, it's less of a certainty. But this house proudly rejects all that sort of modern nonsense. In Haven's library, the books are made of paper, ink, glue. Jeff, who never quite took to Kindles though he owns one, can appreciate the place.

What he can't do is judge Gussie by its contents.

The book collection here is an uncurated mess with nothing resembling order. At home, Jeff alphabetizes his books by the author's last name, while his wife seems to arrange hers by size and color.

If the Doyles were readers, Jeff would imagine this place as a repository for everyone's tastes; family members leaving books for each other the way people do in hostels. Since that isn't the case, all he can think of is that Gussie simply didn't want to be known by her books, and thus she took the kitchen sink approach to stacking her library, focusing on no particular genre or authors.

The library is connected to the parlor by a pair of large glass doors kept open, so that even as Jeff peruses the selections, he can still look up and lock eyes with Gussie. Well, her portrait, anyway. But it's so vivid. He feels Gussie's gaze following his progress from shelf to shelf until he settles on another biography and drags the hardcover with him to the chesterfield sofa.

Nero was a piece of work. A debauched tyrant who taxed his nation to sponsor his artistic pursuits. No one had good things to say about Nero; historians like Tacitus and Suetonius decried his compulsiveness and brutality. The Roman Empire declared him a public enemy. His personal life was a nightmare; the women in his life, be it mother or wife, had the brief, murder-bound life expectancy of the *Game of Thrones* side characters. And then there was the fire. Rome burned on Nero's watch, and he managed to blame it on the Christians, giving his penchant for torture and cruelty another outlet.

And yet, all these centuries later, people still read about Nero. However derisively his name is used, it is still known. The thought bewilders Jeff. Holds a certain dark fascination for him.

Someone like himself—a mild nonentity of a man—will be gone and forgotten like dust in the wind. But these . . . these horrid villains remain, haunting history, the never-ending ripples in the pond of time.

It's why Jeff reads these books. Why he can't get enough of them. Why he now pulls a biography of Caligula from one of Gussie's shelves.

It is Jeff's only flirtation with darkness in a life otherwise perfectly, blandly beige, like the color of his khakis.

He runs his hand over the embossed letters of the title, the worn leather cover of the book, wondering if Gussie ever read it.

He thinks about her more and more each day, their mysterious benefactor. It has to be the portrait, the unspoken challenge in her eyes that seemingly says, "Get to know me, I dare you."

He ought to ask Ansel or whatever his name is, but he hasn't seen the man since their arrival. The groceries have been dropped off at their front door, carefully packed in reusable polypropylene bags. Just how Jenna likes.

The vacation is on week two and Jeff thinks it's going well. Pleasantly low-key. He's grateful Jenna seems to have abandoned her recreational plans in favor of staying put and relaxing. But there are things about their day-to-day interactions that leave him . . . wanting? He isn't sure that's the right word for it.

Jeff just wants more. It seems that every conversation he has with his family is shallow, surface-level only. They speak of food, of what movie to watch (they can barely agree), or what game to play (it's always Monopoly), but never anything real.

Jeff wants to ask his family if they are happy because he suspects they might not be, and he suspects that unhappiness might be what drives Jenna's incessant workouts, Jessie's social media obsession, and JJ's weight. But then again, it just isn't the sort of thing one asks. And what if the answer is no, and the reason is him? What if he isn't doing enough as a father and a husband?

Jeff wants to ask his wife what happened to their sex life. He wants to offer his kids something more important, more exciting than social media likes, gadgets, and food. He wishes for a life with greater depth, intent, purpose.

He tries to remember the last time he had a real, meaningful conversation with someone—anyone—about anything. When he asked all the right whys and meant it. All that comes to mind are drunken college debates. That can't be right, can it?

By the time his relationship with Jenna got serious, Jeff was seasoned enough to know what to say, and more importantly what not to say, to impress a woman. The self-editing software that guides all adult lives was already firmly in place and switched on.

And with kids, sometimes, it's impossible to know what the right words might be. They are so delicate these days, precocious but fragile. You never know what might traumatize them, and sometimes it's easier to say nothing at all. Easier, more peaceful that way, sure, but it results in not really knowing the people in your life. You might learn their favorite color, food, etc. but not the inner workings of their minds, not the deepest wounds of their hearts.

The polite, policed, protected world will not allow it.

Jeff shakes his head. He doesn't know where these thoughts are coming from. Everything's fine. Everyone's having fun. The vacation is relaxing; he's away from work, away from Richie's oily mug, away from the world's needs and demands.

Everything's fine, he repeats, glancing up at Gussie as if daring her to defy him. She doesn't, but the smirk in her eyes says she might consider it.

Jeff opens the book and descends once more into the Ancient Roman Empire's caliginous politics.

He must have dozed off without realizing it because when he comes to, it's dark. The text on the pages of the book splayed open in his lap is impossible to make out, and he is not alone.

A feminine shape slides the book away and replaces it. Her warmth seeps through the fabric of his clothes right into his skin. In the darkness, she could be anyone, but of course it's only . . .

"Jenna." He sighs and wraps his arms around her, pulling her into him.

His wife seems to have something else in mind. She pushes him back into the couch and straddles him. The suddenness, the decisiveness of the motion confuses him. He was under the impression Jenna preferred for him to make the first move. They used to joke about her old-fashionedness. And yet, Jeff likes it, this change. He feels himself respond. Jenna's hands traverse from his shoulders to his waist, and he feels momentary shame at the tire of extra weight there, but the moment passes, burns up in a fire starting up between them.

She undoes his pants with eager fingers, takes a hold of him, and soon he is enveloped in the exquisite warmth of her.

She moves with the frantic desperate urgency of new lovers. He can't remember the last time she had such a hunger for him. He wants to reach for her, to kiss her, to bury his face in her hair, but she keeps pushing him back until he succumbs to her wishes completely.

Jeff idly worries about the time, about whether she locked the door, about the kids walking in or hearing them, but then Jenna wraps her hands around his neck, and he lets the world go.

It's been too long to sustain an impressive performance, but he tries. Tries to hold on, to match her pace.

He feels it building, the way her body tenses up, the way her fingers tighten then release as if forgetting their purpose. She comes shudderingly but quietly. He follows almost immediately. It leaves them exhilarated, exhausted, gasping for air like marathon runners just through the finish line.

"That was . . ." he starts, getting his breath back.

She lays a finger on his lips, then drags it down as if zipping his mouth vertically. Her nail feels long and sharp, talon-like.

There's a noise in the room, like the flapping of wings, or a clapping of hands.

It startles Jeff; he feels himself shrink, slip out; the briskness of night's air is a shock on his sensitive skin.

Jenna stands up, finding a graceful way to do so from a kneeling position. The space around them is made up of shadows, and all he can make out are shapes. It's surprisingly erotic.

He gets up too, doing up his pants, looking around for the source of the sound.

"What do you think . . ."

Jenna hushes him with a kiss. Almost a peck but for the way she briefly bites his lower lip. Then she leaves.

Jeff can't tell if he ought to follow. The encounter has left him spent, unbalanced, deliciously heavy. He sits down, just for a moment, just to get his bearings. Just to let this fresh warmth suffusing his blood linger a while longer. Next thing he knows, it's morning. The sun is doing its best to penetrate the parlor's gloom, and Jeff has a hell of a crick in his neck from having slept on a stiff pillowless couch.

His book is splayed beside him on the floor, spine out, like a wounded bird. Caligula's sightless visage is staring back at him, his expression accusatory.

Jeff feels hungover, dizzy, disorientated. He looks up at Augusta Doyle's portrait and swears that for a second, it looks like the woman winks at him.

In the dishwater-dull light of day, last night doesn't feel real. Jeff feels vaguely unreal himself.

JENNA

JEFF'S ACTING WEIRDLY. Jenna can't figure him out, and it's starting to piss her off. She isn't the sort of person to ask him about it directly; theirs isn't the sort of relationship that is threaded together by deep talked-out understandings, and so she lets it be. Cautiously.

If her husband has a secret, it would be a first, she believes. Jeff is an open book of a man—one of his most attractive qualities.

Frankly, she doesn't care for secrets. She'd rather have help putting away the groceries. But then there'd be annoying jokes and unwelcome remarks about her selections.

Yes, she knows neither quinoa nor tofu is naturally tasty. That's why there are sauces and spices. If it was up to Jeff, he'd just douse everything in cheese and call it a day.

And sure, her husband is in decent shape, especially considering some men his age, but still . . . cheese?

Jenna has tried just about every alternative cheese on the market and is yet to find a substitute her family would deem acceptable. Unlike all the quality fake meats now available, the cheese business is lamentably lagging.

The food delivery just appeared on the doorstep. Angus is nowhere to be seen. She would have welcomed company outside of her family, but the man must be busy. Or private.

Jenna can appreciate a man who just helps out and leaves. A nice change.

She sometimes feels like food is taking up entirely too much of her life, of their lives.

The acquisition of it, the putting away process, the cooking, the eating, the washing up. At home, there's also composting and recycling of food packaging. It's never-ending. Exhausting.

Entirely too much of their conversation revolves around it too. What are we eating? When are we eating? How many calories are in this?

Surely there's gotta be more to life than that. According to the books she's been reading, there's murder.

What about something in between the two extremes?

Sometimes, she misses work. It's an idle, undefined missing, not one likely to prompt any changes. A distant craving for a day full of varied interactions, achievement of shared goals—if lucky, intellectual stimulus.

Her college degree feels like a waste; an expensive paperweight, a box checked, a level ascended in the game of Life, but all to what end?

Lacey, her favorite cousin and arguably the most interesting Doyle, never went to college, setting up a party planning business instead. She later branched out into weddings and now has a productive, thriving career. Lacey always has the best work-related stories, plus, financially, she's doing great. Just bought a freaking Tesla.

Not to save the environment, either. Lacey doesn't even recycle regularly. It's just a trophy. Something that says, "Look, I have arrived. By the power of the sun. In Deep Blue Metallic."

Lacey's a show-off, but she's fun. And the wine she serves is never from a box.

Lately, there might have been too much vino, actually. Her husband is doing a second stint in rehab, and the D word has been mentioned.

They seemed happy enough last Jenna and Jeff saw them at their anniversary party back . . . when was it? Just after they got back from their own Haven vacation, wasn't it? Yes, that's right. Jenna remembers it was at Lacey's insistence that she finally decided to take up her family legacy and reserve August for them.

So far, Jenna's happy with her decision. She barely thinks about the list of activities she had originally put together for them. Things are going just fine without having to go anywhere. Her kids are getting outside. JJ seems to be enjoying the lake, and Jessie is getting some sun. Jeff . . . well, Jeff's happy enough. The parlor here is like a man cave he's never had.

Jenna doesn't care for it. The light is uniformly muted no matter what time of the day it is, the furnishings are drab, and that portrait is downright creepy—the way the eyes seem to follow you around.

In college, she took some art history. There's a way to describe it. What was it? Ah, yes, "the Mona Lisa effect." Of course, Gussie's no Mona Lisa, but the mystery is still there.

Jenna remembers another thing from her class: Trompe-l'œil. A way to make two-dimensional art appear three-dimensional. Whoever did this portrait certainly mastered that trick. The result has a peculiar uncanny valley realism that unsettles Jenna.

She wishes she knew the woman in the image but wonders if she'd like her. Jenna doesn't like secrets, and Augusta Doyle seems to have been a woman full of them. Her mind segues from art to sex with disturbing alacrity. She contemplates the fancy underwear still languishing at the bottom of the dresser drawer. The time just hasn't been right.

Historically, she has always preferred for the man to make the first move. Most associate it with shyness, but in all actuality, it stems from a desire for certainty. Jenna needs to know she is wanted. It's better than foreplay. With their sex life dwindling to special occasions, they've become estranged in a way. Intimate strangers. That seems like the title of one of the thrillers Jenna reads. In fact, it might be.

Either way, the comfortable assuredness they've cultivated out of longtime togetherness seems to have turned into a form of congenial impasse, steadily increasing the distance between them. The seesaw horse of their sex life is paused in the middle; without reaching for one another they are stuck.

It's only their second week vacationing, Jenna tells herself. There's plenty of time. She's glad they booked an entire month.

Plus, sex isn't everything. Maybe for some couples—and here her mind uncharitably drifts to some of her cousins' cheating dramas—but not for them. Jeff seems content enough with his books and his swimming. If she ever learned to bake like Angus, he'd be over the moon.

To be fair, she bakes, but by the time she has substituted for eggs and sugar and butter . . . well, the final product isn't a resounding success with the family. Jeff says she substitutes all the deliciousness out of it, but it's her life, it's her body these things are going into. One of the few things she can control as rigorously as she likes.

Doyle women seem to veer toward a certain rotundness Jenna associates with prolific childbearing, ales, and cheese.

If this is the only way she can stand out amid her family, she'll take it. She'll happily be the fittest Doyle. Not that she's even a Doyle anymore. She is, ironically, a Baker.

Jenna is tired of the kitchen. She takes a walk around the house to see what her family is up to.

They are delightfully predictable, this bunch, she thinks with affection. Jessie's on her neatly made bed with the door open, furiously typing away at her phone. JJ's in his room, door ajar, the place already a mess, bobbing his head to a soundtrack she can't hear but knows all too well to be techno and gunfire.

Jeff is in the parlor, as always, becoming one with the couch. Yet another dead Roman is peering at Jenna from the cover of her husband's book.

She tells them all that food will be ready in half an hour, feeling like a cliché and not minding it.

Jeff's the only one who responds.

"Thanks, babe."

Babe, she thinks. *Babe?* That's new. Or rather a blast from the past. They were never really one of those honey, sugarplum couples, but babe was universal enough to stick around for a while before parenthood firmly returned them to the appropriateness of formal names.

She feels she ought to come back with something.

"How's the book?"

Jeff closes the hardcover with his finger as a bookmark and looks up. Smiling.

"It's good. Ancient Romans being ancient Romans."

Jenna reads the title. Tries to think of a single thing she knows about Caligula.

"What was he like?"

"Oh, you know." Jeff waves his hand. "Mad, bad, dangerous to know. Quite literally, too, on all accounts. Cruel, murderous, incestuous, with wild appetites and delusions of grandeur."

"That sounds like most of them."

"Kind of is, I suppose."

"So, who's reading the same books now?"

"Ouch." Jeff laughs. "Touché."

"You're in a good mood today."

"Aren't you?"

Jeff smirks and does a weird thing with his eyebrow like an aborted wink or a poor man's imitation of The Rock, and it takes willpower for Jenna to not outright ask what he's thinking. Talking about books and food is so much easier.

There's a pause that threatens to get awkward if it goes on for much longer.

"I just want you to know—" Jeff starts.

"Shit," Jenna interrupts him. "Sorry, I just realized I left the oven on. The baked tofu is going to come out all chewy if I don't hurry. Can we pick this up later?"

"Sure, sure."

Jeff gives her another smirk and goes back to his book. Jenna races to the kitchen and makes it just in time. Her family might hate her tofu, but at least it'll have the right texture.

She wonders about the hold these horrible dead Romans have on her husband's imagination as she starts chopping vegetables for an appetizer of crudités. But the thought runs out of steam, and Jenna puts on Adele. She wishes Adele would put out albums more often. It's been several years since *25*. Jenna doesn't love the latest, except for maybe "When We Were Young." But the voice is the same. She even allows herself a sip of wine to the tune. Then another.

That night she falls asleep earlier than usual and dreams of murderous emperors. In the morning, she blames it on Jeff's books, but secretly, shamefully, she admits to herself a certain level of excitement at the debauchery of it all.

It feels warm and wrong; the way it did when once, as a kid, she found and watched in secret a tape of an old movie with that guy from *Clockwork Orange* without knowing anything about its scandalous reputation. It was the first time she had seen such graphic depictions of sex and violence on screen, and it left an indelible impression, forever stirring her viewing tastes toward sunnier vistas.

In fact, until now she had all but forgotten about that. Should she tell Jeff? He'd get a kick out of it, probably. But it feels too intensely private, too intimate to share somehow. Maybe as a joke. Maybe.

He isn't even here, in bed with her. Either he got up uncharacteristically early or, more likely, passed out reading in the parlor.

Jenna gets up and stretches, begins to plan out her morning workout. Through the window, she can just about see the lake shimmering in the distance. The mucky visceral feel of its eerily still waters put her off up close, but aesthetically, from afar, she can appreciate its appeal.

Another day in Haven, she thinks. Lovely.

JJ

THE STACCATO SOUND of gunfire is music to his ears as he nears his goal. This has been by far the most challenging installment of his favorite shoot-'em-up games, and he is so close.

The body count is going up; blood, blood is everywhere. It looks hyperrealistic, just like it does in the movies. Even the creatures do. In fact, playing this game is kind of like being in a movie—one where JJ is the star.

He wishes his family wasn't so lame, that they would share his passion for horror. What's wrong with it anyway? As far as JJ is concerned, it is the most lifelike of all genres out there.

Life isn't all fun and games the way it is in comedies. No one really acts like that.

But people do terrible things to each other all the time. He overhears enough news to know the truth.

The low battery signal blinks at him. Shoot. JJ hits save. Early into his gaming days, he made the mistake of not saving a game and never managed to ascend to the same level again. Now he is religious about it. Any progress, no matter how small, gets saved.

He looks around for a charger but doesn't see it. He could swear he left it sticking out of the wall, impressed the place even had modern three-prong plugs. Then again, his room is a mess. An abyss. Just like at home. Things do tend to disappear.

Before he commits to doing something drastic like cleaning up, he decides to check downstairs.

"Mom, you see my charger?"

"Which one is yours?"

"The green one?"

"No, I don't think so."

"Dad?"

"No, kiddo. Sorry."

And here, he thought a bright neon cord would stand out for sure. There's always Jessie, of course. Perhaps she has extended her pilfering to electronics?

He doesn't want to have to ask.

Someday in the future, their parents assure them, they'll be as close as siblings can be and their two-year difference in age will be nothing. Whatever.

Right now, it's everything. They look, think, and act nothing alike.

Jessie, like most girls, is a mystery to JJ. He's pretty sure she doesn't regard him as one; mostly she just seems disgusted by him.

Not enough to keep her hands off his shit, though, apparently.

He checks the outlets around the parlor and kitchen, then sighs, and goes to knock on his sister's door.

"What?" an annoyed voice replies.

"I can't find my charger."

"Not my problem."

"Oh yeah, not like my candy?"

The door is ripped open with such ferocity that JJ backs off.

His sister is glaring at him with undisguised fury. He must have caught her mid makeup tutorial, because her face is only half made-up, giving it a disorienting unevenness. He chuckles involuntarily.

"What's so funny?"

"Your face . . ."

"Well, guess what? My face will be done in about ten minutes, and it'll look perfect. You'll still be ugly."

JJ blanches. They've fought before, numerous times, but Jessie sounds meaner than usual. JJ regrets bringing up candy but can't seem to stop himself.

"I know you take my things."

"What are you even talking about?"

"My candy bars."

"As if I'd ever eat that garbage."

JJ can't tell if she's lying, only that she's mad. The stronger emotions bury the lighter ones. It's a fight he's unlikely to win, a battle he isn't ready to wage. Besides, he still has plenty left in his stash.

"Whatever," he mumbles, dropping eye contact.

She slams the door in his face.

Back in his room, reluctantly picking up dirty shirts and plates, JJ wonders what set his sister off like that. She said he was ugly. That was harsh. Ugly is such an ugly word.

This vacation is supposed to be mellowing them all out. Maybe if Jessie ever took a vacation from her phone . . .

He's seen her social media feeds. His sister is a try-hard. She copies popular trends but never really does anything original. And she doesn't have that many followers. Not like some other people on there. Not like his favorite gamers.

JJ doesn't ever want to put himself out there like that. It's like asking for abuse.

Sometimes, if someone pisses him off, he'll find them and leave a nasty comment. Always anonymously. He doesn't think of it as trolling because he doesn't do it often. And anyway, what's wrong with trolls? Trolls are huge, awesome, dangerous.

All he knows of trolls is from the *Lord of the Rings* trilogy. And he likes it. He's watched all the movies a bunch of times. Tried the books once but found them unreadably dense. The movies, though, all those hero quests. Now that's a life. Miles better than the dull drudge of his existence.

The charging cord is nowhere to be seen, and JJ begins to feel the first tinges of panic.

What if he lost it? What if his beloved screens go dark and there will be no more games, no more nature shows? What would he do with all that nothingness, with all that silence, with all that empty time?

It's not like there's a store nearby like in the city, is there? He hates asking his parents for favors like driving. His father is a huge believer in even exchanges and is likely to counter with some chore or other to balance things out. But at this rate he might have to.

This freaking house, JJ thinks angrily, his shit never went missing at home. Not like this.

He huffs and puffs and kicks at his freshly arranged messy piles until their contents are strewn across the floor once more.

Then he changes, grabs his towel, and heads out to the lake. One decent constant in this never-ending month.

JESSIE

ONE STEP AFTER another, one tree after another. Hiking is supposed to be fun, but she isn't getting the appeal at all. So much for doing something different, for trying something new. Yeah, she was upset by the confrontation with JJ, but the little shit shouldn't have the power to push her into this. Jessie is hating the woods.

She keeps getting bitten. Nature here abhors intruders, it seems. Eats them alive. And what sort of activity is hiking anyway? Why don't they just call it what it is, which is uncomfortable walking?

Jessie has tried to redeem her time by posing for selfies and thinking up cute hashtags, but nature, on top of being hostile, is also not that photogenic. The light is uneven and shifty; the trees are strange, contorted in ways that appear freakish and unpleasant to look at.

She knows some of the InstaStars she follows would have spun this opportunity into gold, but photo after photo shows her looking sweaty, tired, annoyed. Her makeup is melting off her face. The sunscreen-fortified face cream is stinging her eyes.

Where is this guy? Arthur? No, not Arthur. She isn't good with names. She's only seen the man once, and his face didn't fix itself in her memory either. People, in general, don't seem very real to her unless she has scoped them out on the internet. It's the reason Aunt Gussie seems kind of mythical too.

Jessie once read that her generation is the most photographed one in the history of the world. That seems significant to her. She can't quite imagine the world that goes by unrecorded and uncurated. Does that make it unobserved? Jessie has taken a photo of every important moment in her life for years now. She wishes she had a photo of kissing Ainsley. It would make it seem more real. Instead, as time passes, it feels more and more like a dream.

Ainsley would make this place work for her. Put on some cute outdoorsy outfit and post some charming comments.

Maybe if Ainsley was here, Jessie wouldn't care about any of this dumb crap. Maybe she would just be happy.

This place, this vacation, is starting to get to her.

JJ, for one, is completely losing his shit. To come in and accuse her like that. What was that?

The thing she's most mad about, if she were to be honest with herself, is that he knows about her nighttime candy raids. Why, she wonders, hasn't he told their parents? What's his angle?

Jessie looks around. She should have marked these freaking trees or something, because they all look the same, and she feels like she might be lost. She tries to pull up a navigation app on her phone and can't find reception. A twinge of panic tugs at her stomach.

Paying closer attention to her surroundings, she carefully proceeds in a straight line. Surely it'll lead her out. No one gets lost in the woods. Not really. This isn't some stupid fairy tale.

Her shoes weren't meant for this. Her adorable white Adidas tennis shoes, made from recycled materials to demonstrate her commitment to fighting climate change, are not at all suitable for hiking in the woods.

Jessie trips on something and bends down to examine it. It's a twig or, wait a minute . . . She drops the thing like it's on fire.

Years ago, at a sleepover, she was tricked/peer pressured into watching *The Blair Witch Project*. The movie terrified her. She actually almost peed her pants at one of the scenes. Until that night, Jessie never had any strong feelings about the woods one way or another; afterward, they terrified her.

She thought she left her childhood fears behind, but the object she found, the tiny figurine composed of twisted bound sticks, looks almost exactly like something out of *Blair Witch*.

Take a photo of it, Jessie thinks, take a photo. But her hands are shaking, and she feels like she might throw up, and there is a panicked, terrifying notion in her head that if she photographs this thing, it'll live on in her phone and travel home with her.

Jessie backs away, looking around. Really looking now. She finds another figurine hanging from a tree, about five feet off the ground. Then another, nestled near some gray mushrooms.

She no longer cares about Arthur, Albert . . . Angus, that's it. All she wants to do is get back, safely and immediately.

Even if it's just another tedious family night of Monopoly.

Something crunches under her tennis shoe. Sticks to it. She twists her foot, sneaker sole up to take a look. A Snickers bar. One of those tiny fun-size ones you get on Halloween. What is it doing here?

There's one more. One hits her in the face, then another. They are falling from a tree? From the sky? It's raining candy, except that it doesn't feel like rain. It feels like she's being pelted by Snickers.

Jessie slips on a wrapper, loses her balance, and goes down hard, catching herself on her hands and knees. The forest floor is mucky, muddy, disgustingly alive. Her outfit is ruined, she knows. Her knees are likely skinned.

It doesn't matter. Jessie gets up and continues in the direction she believes Haven lies. She whispers something that may pass for a prayer, wishing for the house's imposing silhouette to make itself visible through the trees, to guide her back.

There's no more candy, but there's a sound now. Like footsteps. But larger, louder. Like something is chasing her.

She starts running. She never runs. The ground is slippery; her tennis shoes offer almost no traction. More than anything, she wants to turn around. That scab-picking itch, the slow parting of the fingers covering eyes at the horror movie, the peeking-into-the-dark-basement feeling has grabbed her in its claws.

Her head begins to turn, slowly, as if not of her own volition. So that when she runs into a tree, the shock and surprise of it cuts her at the knees, and she goes down like a sack of potatoes.

Jessie doesn't see stars the way a cartoon character might. All she sees are leaves, branches, slivers of gray skies above. Then there's nothing.

"Are you okay? Young lady, are you okay?"

Jessie feels her eyelashes unglue themselves, and then there's light.

And a man.

A kind concern in his eyes. A funny hat on his head. It takes her a moment, but she recognizes the caretaker.

"Ugh," she says, rubbing her head. Her hand comes away dirty but not bloody, which is a good sign.

"Wanna sit up?"

Jessie nods as much as she dares to move her head.

The man pulls her up gently until her back can lean against the tree.

"What happened to you?" he asks.

Jessie thinks back, her mind sluggishly retrieving recent events with all the enthusiasm of a post office clerk checking for packages.

It returns slowly, then all at once.

"Were you chasing me?" she asks, eyes narrowed in suspicion.

"Chasing you?" The man laughs. "I didn't even know you were out here."

"Did you . . . did you throw candy at me?" She cringes; it sounds so stupid said out loud.

The man raises his eyebrows comically until they just about meet the brim of his hat. "It's not Halloween yet."

"Right, right," Jessie mumbles, gathering her thoughts. She wanted to find the man, but not like this, never like this. Now he's going to think she's an idiot. A clumsy one too.

"I just . . . I thought I saw something."

"Candy?"

"And these weird . . ." Jessie stops herself. "Maybe I can show you?"

"Sure, okay. You good to walk?"

She stands up tentatively. Tests her limbs. It seems the thing that got bruised the most was her ego. She must look terrible, she thinks, and fights the impulse to pull out her phone and check.

All she can do is smooth down her hair and brush off her clothes the best she can.

"It's back there." She gestures in the direction she came from, realizing she isn't entirely sure. It's so easy to get turned around here.

They walk on, side by side.

"What were you doing out here?" the man asks.

"Oh, just, you know, hiking."

"You're not dressed for hiking."

"Well, I didn't realize the woods had a dress code," she snaps, then feels immediately bad about it, but the man just chuckles.

He is, of course, prepared, Jessie observes. Dressed like someone out of an old L.L.Bean catalog. With that funny hat and sturdy boots.

"It's just that your family doesn't really come out to the woods."

Jessie shrugs. "I wanted a change."

"A change is almost always a good thing." Angus nods sagely.

It seems like this ought to be the place. Surely she didn't run that far before. But there's nothing, anywhere she looks. No freaky twig figurines, no candy bars.

The man stays quiet, allowing Jessie to look as much as she wants, as much as she needs to, and she feels more and more ridiculous with each passing moment. Like some dumb hysterical city princess who got freaked out by some trees.

A thought occurs to her: what if it was JJ all along? How difficult would it be to tie some twigs together and to throw some candy at her?

Maybe this was his revenge. For her theft, real and imagined.

She was really mean to him the last time they spoke. It surprised her. He surprised her. She felt ashamed about the candy, so she lashed out. But still, ugly was so harsh. The kid knows what he looks like and gets enough flak for it in school. She shouldn't have said it, but then she couldn't bring herself to apologize either.

Well, she thinks, looking down at her ruined clothes, imagining future bruises blossoming, now they are even.

"You know, it's fine," she tells the man. "It's really fine. I think I was just tired or something."

"Okay, sure." He accepts the lie so easily. "You want some water?"

Jessie knows enough not to take unsealed liquid from strangers. Is Angus a stranger? Technically, all the food and drink they have in the house is brought by him. And she is thirsty.

She accepts an old-looking metal water bottle and drinks greedily from it.

"Better?"

She nods her gratitude. The water is rumbling in her empty stomach.

"Hungry? I got some sandwiches." Angus reaches into his bag and brings out a couple of neatly wrapped squares. "Let's see. PB 'n' J and ham and cheese."

"I'm a vegetarian," Jessie says automatically.

"PB 'n' J it is, then." The man smiles and offers her one of the squares.

She doesn't know why, but she accepts it, unwraps it, and eats the entire thing. Thoughts of invading calories swirl in her mind, but she banishes them. The creaminess and richness of peanut butter balanced out by the perfect sweetness of strawberry jam—it's so good, she wants to moan with pleasure. She practically swoons.

Angus watches her, amused, as he slowly eats his sandwich.

"Wish I had another one for you. You look like you could use it."

Is that a weight slight? Jessie wonders. Those always feel like a backhanded compliment; they offend and flatter at the same time. But then again, Angus looks sincere.

"Thank you," she says, brushing the crumbs off her ruined shirt as if it mattered.

Angus takes the paper wrap from her, folds it neatly, the same way he did his, and puts it into his bag.

Leather, she notices. The man is definitely not a vegetarian. The sandwich, the bag. His boots, too, by the look of them. It occurs to her that he may not know her name. Didn't he call her a young lady earlier?

"I'm Jessie," she offers.

"I know who you are." He smiles.

There's no telling his age. Older than her dad, she figures.

Most older men, in Jessie's experience, are creeps. Including some of her friends' dads and even some of her teachers. In fact, the only non-creepy teacher they had was Mr. Travis, geography. Mr. Travis made eye contact, spoke with friendliness and confidence, didn't patronize. And then, Mr. Travis got fired for inappropriate behavior, so, you know, so much for all that. But Angus seems genuinely different. Jessie feels completely comfortable around him. He's like her dad but less weird. Like one of her uncles or granduncles, though much less rude and obnoxious.

Jessie wants to tell him she's been looking for him, that it's one of the main reasons she's in these creepy woods, but she doesn't know how.

"How's your vacation going so far?" he asks.

"Fine. It's fine, I guess."

"Ah, high praise."

Once again, she wonders if he might be joking at her, but it seems to be the joking *with* sort of thing. His smile is too kind. So are his eyes. She feels herself relax. Her hunger, for once, abated.

"It's not really my scene, you know."

"City girl through and through, huh?"

"Something like that."

"So then, why the hike?"

"I was . . ." She almost says, "looking for you," but then shifts, blurting out, "Did you know her?"

"Did I know who?"

"Gussie, Aunt Augusta."

"Ah, right. Not much."

What sort of an answer is that?

"She wasn't an easy person to know," he adds cryptically.

"What was she like?"

Angus sighs, rubs his forehead, then pulls his hat back down.

"Complicated, interesting, generous. Whip-smart. Razor-sharp sense of humor."

Jessie likes the sound of that. She can just imagine Augusta Doyle's social media page. The portrait for the main picture and those adjectives below it. Iconic.

"Why do you ask?"

"I was just curious, you know. I tried looking her up on the internet and didn't find anything."

"Well, she was very private."

"Right."

"I know your generation doesn't put much stock in privacy."

"No, I get it, like she had her secrets."

The man laughs at that. "You know the best thing about being a private person?"

"Is that like a riddle?"

Angus holds up his hands, palms out, the gesture of innocence.

"Honest question."

"So, what is it?"

"No one knows what to expect of you. Anything you do can be a surprise. A revelation."

Huh. Jessie contemplates that. "I've never thought of it like that."

"Well, now you have." Angus winks.

"Did Aunt Augusta surprise you?"

"You've no idea."

Jessie senses there is a story there, more than one, a treasure trove of them. She feels questions brewing up.

"It's getting dark," the man says. "Think you can find your way back?"

She desperately wants to be the strong-spirited woman on the motivational memes who answers yes, whips out a compass, and trailblazes her way. But she's tired, her memory of earlier events is too fresh, and she just wants to get to her room, take a shower, and crawl into bed, so she shakes her head no.

"All right, I'll walk you. It isn't far."

And they walk. More small talk. It's easy, so easy to talk to this man. He seems distinctly real to her in a way she isn't used to. But there's a certain vagueness to the way he speaks too, to the answers he gives.

"Do you live around here?" Jessie asks.

"Close enough."

"You like it?"

"Sure do. It's quiet. I get my best thinking done."

"Do you take care of other houses in the area?"

"No, Haven keeps me busy."

Does it? Jessie wonders. It's just one house, and Angus only seems to be dropping off groceries lately. Maybe there are other aspects to the caretaking she isn't thinking of.

The house comes into view, and she's happy to be close but sad their conversation has to end. "I'm interested in Aunt Gussie," she tells him. "My family never talks about her. Will you talk to me about her?"

"Maybe sometime," he says noncommittally, "but now you best go on in. Your parents must be worried."

"Ugh, please. They probably haven't even noticed I was gone."

"You'd be surprised what parents notice."

Unlikely, she thinks. Does that mean Angus has kids? She'll ask next time.

He says goodbye at the door like a proper gentleman, like someone out of Jane Austen movies.

Jessie lets herself into the house. Her parents are in the kitchen, cooking. Well, her mother is cooking, and her father is handing her things. JJ is nowhere to be seen.

Jessie slips by as quietly as she can and heads upstairs. The squeaky steps betray her.

"Jessie, that you?" her father calls up.

"Yes, Dad."

"Were you out?"

Told you so, she thinks. Angus doesn't know her family like she does.

"Yeah."

"We're eating in twenty."

"Okay." With that, she stomps up the stairs, ending the conversation.

JJ's door is open; his room is as disgustingly messy as ever. His back is to her, and she shoots mental daggers into it.

The confrontation will have to wait. First, there's going to be a shower long enough and hot enough to make her feel like herself again.

Afterward, getting dressed, powdering her emerging bruises into nothingness, she realizes that she never asked Angus how to find him again. Also, that she never purged her sandwich and doesn't really want to. And then, there's the fact that despite meeting the man and asking about her aunt as planned, there are still more questions than answers. The mystery remains.

AVA

THE CITY

The club had no name. She wasn't even sure the street it was on had a name. There were no signs. It was hardly a street, more of an alley.

"Are you sure it's safe here?" she asked. And James laughed as if the thought of him putting her in danger was too preposterous to entertain.

"It's fine." He squeezed her arm reassuringly. "Perfectly fine, dear. Ready to celebrate your birthday?"

James knocked on a door that almost completely blended in with the rest of the wall. When an eye-level mail slot opened, he showed a card and said a sentence that made no sense.

With a screech, the door opened, admitting them in. If the entryway reminded her of Open Sesame from an Aladdin fairy tale, then what lay within was the cave of treasures indeed.

Augusta had heard of such things but had never really imagined them to be real. The atmospheric lighting revealed shapes intertwined, drinking, swaying to the music. Men with men. Women with women.

Men who looked like women. Women who looked like men.

The place was thick with aromas of cigarette smoke, perfume, sex.

Her first reaction, much to her shame, was to leave. Just turn on her heel and flee. This was too strange, too foreign, too much.

But James held on to her arm like an anchor, steadying her, until her anxiety drained away, and the only thing left was excitement for a new adventure.

They made their way to the bar.

As her eyes became accustomed to the low lighting, as the smoothness of gin suffused her veins, she started to look, really look around.

The men here reminded her of James. So good-looking, so well dressed, so . . . soft. So unlike the Doyles.

And James . . . James came alive in a way she had never seen him do. Breaking through the carefully constructed carapace, he emerged so much freer, livelier, happier.

She knew it, this feeling. It was the way she had felt around Lani. So very much like yourself. As you were meant to be, as things were meant to be.

The look he gave her that night, a shy uncertain look, so unlike him. So vulnerable.

Every close relationship eventually reaches a point when people reveal themselves to each other, their truest nature, their most carefully hidden selves. This, she recognized, was theirs.

For her birthday, James was giving her the gift of honesty. She smiled and accepted it. Later, watching him dance, Augusta couldn't stop smiling. It had occurred to her that perhaps she ought to feel betrayed or lied to, but she searched her heart and found none of it.

For half an hour or so, James disappeared, then came back buoyant as they shared another drink. They danced together, and they danced with others. All the men here were such good dancers. The one who asked her to a slow number was tall, with brilliantine-shiny, slicked-back hair and a snazzy suit. It took Augusta until mid-song to realize she was dancing with a woman. The surprise of it stopped her still.

"What's the matter, darling?" the woman asked her in a low, velvety baritone.

"Nothing, nothing at all." Augusta smiled and swayed to the music, picking up the rhythm. Relaxing, she pressed into a strange body. There was such comfort to be found there.

Later there were so many strange bodies. To be sampled, to be enjoyed. Once or over time. None of them were Lani, but that was fine.

A heart can only take so much. A body, on the other hand, seemed to be a perfectly resilient machine built for pleasure.

James and Augusta started the night together and often went home together. What they did in the intervening hours was nobody's business but their own.

There were so many of these hidden clubs, these clandestine bars. So many nameless destinations and strangers.

And sure, there was the ever-present threat of police raids, but somehow, they managed to avoid the worst of it.

It was almost a thrill, all this sneaking around, like being in a spy movie. It made her feel wild, alive, excited. Exciting.

And if their dalliances ever cut deeper than skin, they'd comfort each other. Best of friends, partners in life.

"You'll always have me," James would say, wrapping his arms around her, kissing the top of her head. And foolishly, she had believed him.

For a while, it seemed, life was good.

A mild-mannered, employed couple by day, sexual adventures by night, why, they could almost be comic book heroes, James would joke.

But every comic book hero has a villain. Sure as night follows day, the darkness found them.

⁂

Ava cringed and dropped the pen. Some memories were so violent that even their ripples decades later were strong enough to cause a physical reaction.

She rubbed her hand, then her wrist, her fingers lingering on the scars there. For the longest time, she took such great care covering them up, with long sleeves and jewelry, and now it didn't even matter. The old skin was as good of a camouflage as any. Not that anyone even looked.

Old age was like an invisibility cloak. Had she had the energy or the need of money, she could probably walk into the bank and rob it, and no one would ever suspect her or even notice her.

Where there are no loved ones to behold you, the years get even more voracious, devouring you, disappearing you from existence.

Soon, Ava thought, soon, there would be nothing left. Nothing but some money, nothing but some words.

Words.

The next ones wouldn't be easy to write, but she steadied herself, picked up her pen, and proceeded.

HOMECOMING

The Doyles had found them. What were the odds? The Doyles who never came to the city, who frowned upon it, who considered it a citadel of sin. All it took is one of them, who saw the Sullivans on the street and followed them to their destination, thinking of springing a surprise on them. It was a strange sort of bar, Tommy Doyle thought, one that appeared to require a password, so he pretended to tag along with a small rowdy group of men to get in.

And then the surprise was on him, steadily turning into shock as he looked around the place, and the realization slowly dawned on him. For a while, Tommy just sat there, dumbfounded.

From a shadowy corner, he watched Gussie and James flit around like social butterflies, as comfortable as comfortable could be in these sin-laden walls. The place mesmerized him with its strangeness. Outside of the army he had never seen or imagined such things. And here, in the middle of the city, amid all these decent people going about their business . . .

A slim, handsome man sauntered over to him, winked, and offered to buy him a drink. Tommy had almost thrown a punch right there and then, but he didn't want to draw attention to himself just yet.

Better to leave unseen. And leave he did, turning down a free drink for the first time in his life, the thought of what strings it may have come with making his skin crawl.

Even the air outside tasted unclean to Tommy as he took great big gulps of it. Disgusting. Shameful. It was one thing after another with their sister, wasn't it?

First, she had wandered astray, now she had led her husband along with her. James was a good guy, Tommy remembered him from work with fondness. Now he was a pervert, just like her. That girl was poison. She ruined everything she touched. He had to tell the family. He couldn't wait to tell the family.

The family, however, did decide to wait. A move uncharacteristic of them. Strategic.

No one had said anything until the Sullivans made the trip upstate for Thanksgiving.

Only then and there, across from the overcooked turkey and butter-glistening side dishes, the accusatory staring daggers turned into words.

"Tommy was in the city coupla months ago," the Doyle patriarch growled.

"Oh, you should have looked us up. We would have been glad to see you, show you around," James said, smiling.

"I seen plenty," Tommy mumbled. "Seen plenty on my own."

"Where'd you go?" James continued unsuspectingly, overlooking the tone.

"Small club. Offa Sixth Avenue. Down the steps, basement entrance."

James looked up, and Augusta could see the color drain from his face. She didn't think such a thing was possible, having only ever encountered it in fiction, but there it was. Her beautiful husband pale as a sheet.

No one said anything for what felt like ages. The atmosphere was as thick as the meat on a giant serving plate before them, requiring the sharpest of knives to get through.

Then Doyle Sr. cut in once again. "Care to explain yourselves?"

His stare was pure venom. Augusta knew just as James did that no words would suffice.

Sometimes retreat isn't just the best option, it's the only option.

"Perhaps, we better leave," James said mildly, getting up.

"Sit," the old man growled.

"We don't want to cause any discord," James said, folding up his napkin and putting it over his plate.

"I said, SIT."

With that, the Doyle brother nearest to him, Liam, laid his huge construction business-hewn paw on James's shoulder and shoved him back down.

"NOW you don't want to cause any discord?" the Doyle patriarch spat at him. His face had taken on a distinct beet-red shade of fury, making thick veins stand out in sharp, angry reliefs. "NOW? You've brought shame on this house, you've disgraced us. Wasn't one scandal enough? You couldn't control your wife? You couldn't control yourself?"

"Now wait just a minute . . ." Augusta was proud of James for speaking up, but on the other hand, she desperately wished for him to stay quiet, to not add fuel to a fire already gearing up to be an apocalyptic inferno.

"We are all out of patience. With both o' yous. Had enough. Think you're too good for us? You ain't nothing but a pair of perverts. We are ashamed to share a table with you, to share blood with you. We are good and decent people. What sort of abominations are you?"

"Daddy, please," Augusta said, hating how small her voice sounded.

"Daddy please nothing. Done pleasing you. Ain't no pleasing you. Should have stopped at eight. Stuck to boys. You've done nothing but disappoint, Gussie. Nothing but disappoint."

Her mother came over to her side of the table and slapped her. Hard.

It was like the years fell away, all the years of life spent away, marching to the beat of her own drum, all her accomplishments, everything . . . withered and vanished beneath the hateful gazes of the Doyles.

They should never have come, no matter how sincere the invitations sounded. There was evil here within these walls.

It had chosen to masquerade itself with sanctimony the way the wickedest do, but Augusta saw it then. And swore to herself that if she ever left the Doyle house that night, she would never, ever come back.

And James. Poor, kind, decent James tried to rise, tried to come to her defense.

Only to be met with fists, and angry words, and more fists. Doyles have never been good at stopping once they got going. For a while, she couldn't even see him from where she was held as she struggled to break free, only a sea of flailing limbs, the splatter of blood.

She was trying to listen for James's voice, even a moan, even a groan, anything to pass as a sign of life, but there were only the ugly sounds of bodies destroying another body.

It took an eternity. It was over so quickly. What did time matter anymore?

When they finally parted, the bloody mess on the floor hardly resembled a human being, let alone her wonderful James. Her Saint James.

She didn't have to reach for him, to touch him to know he was gone. What was left was only flesh.

Her family had always had violence coursing through their veins, but it had usually released itself in smaller, tolerable ways: slaps, fisticuffs, casual cruelties. She had never imagined this. By the look of them–slightly dazed, as if coming out of a violent dream–neither had they. But whether this was intended or not, it was much too late. Much too late for all of them.

They released their hold on her, for there was nothing they could have done to her then. Nothing left to destroy.

Augusta kneeled next to James's ruined form and whispered apologies, words without meaning because they were much too late coming.

It was all her fault. All her fault.

She would have stayed there, kneeling at his side forever, atoning for her sins without a hope of forgiveness, but those strong Doyle arms reached for her and dragged her away.

How quickly they came to, snapping right back into horrible practicality.

"You're stayin' here, where we can keep an eye on ya, where you can embarrass us no longer," her father sneered at her.

It wasn't until later that one of her sisters-in-law took pity on her and told her they had buried James in the nearby woods. Sold the car for spare parts to the local man who paid cash in hand and avoided the law at all costs. That simple. No body, no crime, as they say.

Outside of James's coworkers, who likely didn't particularly care, who would report him missing? The person he mattered to the most was her, locked up and useless.

For five days straight, she thought of nothing but her James, her guilt, his unmarked grave. On the sixth day, Augusta Sullivan slit her wrists.

She did it the right way, north to south, not east to west, though she couldn't recall how she knew that.

There was so much blood.

It was purely a matter of chance—her being found in time. Her sister-in-law misplaced an earring and came back up to look for it.

Then there was the screaming. The rushing around. Towels pressed tightly to her wrists, cheap terry cloth changing color from white to red.

Then there was the Facility, as she had come to think of it after a while. A building almost gothic in proportions and atmosphere. A place to lock one's shame away. The concept of it, the . . . everything of it, felt positively medieval.

Augusta didn't know such places existed still. Hadn't realized how easy it was to end up in one. To relinquish all autonomy, all rights.

Amid the institutionally beige walls, unseeing eyes, and unhearing ears, in a cloud of forced-down sedatives, in a milky light streaming weakly through the thickly barred windows, Augusta lost herself.

Everything she was—person, woman, dreamer, lover, friend, wife, reader, worker—fell away, and what was left wasn't worth fighting for. She would have stayed forever in that wretched place if she hadn't met Max.

❧❧❧

Ava took a sip of tea and regarded what she'd written. It was almost as if it was all a game, she mused, with her playing at being a writer of fiction. Creating a character. Wasn't it all fiction after a while anyway? If every recollection can alter the memory itself, then eventually isn't your entire life no more than a story?

The tea was strong, just as Nina used to like it, just as Ava had come to appreciate all those years ago. Milk, cream, sugar to Nina were no more than meek affectations. She was a purist, that woman, through and through. The most she'd agree to was lemon, and only because its bitterness pleased her.

"It's a Russian thing," she'd explain, shrugging. "We like strong flavors. Bitter, tart. Like life itself."

Funny what her cosmopolitan, multinational lover chose to hold on to.

Ava closed her eyes, summoning an image, any image, of Nina. A visitation, a comfort.

And there they were, on a huge bed—one had to prioritize—in a tiny apartment in Paris. Ava giving her lover's poor feet a rub—the one thing a ballerina, even a former one, can never have enough of—and Nina smoking and singing, terribly off-key, and laughing. Her beautiful face relaxed, peaceful, stylishly framed in cigarette smoke.

The smoke swirled and devoured the memory. Ava came back to reality with a jolt and sighed heavily. They never stayed, all those lovely memories. Seldom came to her when she slept either.

The nightmares, on the other hand, the nightmares haunted her. It was as if all the ugliness of her past had been lying in wait, just biding its time until Ava was alone, and now had pounced on her like a predator on prey.

Maybe, Ava thought, if she wrote it all down, the nightmares would be somehow appeased. Maybe then, she could rest.

5

JEFF

AS FAR AS he knows, there are no cards made with something like, "Our last sex was great, let's do it again," for a sentiment. And subtlety has never been Jeff's strong suit. He wants to reach out for his wife, but every time he does, it seems to only highlight the distance between them.

Once he even does it at night, hoping for a sleepy fumble in the dark, the way they used to before the kids. Before life began to make them so tired that going to bed became primarily a sleep-only destination.

Jenna pushes him off so violently that it bruises his arm. Though not as much as his ego.

He turns away, dejected; frankly, pissed off.

It feels like she's playing a game with him. Jeff hates games. It's what soured dating for him back in the day; it's stupid, petty.

The funny thing is that outside of their sex life, or lack thereof, everything is going great.

The kids aren't being too difficult; the weather has been cooperating, providing one perfectly sunny day after another. Angus keeps them in food. There are movies, books, games. This vacation has been genuinely relaxing. Jeff tries to concentrate on the positive. He's nearly through with Caligula, and this morning he is perusing the library shelves idly, looking for his next read.

The incoming phone call jars him, shrilly ripping apart the soft fabric of the early hours' quietude. It's been so long since he received one that the sound takes a minute to place. Work knows Jeff's away. There is, sadly, no one else who'd reach out. He's been carrying the phone around like an oversized pocket watch.

Fumbling with it for a moment, forgetting to check the caller ID, he finally presses the accept button and pushes the phone against his ear.

"Hello?"

"Mr. Baker?" a woman's voice comes through.

"Speaking."

"Please hold for Mr. Bonneville."

Jeff feels all the forced merriment of his morning dissipate as he waits for his boss to come on the line. He imagines the man right now: the tailored suit a size too small, creating the effect of a man powerful enough to burst out of it anytime, Hulk-style. The arrogant jowly face. The dark unblinking snake charmer's stare. The fake man-of-the-people timbre of his voice.

Charles "call me Chuck" Bonneville is not a man of the people. He was born into privilege, and his main accomplishment has been not squandering it all away. And no one ever calls him Chuck but ass-smooching Richie.

"Jeff, my man, how are you?"

"Doing well, sir, and yourself?"

"Sorry to bother you during your vacation." Charles Bonneville is not sorry—Jeff knows that for a fact. In all the years he's worked for the man, Jeff has never heard a sincere apology out of his mouth.

"It's quite all right," Jeff lies.

"The thing is we've been restructuring a bit, and I didn't want you to return to the office uncertain of the lay of the land, so I figured I'd give you a heads-up."

Jeff hates the sound of this. He can feel the anxiety gathering itself into a tight ball in the pit of his stomach.

Bonneville's voice flows into his ear like poison. "As you know, we've had Richie advance the ranks a bit, and well, we've been reexamining the account load and thought a bit of redistribution might be in order. Just to even things out. Nothing crazy. Few things from column A to column B and vice versa."

Jeff hears all the words his boss isn't saying, feels them like a thousand paper cuts.

He thinks of Caesar at the Forum on his last day. The way it must have felt to find the woven tapestry of his world ripped out from under him.

"So, you mean some of my accounts—"

"Yes, just a few here and there, nothing major, you'll still have plenty to do. We'll be giving you some of Richie's."

"May I ask which ones, sir?"

Charles lists the accounts, sounding like he's reading them off a screen in front of him.

It's just as Jeff suspected. His most lucrative accounts gone, moved to Richie. What he gets in return are a few smaller and more tedious clients. Potentially less money, certainly more work.

It feels to Jeff like an evil Richiesphere has been formed at his workplace, and it is slowly eating into his livelihood, into his life.

He makes a fist out of his free hand and pushes it to his mouth, afraid to say something stupid, something rash. Jeff counts to ten, slowly. Thinks about how much he needs his job, how much his family needs it. Muting the phone for a moment, he slowly releases a deep jagged breath.

"Still there, my man?"

He hates the rich baritone on the other end of the phone. What did he ever expect from a man named for a midsize sedan?

Jeff once saw a Pontiac Bonneville from the late 1950s at a classic car show; it was a thing of beauty. His boss is the bland '90s variety of the line. So generic, so unimpressive that it got shitcanned midway through the decade and no one has missed it since.

If only Charles Bonneville went the way of the car and vanished. But then, who'd be his boss? Richie?

Jeff hits unmute. "Yes, sir, I'm still here."

"And you're all right with all this, I trust?" A rhetorical question if ever there was one.

"Certainly, sir, thank you for letting me know."

"All right, then. Enjoy the rest of your vacation. Give my best to the family."

The phone call ends, and Jeff drops his phone on a nearby table like it's a venomous snake. Why'd he have to answer it? Why didn't he just turn it off for the duration of their stay?

The dumpster fire of a new setup would still be there when he went back to work, but he would have had two more weeks of blissful ignorance. Would it be worth it?

There's nothing he can do, no way to prepare for this, to make it okay. Just grin and bear it. Go on like everything's fine.

The Confucius method doesn't seem to work. He can sit by the river all he wants, but his enemies are not floating by. They are very much alive, happy, and thriving.

Maybe Jeff's the one who should take a dive.

He feels a white-hot blinding rage that, finding no outlet, seems to scour his insides. If only there was something to break, something to punch. But this isn't his house, and he isn't that type of man.

Jeff continues to pull books out and put them back on the shelves. The motion is automatic, he's barely registering the titles.

Then he hears a low screech, the sound of a basement door opening in a horror movie. Looking around, he sees that a hidden compartment has been unveiled. One of the books must have hidden a secret pulley mechanism. How delightfully cinematic.

The newfound cubby is made of glass or something glasslike and shimmery in its manipulation of ambient light. It contains a few shelves of what looks to Jeff to be top-notch liquor.

Ah, just what he wanted. Perfect. Thank you, Gussie.

Sure, it's early to drink, but Jeff's on vacation. And if there was ever a morning to get wasted . . .

Jeff pours himself a shot of scotch. The Macallan. He's only heard of the brand, never had the actual pleasure.

The liquid burns its way down like the most delicious of fires. To his undemanding palate, it tastes almost like dessert. Something like a warm bread pudding with raisins. Can that be right?

He considers reaching for his phone and looking it up, but the phone is still banished as the bearer of shit news.

Jeff takes another shot instead.

This is better than breakfast.

He toasts the portrait in appreciation of the gesture. This was exactly what he needed. This and some fresh air. He feels like he's been cooped up in the house for too long.

They've been idly discussing driving out somewhere, but the nearby towns are not that near—Gussie must have loved her privacy. Plus, once they drove all the way out there, they'd have to agree on activities and dining options; it always just seems easier to stay put.

Besides, driving with the family is a chore. Jeff misses driving for pleasure, with no one kicking his seat, asking him if we're there yet, making fun of his music.

Jeff takes another drink. It's so perfectly smooth. Now he understands why people pay good money for top-shelf liquor. He used to think it was an indulgence, but now he knows better.

It's to feel like this: like a king of the world. Well, a very small world and a very brief reign, but still.

A shot—and the family noises trickling in fade away to the background.

A shot—and his job woes follow.

One more—and he's the king of the castle with the road ahead unfurling like a red carpet.

Or . . . The metaphors mix and match themselves at leisure. The world spins around, and Jeff catches himself on the bookcase. The secret hideaway bar's door swings shut.

The transition is seamless, like the thing was never there to begin with. Jeff tries to remember which book triggered the opening mechanism. He can't. His hands are clumsy; the books are falling to the floor. He's making a mess and he doesn't care.

He still has the Macallan bottle in his hands. The party isn't over. He won't let the frustration take it over. The hideaway bar will be found again in due time.

Gravity pulls him down, and the chesterfield's leather rises up to meet him. The couch is too low to put his head back; he lies down, but it makes him dizzy. Sitting up again, Jeff looks around.

It's still early. The day is young.

The stupid phone call that nearly ruined it feels hours away, days away.

He hates his job. Everyone hates their job. He can work himself to the bone and never be able to afford a place like this. Why even bother?

His wife is a cockteasing ice princess. His kids are distant, screen-addicted, and will soon flee the nest anyway. He doesn't have any close friends. He's done everything right in life, and where are his rewards?

He is spiraling and there's no reining it in. Self-pity, and a well-deserved one at that, he feels, has got its claws into him.

The bottle slips from his hands, and scotch begins to pour out onto the rug. Persia meet Scotland, he thinks bemusedly. For a moment, the liquid pools in a manner too artistic to interrupt. Something about the way it attracts the light.

Then, he catches himself, grabs the bottle, and rights it to save its precious contents.

"You're good company," he tells the woman in the portrait, "but I need some air."

What Jeff believes he needs right now is a drive. Not far, just enough of a distance so he can be alone for a while, without the constant threat of interruption.

He can't remember the walk from the parlor to the Subaru, but the next thing he knows he's in the driver's seat. The ignition keys are in, swinging hypnotically, beckoning him. Why not, he thinks, why the hell not?

Somewhere sometime through the thick haze currently clouding his memory lane, Jeff remembers reading that the newest model of his car can get up to 127 miles per hour. He has never driven anywhere close to that. In any car.

It sounds dangerous, but also, kind of exciting.

The bottle next to him whispers shimmering golden encouragements. Jeff feels his foot pushing down, heavier and heavier. The road rises up to meet him like a tsunami wave, obliterating all else in sight.

It feels like freedom, it feels just like flying.

JENNA

SHE KNOWS WHAT she ought to be feeling: pity, compassion, etc., but it just isn't there. Jenna digs in deep to look for it beneath the layers of anger, annoyance, and disappointment.

It takes all her strength to hold back the "How could yous?" in front of the kids. Not that they don't understand what's happening; both of them are old enough to know.

Yes, kids, your daddy got wasted and crashed our family car into a tree.

It isn't even a sexy James Dean sort of crash; this is a sloppy, slobbery drunken folly that even Jeff seems to be embarrassed by.

He insisted on not calling 911, and eventually, Jenna complied. So now she's staying up with him to make sure he doesn't have a concussion or, heaven forbid, some internal bleeding that is slowly killing him.

To an untrained eye, Jeff's injuries are superficial. The airbag took the brunt of it. Well, technically, the tree did.

There are bruises, sure, but all the bones appear to be intact. He'll live. It's more than they can say for their Subaru.

Jeff isn't talking; he's just sitting there, sullen as a teen, sulking, stewing.

It was Angus who found him and brought him home. Wherever her husband was going, he didn't get very far. Angus was also the one who arranged to have the Subaru towed to the nearest mechanic. Jenna cringes imagining the future car repair expenses. If it is even salvageable. Angus thinks it might be.

Jenna finds herself appreciating the appeal of a quiet, unpresuming man. She had always liked them tall, with good hair, outgoing within reason. But that fades. One look at Jeff bonelessly spread out on a chesterfield confirms it.

She knows there are layers to her resentment. Things that have been on her mind, simmering there, unaddressed, and made raw and abrasive by the silence.

The way Jeff has been reaching for her at night. So crudely, so proprietarily. Not at all like him. Not at all like anything in their love life over the past two decades.

Night's darkness magnifies all things. In those quiet hours, a thought can become an obsession, a voice can become a scream, and a hand can become a weapon.

The way Jeff has grabbed at her at night felt like an assault. She's shoved him away time and again. Gently at first, then roughly. The strange thing is that he doesn't persist. Just rolls over and falls asleep. Leaving Jenna wide awake, upset, discombobulated. Leaving her to contemplate how large and strong his hands feel in the dark, not at all like the soft, hard-labor-averse hands she has come to know as well as her own.

Night Jeff is a stranger to Jenna. His features obscured by darkness, his needs made ugly by the force behind them.

She goes to bed and wakes up to the same man she's known for nearly half of her life. The hours in between are spent with someone she struggles to recognize.

It isn't the sort of thing one brings up, either. Like strange dreams, night things are best left to the night. In the light of day, they seem implausible, impossible. Tricks of the mind.

When she finally mentioned something to Jeff, the conversation went as awkwardly as she might have predicted. She can still recall it in every cringing detail. Play by play, like something out of a movie watched over and over.

"Did I do what?"

Jenna holds her coffee mug as a fortification device and plows on. "Grab me? At night?"

She hates the way her uncertainty is turning her statements into questions. She sounds like Jessie.

"As far as I know I slept through the night like a proverbial log."

"Are you saying I'm making it up?"

Jeff holds up his hands in that "Whoa, Nelly" way and says with what sounds like perfect sincerity, "Babe, no, absolutely not. But is there a way you might have, you know, dreamt it?"

And the thing is, she can't say she's 100 percent sure she didn't. That's the worst part of it. That's how the night gets you. It's the best worst trick.

"I don't think I dreamt it," she says, but suspects he can probably hear the weakness in her voice.

"Look, I would never . . . You know, I would never, right?"

And she does, doesn't she? Otherwise, she doesn't know him at all.

A few days later, Jeff shows her a bruise on his arm. "Look at this," he says. "I went to cuddle you last night, and you hit me."

"Cuddle?"

"Yes, sheesh, just cuddle. I mean, I think you didn't even wake up. I think you did it in your sleep."

The bruise has a fresh blueish tint to it, decorating her husband's upper arm like a tattoo.

"Maybe you thought I was grabbing at you?"

"Maaaybe." Who are they? What the hell are they doing to each other in their sleep?

"Look, I can sleep somewhere else for a while if that helps," Jeff offers.

"No." The objection flies out of her mouth before she can fully consider it. "No," she says slower. "It's okay."

She doesn't want to have to explain it to the kids. They already know too many divorced parents. She just wants a perfect vacation. If it means some interrupted sleep, so be it.

They continue to share the bed. The unspoken tension is thick enough to cut with a knife. It puts any thought of sex firmly on the back burner.

Just when they both start sleeping through the night again, this happens. Ugh, as her daughter would say. Just . . . ugh.

She studies her husband now, trying to see him as a stranger might. Tall but soft, with strong enough features but too mild of an expression, Jeff is a man solidly in the grasp of the middle-age doldrums. He's been many things over the years, mostly good things; at the very least, understandable things—a faithful husband, a decent provider, a steady co-parent. But he had never been reckless.

He says he's fine; he looks like Sisyphus finally crushed by his boulder. Good thing the house is large enough to keep its secrets. Good thing the kids are too absorbed in their own world to see him like this. Good thing Angus came along when he did and acted as swiftly as he did. The man is the soul of discretion, the way he conducts himself.

"Like nothing happened." He smiled at her before his departure, and she almost believed him. Why not? This too shall be bandaged; this too shall pass.

Who knows how many of the Doyles' careless blunders he has covered up over the years?

Jenna likes to think theirs is only one of many—and by far, the least severe of them.

Jeff starts to doze off, and she goes over and gently shakes his shoulder.

"I'm awake," he moans, "I'm awake."

To be perfectly honest, Jenna resents playing the caretaker to the man who has just wrecked their only available vehicle, their only way out of there. But then again, when she thinks of the expenses they would certainly incur by taking Jeff to be seen, she accepts the responsibility a bit easier.

"Talk to me." Jenna read up about concussions on her phone. "Talk to me to stay awake."

Jeff tries to shrug and winces. "Nothing to say."

"Seriously? Nothing at all?"

Silence.

"Don't want to tell me what you were doing out there driving drunk?"

"A couple of drinks."

"A couple?"

"Few."

"Few drinks of what?" A few glasses of wine wouldn't get him in this state.

"Scotch."

"We have scotch?" She prefers gin or vodka but feels like either way, that's something that should have been mentioned.

"We have a full bar."

"Where?"

"It's—you'll love this—hidden in the library."

"Hidden how?"

"Among the books."

Jenna gets up, goes over to the bookshelves, and looks. Same dusty tomes, nothing out of place.

"I don't see anything."

"That's what hidden generally means."

She resents his snippiness, figuring he's lost all privileges of having an attitude for a good long time.

"But you found it?"

"Yeah, just pulled on a book, and a door opened up, and there it was."

"Sounds like something out of a movie."

Another failed shrug.

"Can you find it again?"

"I don't know. Maybe?"

"And where's the bottle?"

"Huh?" He doesn't look like he has a clue, and just like that, an already highly suspect story starts to come apart. There is, of course, a chance that Angus took the evidence away, to perfect that "nothing happened" scenario. But what if Jeff brought booze with him? That seems plausible. Not very much in character, but not that far of a stretch either.

Maybe he carries it along, the way their daughter does her weight scale, or their son does his snacks—a known but undiscussed for peace of mind's sake thing. A pacifier, of sorts; a security blanket. Maybe Jeff was just sober enough to throw the bottle away before being brought back to Haven.

So many maybes.

"Where were you going?"

"What?"

"Where were you driving to?" A wild thought crosses her mind: what if Jeff was leaving? Leaving her, leaving them? Would he?

"I was just"—he waves his hand nebulously—"just driving. No destination. Just . . . out."

Out sounds like *away* to Jenna, but she doesn't push it. Doesn't want to. Doesn't dare to.

And holding back makes her angrier still.

"Are you happy now?"

"Happy?" Jeff laughs, a sad ragged sound. "No, Jenna, I'm not happy. I feel like Mike Tyson used me for a punching bag. I'm pissed about the car. I'm wrecked, I'm mad, I'm sorry. I am categorically not happy."

Was that an apology in there? she wonders. Because he has yet to offer one. And she believes she's entitled to at least that much.

"We'll be lucky to get the car back when it's time to leave. Until then, we're stuck here, thanks to you."

"Not like we were going anywhere anyway," he counters. Venom on venom.

"We were going to," Jenna says without conviction.

"What? Where? All we need is right here. All we need for a perfect family vacation."

She senses sarcasm in his voice, and it's pouring gasoline on her fire. Their vacation is perfect, will be perfect. As perfect as vacations get. Certainly miles better than her family members' vacations.

Jenna deserves it, and she won't let anyone, not even Jeff, ruin it for her. She knows this in her heart and refuses to be proven wrong.

Their family may not be perfect, but this vacation will be. She throws that at Jeff like a glass of ice water.

He says nothing, his eye contact weary, watery, over too soon.

"You know what?" she says letting go of all inner tranquility, "I don't care if you do have a concussion. Fall asleep, do what you like. It's all you want, anyway, isn't it? Just stay here with your stupid dead white men books and your imaginary secret bar and . . ." She flicks her fingers at him as if they are wet. "I'm done. I'm going upstairs to get some rest."

"Love you too," he calls after her, and the urge she feels to turn back and sink her perfectly polished nails into his insolent, unshaven mug scares her with its intensity.

She leaves before they do or say any more things they might regret.

JJ

THE CHARGER CORD is back. Just like that. Like it was never gone to begin with.

JJ knows his room is messy, but he would swear—he would bet money on it—the thing was gone. And as glad as he is to have it back, it kind of makes him feel like someone is messing with him.

It might be his parents trying to teach him a lesson, but it doesn't strike him as their brand of instructional guidance. They are more likely to cut his allowance than anything. And only if Jenna insisted. Jeff is a bit of a pushover.

Ansel or whatever his name is never seems to come into the house. Presumably, as the caretaker, he has the keys, but JJ has never seen him use them. Besides, why would the man mess with him? They don't know each other, have never spoken, likely to stay that way until this shitty vacation is over.

That just leaves Jessie. JJ suspects her but, lacking proof, isn't quite sure how to proceed.

All he has is his anger—the anger he believes to be righteous.

It sucks being a kid, being the youngest. He feels small, a toy in anyone's hand, a leaf at the mercy of anyone's wind.

There are four long years looming ahead of him before he can have any sort of agency of his own. Any sort of freedom.

Considered as a block of time, it feels daunting.

Four more years of humiliation at school. Four more years of his parents' rules and his sister's whims.

No, wait, he thinks, only two years. With any luck, some college will whisk Jessie away, and that'll be that.

It still doesn't give her the right to be mean. And it doesn't inspire him to forgive. Two years is a long time.

He wants to do something wild, something reckless. To get her back but creatively. Not just by stealing her things. JJ needs a master plan.

So he thinks. He stews. He plays his freshly charged video game, replacing the faces of his on-screen victims with those of people he knows.

It was quieter before when the charger was missing. He floated around in the lake until his skin pruned. Sometimes he narrated his surroundings to himself, pretending to be his very own David Attenborough.

His accent was atrocious, but he thought his observations were right on the money. But then, that wasn't him. That was some other version of him. A Vacation JJ.

This, here, in this stale dirty room, immersed in a shooter game, this is him. Taking control of things. Planning his revenge.

He scratches his head, ignoring the snowstorm of dandruff it stirs up. The lake water is doing something funny to his hair, it's softer, more manageable. All JJ wants is to drape it down his face like something out of a Japanese horror movie until the tiny angry volcanoes dotting his skin calm down.

The worst thing to happen to Jessie would be to look like him for a day, he thinks. Poetic, but impossible. He'll have to come up with plan B.

There's some kind of drama outside, and he's missing it. The sounds of it are drifting to him, faint through his headphones, like messages from a distant planet.

JJ considers shutting the window, but the air feels nice on his sweaty face.

He's so very close to finishing the game. He can almost envision the final screen, the music score rising up in volume to sound triumphant, congratulatory.

It will be an accomplishment, he doesn't care what anybody thinks.

The movie from a few nights ago is idly cycling through his mind. One of those stupid '80s comedies his parents deem family-friendly. It's only nostalgia, JJ figures. They just miss being young, the age they were seeing those movies for the first time.

JJ will never miss being a kid. Ever. Once he reaches adulthood, the tedious years preceding it will be boxed up and locked away in the deepest, darkest corner of his mind, somewhere he'll never go.

Maybe they all forget just how awful it is being a kid, he thinks. Maybe they just remember the good parts. Like the way all he'd ever want to remember from this vacation is the lake.

Does it work like that? Does memory work like that when you're older?

In the movie he's thinking about, one person gets mistaken for another, two very different people, and hilarity ensues. There's something there, something about the concept that sticks with him. He lets it simmer, and soon enough plan B is born.

He'll need access to Jessie's phone. A nearly impossible task since his sister is virtually glued to it, but worth a shot.

The rest he can do, he's certain of it. He's spent enough time on various social media websites—not trolling, just . . . checking things out—to know what to do.

For the next couple of days, JJ dedicates his time to sneakily taking the ugliest, most unflattering pictures of his sister. It makes him feel like paparazzi. Except that would make Jessie famous, and she is categorically not. And soon, she'll be . . . whatever the opposite of famous is. Laughed at?

Jessie won't go in the water, so that's out. She takes her phone with her to the bathroom every time, annoyingly enough.

In the end, it just leaves outright stealing. If only temporary. The way she filched his charger cord.

JJ lifts the phone while Jessie's in the kitchen pretending to share a snack with Jenna. It's all veg and dip, but she'll still throw it up later, JJ knows.

He'll have to pretend to be social, to create a subterfuge. Check him out. He smirks to himself. A hero of his own story, a superspy. JJ plops down on one of the padded stools along the large breakfast bar.

"Hey, hon," Jenna says. "You hungry?"

Jessie rolls her eyes at him as she says, "Ugh, like you have to ask."

You'll pay for that too, Jessie, JJ thinks.

"I could eat," he says with a shrug.

"Want some veggies?"

"Um, do you have anything more, you know, more?"

"I can make you a sandwich?"

"Sure, okay."

Jenna goes to the well-stocked fridge to take out cheese and lettuce and tomatoes. JJ watches, hoping for the addition of bacon or something substantial.

A carrot stick hits his head. "Can't you make your own?"

"I don't know. Can you even eat a sandwich?"

Jessie flinches then regains her composure. "Can you even not eat one?"

"Kids."

"Mooooom." All these years later, and they can still do that in perfect unison.

Jessie rolls her eyes and laughs.

"Sorry, little brother." There's nothing even resembling an apology in Jessie's smile. "I know you need your calories. Just be sure you can still fit into the back seat in a couple of weeks, or we'll have to leave you here."

"No one is leaving anyone here," Jenna says automatically without turning around.

Whatever she is adding to his sandwich doesn't smell at all like bacon. It's probably some garbage like seitan or tofu, none of which are good or even adequate substitutes.

"Oh yeah." Jessie is slowly working over a small piece of broccoli like a cow with her cud. "Actually, we might all be staying here. Did you hear what Dad did to the car?"

"Jessie," their mom says with caution in her voice.

JJ feels out of the loop. It's disorienting. Sure, he's been in his own world, but how did he not notice the absence of the Subaru in the driveway?

"What did Dad do to the car?"

"He crashed it," Jessie says triumphantly, spitting it out like a piece of good chewy gossip. "Into a tree."

"No shit?"

"Language, JJ."

"Sorry, Mom.

"Seriously?" he rephrases.

"Yeah, seriously."

Jenna places the plated sandwich in front of him, and he looks up at her for confirmation.

"Your father had a slight driving disagreement with a tree. The car will be fine. It's being worked on. We'll have it back in time for the end of the vacation."

"So, we're, like, stuck here?"

"Yeah, kiddo. You're stuck in this giant awesome house with all this nature and the lake and your loving family. You poor thing." His mom smiles and ruffles his hair. A trail of dandruff drifts down to his food. She pretends not to notice, but Jessie says, "Gross."

"Whatever."

"They have shampoos for that, you know."

"Yeah, let me waste all my time grooming the way you do."

"Right, why would you? Not when you can waste it playing video games instead."

"Exactly," JJ says and takes a bite out of his sandwich. It's too good-for-you to taste good, but it'll do.

JJ's tired of sparring with Jessie. She's getting meaner. Sharper, somehow. Probably just hungry.

He can't believe he didn't know about the car. Too late he realizes he didn't even ask about . . .

"Your dad's fine," Jenna says as if reading his mind. "A few bruises."

"Oh, right. Good. Okay."

"Well, I'm going to go read. Can I trust you two not to kill each other or burn the place down?"

JJ just nods, but Jessie hurries after Jenna to ask something. Leaving her phone behind on the counter. JJ had almost forgotten what he was doing there in the first place. The food and the bickering and the news distracted him.

But now he reaches for it, as stealthily as that *Mission: Impossible* dude, and puts it in his pocket. Then he crams the rest of his sandwich into his mouth, waves something like "thanks, bye" to Jenna, and rushes back to his room.

He knows Jessie will come knocking sooner than he'd like, and he has things to do on her phone before that happens. Things that will make his sister deeply, deeply unhappy. "Payback is a bitch," he says to himself quietly, savoring the thought, relishing the statement. Then he turns the screen on.

The apps come right up. One good thing about his sister living on her phone is that she's never away from it long enough to get logged off.

JJ sets off about his business, typing furiously. There's still some oil on his fingertips from his food, and the idea of desecrating his sister's immaculate bedazzled phone gives him a delighted shiver. She's going to be so mad. Furious. It's going to be so much fun.

JESSIE

THIS IS BY far the worst thing that has ever happened to her. Worse than when her best childhood friend moved away to Fresno, California. Worse than when she got caught shoplifting on a dare at the mall. Worse even than that time her period started when she was wearing white jeans at Allie's party.

Jessie stares at her phone in disbelief. What she sees there is so hideous, so . . . wrong, that it almost doesn't seem possible. It's like some terrible dream she's going to wake up from any moment.

She wants to stop time and then rewind it to before, when her only concern was getting more followers. But time won't listen to her, won't stop barreling toward a terrifying new future where Jessie is a laughingstock.

She watches the numbers crawl. Her followers are disappearing, but her photos have more comments than ever before. All of it is negative. All of them are mean. Some creatively so. She doesn't know if that's better or worse.

It occurs to her that in a way, this is the most popular she's ever been. In a very, very wrong way.

There is her picking a wedgie by the lake. The bathing suit she's wearing is an almost impossible contraption of straps and ties—wedgies are unavoidable. There's her rolling her eyes. She really looks that ugly when she does that? Sheesh, she needs to stop, to never do that again.

Her without makeup. A plain, washed-out face no one would look at twice, she thinks, studying the image. Thank goodness for makeup. A bedhead hair picture is particularly popular. Leftover product always makes her hair do crazy things first thing in the morning before she tames it into the perfection of smooth, ironed-down tresses.

She can't stop reading the comments. She knows she should, but she can't. It's like prodding a bruise. Like picking a scab.

Ugly, ugly, ugly the comments chant at her. No one ever said she was pretty with the same insistency.

Why is it, she wonders, so much easier to tear someone apart than to build them up?

Her brother does it too, leaves nasty comments for others. Her brother . . .

It hits Jessie like a slap in the face. Of course. That little shit.

Who else would be behind this? Who else would have access to her private moments like this?

With the realization comes a steady calming wave of hatred so pure that Jessie can feel it burning white-hot in her veins.

He did this to her. And for what? Some stolen candy? What sort of a person would do that?

A greasy friendless creep, that's who. Oh, he'll pay for this, she thinks. He. Will. Pay.

She just has to come up with revenge adequate to the damage done. And the damage, she knows, is significant. Pictures on the internet never go away. You can be famous for a day and forgotten soon after, but infamy lasts much, much longer. She will be forever branded by this like that woman in the book they had to read for English Lit. This is her scarlet letter.

One after another, she deletes the images, the comments. Until she's given herself a blank slate.

She knows it won't last. Someone somewhere must have grabbed a screenshot, saved it—that's all it takes. This shame turd will cycle the drain indefinitely. And even once it gets forgotten or, likely, replaced with the next salacious, scandalous thing, it'll still be there with endless potential to resurface and haunt her. The monster that is dormant but not dead.

It wasn't just the images either. It was the words. Each photo has a title, a description, a story. Nasty, evil, creeping truths stolen from her private thoughts, private notes. Things she would have never shared.

Her brother must have gone through her phone. It feels like a major violation. More than the time she told Rick Yolan to stop, and he kept going. It's personal, a destruction of a sacred space.

She could, of course, tell her parents. Their reaction would be so predictable, Jessie can imagine every minute detail of it. From sincere outrage to serious conversations about privacy to telling her it'll be fine, it'll blow over soon, to some inane punishment for JJ like allowance withheld.

All well-meant. All woefully insufficient. All proof of just how different their world is from hers, of just how little they understand her.

For some reason, it makes Jessie think about Augusta Doyle. Banished by her entire family, the woman had more cause for revenge than most, and what did she do instead? She left them all a vacation home. Way to turn the other cheek, Aunt Gussie. How does someone even do that? Jessie can't foresee any way she would ever let this go, any way to forgive her pizza-faced little shit of a brother.

She had never thought him evil before, not even particularly mean for that matter. Just kind of a loser. An ineffectual, lazy slob addicted to his moronic video games. She'd never suspected such viciousness in him, never glimpsed it. It's almost impressive. Now she knows. She's glad she knows. It's like seeing someone's true face for the first time.

JJ thinks he has exposed her unmade appearance to the world, but in doing so, he has shown his true colors. Maybe that's just how it works. Maybe we are the truest versions of ourselves when we lash out.

Jessie's tired of contemplating these things. She feels heavy in a way that, for once, has nothing to do with weight. She wants to go to the kitchen and eat until she can't eat anymore. Until she can't feel anymore.

She might do just that.

Her mom and dad aren't around. If there's one good thing about this weird house and its impossible design, it's privacy. The rooms are spaced wider than they are at home, and the walls appear to be made of something sterner, tougher, thicker.

She's alone in the kitchen, just her and the gleaming fridge. Its contents beckon.

Jessie starts with carrot sticks out of habit, but it does nothing, and she discards them. There's yogurt but it's her mom's, fat-free, flavor-free. Jessie fishes out ice cream from the back. Its fat content is low, but it's enough to make her swoon. She finds a loaf of bread in the cupboard and shoves slice after slice into her mouth. Then she spies a jar of peanut butter. It's been so long. Too long. She eats it with a spoon. It's so rich, so creamy, so good that she notices tears dripping down her face. She tells herself she's only crying over breaking her diet. Nothing else.

It's just calories. She'll purge. She'll be thin and pure again. If only everything in the world was that easy.

When the food comes back up, it's a tidal wave. Jessie is used to throwing up, but she usually has to force it. This thing is forcing itself out, like some perverted birth. She barely makes it up the stairs to her en suite bathroom. The vomiting takes forever.

Afterward, she slouches on the floor, the rim of an old-fashioned claw-foot tub digging into the back of her neck. There's not enough energy left in her to get up, rinse her mouth, make sure nothing got in her hair. She is spent.

A feeling comes over her—a perfect emptiness of mind and body—and she lets it envelop her. It's clean, pure. A steadying calm. And in it, a plan begins to formulate.

It'll have to be multilayered. Complex. JJ's offense deserves no less. And while nothing may ever even the score, Jessie's going to try to come close. She knows just where to start.

AVA

ℬ ℬ ℬ

THE FACILITY

There are few introductory phrases as overused as "not like anyone they've ever met." It's all too obvious, isn't it? Almost a given. Everyone you meet is, by definition, not like anyone you ever met. Still, though, Max stood out.

And not just due to being well over six feet tall. There was the long straight dark hair trailing every move like a blackout curtain. The deep-set piercing eyes. The booming voice.

Max was thin as a shadow, nearly two-dimensional in appearance, but never seemed weak.

Augusta thought Max to be fascinating, and not a little scary. In fact, she believed most people in the Facility, including the staff, were a tad frightened of Max.

There was never any violence that she had seen, but then again, the place came alive after the lockdown, it seemed, if she were to believe the howls and screeches of the restless souls. There were a few of those around, but mostly, Augusta was surprised to find the majority of people around her to be as sane as she was. Whatever sanity meant to her anymore.

They were trapped here, same as her, by their family's prejudices, unfortunate circumstances, the manifold vicissitudes of life. But through the tired looks and sedated gazes, one could observe a certain clarity of mind, the outrage at the unfairness that had landed them here.

Some had tried to take their own lives as she did. So many people, she thought, with nothing left to live for.

Not Max though. Max had the wild, indefatigable energy of someone bursting with life. Restricting such a person by these blind walls was like caging a wild animal for private amusement. Terribly, unjustly wrong.

Max fascinated Augusta, cut straight through her despair and sadness, stirred her curiosity. But she would have never said anything, had Max not spoken to her first.

Sliding up casually next to her at lunch as she pushed around limp green beans into grayish mashed potatoes with a plastic fork, towering over her even while seated, Max nodded to her wrists.

"Suicide?" That was the first word exchanged between them. Jarringly to the point.

Augusta nodded back. "You?"

"Oh, me, I'm all kinds of wrong. But chiefly, I'm a warlock."

Augusta didn't expect that. She almost sputtered her weak tea all over the table.

"Do you find that funny?"

"Oh no, no, just . . . unusual."

"Well, who wants to be usual." Max shrugged and stole a bean off her plate. "Ugh, disgusting. You wouldn't think one can mess up something as simple as a vegetable side, but the chefs here are eager to prove you wrong."

Augusta laughed. Then caught herself. She couldn't remember the last time she laughed–it was a strange, stretchy sensation, like using a seldom-exercised muscle.

"So, they locked you up for being a warlock?"

Max sighed. "Among other things. You do know what it is, don't you? Many don't."

"Yes," she said, grateful for her time in the city and all the esoteric knowledge picked up over the years. "It's like a male witch."

"Just like it." Max grinned.

"And are you . . .? Do you still . . .?"

"Practice?" Max nudged.

"Yes."

"Always. The magic is all around us."

"Even here?"

"Even here."

What a hauntingly hopeful notion, Augusta thought. And with that, a new friendship was born. A new start, once again.

Of all the sins Max had committed in the eyes of his family, being a warlock was by far the least. Living his life as a man was the greatest. The most unforgivable one of all.

The family didn't appreciate their only daughter, Maxine, stylizing herself as a man. Over the years, they tried and tried to reshape him into something they could recognize, love, be proud of, but eventually, begrudgingly admitting their failure, they had him locked up.

Max had been through the mill of them, from fancy private resort-style "getaways" to communal Eastern-style retreats. The Facility was merely the latest and longest stop.

"This is by far the worst," he'd say. "But at least, there's no pretense here. Everyone knows and acts as if this is the low-rent loony bin that it is."

"Can't you just magic yourself away from here?"

"First off, it's magick with a K, and secondly, no, sadly, it doesn't work quite like that. Maybe it would, if I were at the top of my powers, but I am but a humble adept."

They started spending all their free time together. Two odd peas in a drab and dire pod.

"Look at me," Max would say. "Don't you think I was born to be a man?"

Given his height, his strong rough features, his flat, thin, curveless body, it was difficult to argue.

"You, on the other hand . . ." He'd squint his eyes as if taking an estimation of her until she laughed.

One thing about Max was he could always make her laugh. And it was that and not the bitter sedatives and the useless therapy sessions that finally began bringing her back to herself, back to the light.

Max was a liar, but the most amusing sort. He made up stories to delight, not to deceive. He fibbed in jest, in kindness even.

"You're not what I would have expected in a warlock," Augusta told him.

"You should see me in my cloak." He cackled madly. "Or on my broom."

"Do they even make brooms for someone your size?"

"Oh, mine is a custom job. Zero to forty in ten seconds flat."

There were clocks on the walls, but few and far in between, and no calendars at all. It made time easy to forget. And with that, one can just as easily forget about the world outside, and worst yet, let the world forget about them.

The Doyles didn't visit. Of course they didn't. She wouldn't have expected them to, wouldn't have wanted to see them, to be seen by them.

Murderers, she thought when she lay awake at night. I do not forgive you.

There was no Max after hours to distract her from her dark thoughts. The nights in the Facility lasted forever.

When Augusta finally told her new friend about the circumstances that landed her there, he went uncharacteristically quiet. Paler than usual.

"I'd hug you, darling, if they permitted such affections here," he whispered with feeling.

"I'd hug you back."

"Don't . . ." Max hesitated, then continued, ". . . don't forgive them. Don't ever forgive them."

"I won't."

"Don't forget it either."

"I can't."

"Good girl." He smiled. "I see the steel in you. You'll shine yet."

Max's age was impossible to determine, but the more she learned about him and his life the older she placed him. Older than her.

Than James. Than her brothers, one by one.

"Don't go counting my tree rings, Augusta. Age is but a number." He'd smirk whenever she asked leading questions.

She wondered if that were true. After all, in her life before this place, no meaningful connection seemed to concern itself too greatly with age. She had thought of herself as an adult who interacted with other adults. That was all.

Ever since that terrible Thanksgiving, she had felt increasingly like a child. Being punished, held against her will, left alone.

"It's the helplessness of it all," she told Max.

"Whether you're a child or a woman, it seems." Max nodded thoughtfully. "Or me," he added with a laugh.

Every so often, as part of the well-behaved group, they were allowed brief supervised walks. The world outside shocked Augusta anew every time. The weather was always different, the sky was ever-changing. Eventually, she started looking at other things, like walls and fences.

Max noticed.

"You can get out of here, you know," he told her quietly.

"I don't know. I was never a good climber."

"No." He laughed, waving his hand dismissively. "Not like that. That's for movies."

"Then how?"

"Legitimately. By proving you are sane and ready to rejoin proper society. Properly. This is a state facility, darling. It makes perfect financial sense for them to kick you to the curb if they believe you're curb-ready."

"Why haven't you then?"

"Look at me. I'm not ever going to be curb-ready enough for their liking."

"But surely you can't just stay here forever," she protested, her voice rising.

"Shhh. Calm down, calm down, love. Forever isn't what you think."

She sighed and steadied herself, lowering her voice back to a whisper.

"What is it?"

"Forever is a legacy. A remembrance. Revenge. I'm waiting on mine. Mastering my skills. Biding my time. My parents will not last much longer, last I

heard. And though they despise me, they are much too conventional to disinherit their only heir."

"Ah. So you do have a plan."

"Darling." Max smiled widely. "I always have a plan."

But for now, it was decided they would focus on her.

Augusta hadn't been applying herself at the Facility. Sleepwalking through therapy, sitting out activities. Now she did it all, attacking every opportunity to prove herself improved with zeal and alacrity.

Eventually, for institutional cogs turned slowly, her efforts became noticed, noted, encouraged. And later still, they began the talks of her release.

The mere possibility of it both excited and terrified her.

"What will I do?" she fretted to Max. "Where will I go?"

She'd never been on her own before. All the independence she had ever acquired had been with someone by her side. With no love, no friends, no money, the world seemed daunting. She craved her freedom, naturally, instinctively, but didn't know what she'd do with it.

"All you need to feel is exhilarated by the possibilities. Trust the universe. Something will materialize."

"Max, that is much too abstract for me, I'm afraid. Are you planning to conjure some magick with a K for me on the other side?"

"You mock? You dare?"

"No, of course not." She smiled, and for a moment made her arms into a life preserver. It was their shared gesture, meaning, "I'm hugging you."

He returned the motion.

Truth was, Augusta didn't know what to believe about Max's claims of exploring powers beyond this realm. She'd heard of séances and clairvoyants in the city, but never took any of it seriously. James had always found it outright laughable.

Then again, James had never met Max, had never been to a place like this.

James, her poor James, would never meet anyone again or go anywhere. She hoped the place he ended up in was a happy one. In here, in this direly unhappy place, warlock or not, Max had been her magic. Her magick too.

He saved her; she believed it with all her heart.

A heart that would tear to leave him behind.

In the end, she did have a visitor. Gerry, the softest of Doyle boys, for whatever that was worth.

She didn't know why she agreed to see him. Was it the "know thy enemy" policy Max extolled? Was it mere curiosity?

Either way, she brushed her hair, washed her face, and made her way to the visitor's room. For the first time in all of her stay.

Gerry looked uncomfortable enough to crawl out of his skin, rumpling his hat in his hands. He also, she noted with some surprise, looked older. Did she?

He stood up at her arrival.

"Hiya, sis."

"Gerry."

"You look well." The insincere compliment dropped to the floor like a bag of flour.

"Let's sit, Gerry."

He plopped down gratefully, letting the furniture take some weight off the conversation.

For a while, no one said a word, but the silence became uncomfortable quickly enough.

"Heard you were getting out?"

"If all goes well."

"The family says hello. Sends you good wishes and all that." He couldn't meet her eyes anymore, his hat taking all of his focus.

"Do they now?"

"Yeah, they wanted me to tell you, no hard feelings, yeah? Bygones and all that."

Bygones. What a quaint way to describe murder and forced confinement. She squeezed one hand with another to avoid screaming. To avoid hitting him.

Temper outbursts were not welcome at the Facility. And she wouldn't dare. Not when she was so close.

She slowly released her breath, steadying herself.

"So, what might you do once you're out?" he asked.

"I haven't decided yet."

"But you won't . . . you won't go telling stories, will ya?"

She almost shook her head. Ah, so that's why you're here. You want to make sure I don't tell on the Doyles. Now that makes perfect sense. To think, for a moment she might have imagined they cared about anything but their own skins.

Truth is, she'd given it plenty of thought. Some days, some nights especially, it was all she could think about. What she came up with was nothing. Nothing she could do. Too much time had passed. There were no witnesses but her, no proof. The Doyles would all stand by each other, and she, with her history, would be made a laughingstock at best or end up right back in the Facility, or worse. Perhaps the Doyles would even take matters into their own death-stained hands, making sure she never told any tales again. Reducing their family to be as Doyle Sr. always wanted: eight kids, all boys.

"No, Gerry." She leveled her eyes at him until they were met. "Tell the family I have no plans of telling stories. And who'd believe me anyway? Fresh out of a loony bin."

"Right, right, good." Her brother nodded quickly, his relief palpable. "Well, look, I won't keep ya. Just wanted to make sure you were all right. And here." He fumbled in his pocket and handed her some bills. "Just something to get you started on your way."

On your way far away from here is what he didn't say, but it was implied. After he left, his broad back receding like a ship in the night, Augusta counted the money. Thirty bucks.

That's all she was worth to them. All her silence was worth.

She wanted to run after him, wad it up, throw it at his back like a snowball. The Doyle boys had always spiked their snowballs with shards of ice when they pelted her. She still had a few small scars here and there.

But of course she did no such thing, only stayed and watched, letting her rage crystallize into pure hatred, to be stored for later. She wouldn't forgive. She wouldn't forget.

Never.

When the day of her release came, Augusta allowed herself one grand indulgence. She walked up to Max and wrapped him in her arms. He was so much skinnier when touched, nothing but bones, almost fragile. She had never thought of her friend as fragile before.

Many things but never that.

Now she worried about him, about leaving him, but he swore up and down that he'd be fine.

"Don't cry," he said, and she wiped at her cheeks automatically. She hadn't realized she was.

"You go on, get out, and live a wonderful life. I promise I'll send some magick your way."

"You are my magick, Max," Augusta said, and now the tears came full force like a dam split open; years and years of grief pouring out.

The orderlies separated them, rudely, unceremoniously. Just doing their job, never mind the heartbreak, the waterworks.

She walked away on leaden feet, afraid to look back. The small suitcase she'd brought in with her, seemingly a lifetime ago, felt light, almost empty. Thirty dollars burned shamefully in her pocket.

It would be enough to pay for a ticket back to the city. A deli sandwich. A cup of coffee.

And then, she was back in the city. In some ways it was as though she never left; in some, it felt like eons had passed.

Augusta wandered the streets of the place she had so loved, and memories lit it up like a Broadway stage set for her, bringing it to life. But in nearly all of them, there was James, and without him, it just wasn't the same.

That was as far as her plan had stretched: coming back to the city. Now she was at a loss.

Caught up in a wave of dizzying, disorientating freedom.

She bought another cup of coffee from a park vendor, a grizzled old man with a proper Neyuuu Yaaawk accent. Then, with the last of her change, on a whim, she added a lottery ticket.

⁂

It was strange to think that a small piece of paper could completely alter the course of one's life. Just some numbers. Ava had never played the lottery before or since. Didn't believe in lightning striking twice, didn't wish to tempt her luck.

She almost lost the ticket back then, to the casual debris at the bottom of her pocket, almost forgot about it. But something didn't let her. She remembered the feeling still, though there were no words to describe it. The peculiar insistence of it. A glimmer of something bright at the end of a long dark road.

Ava decided to stop writing for the night. Her eyes were tired, her soul was weary. The darkest chapter in her life became the darkest chapter in her . . . what? A manuscript? She loathed to think of it as a diary, and anyway, weren't diaries written of their time in their time? Then again, surely not a biography—that sounded too weighty.

To think that once, the very freedom she had always taken for granted wasn't a given. To think that she had been caged.

Ava shuddered and pulled her shawl closer around her shoulders. She was an old lady now, she reluctantly acknowledged, and old ladies wore shawls.

Perhaps not handwoven shahtoosh shawls, but then, they didn't throw their last coins to the winds of chance, selecting a combination of random numbers—Leilani's, James's, Max's, and her favorite ones—and striking gold.

The wind howled outside, but Ava was safe and warm behind the triple-pane custom windows of her house. Lonely, but safe and warm.

And not so old as to forget what it was like to be neither. Still grateful. She settled in her favorite chair, enjoying the view. The water had never ceased to soothe her. She'd pick up the narrative tomorrow, she thought. Bright and early.

JEFF

HE FEELS LIKE a fool. He feels like a fool who got run over by a Mack truck. Knowing he's done it to himself makes it worse.

Must every pleasure in life be paid for so dearly?

The last thing he remembers before being pulled from the car by Alex, no, Arthur, no, Angus, was flying high on Macallan and pure automotive speed.

Maybe that was just his mind telling him fairy tales. He isn't sure where the bottle went; presumably, the caretaker, in an act of discretion, whisked it away.

Jeff knows for a fact he wasn't flying all that far. The tree he crashed into is depressingly close to the house.

Jeff feels a deep sense of shame, but when he examines it, he realizes just how much of it is pure embarrassment.

Jenna's done a great job of keeping the brunt of it away from the kids, but he can feel all of their disappointed looks on him like fingers jabbing into his countless bruises.

He played off the worst of the damage, refusing to call 911. Avoiding a public record of personal shame, avoiding the bills that would inevitably come. His insurance isn't that good. A promotion would have upgraded it. He bets Richie's coverage is stellar.

All Jeff really wants to do is crawl into a ball and lick his wounds. As privately as being a part of a family with kids might allow.

He desperately wishes he could find the hidden bar again because the hair of the dog might be the only thing that'll help. He's tried every book on the shelves, it seems. Nothing gives. It's confusing, disorienting. Jeff knows for a fact he isn't imaginative enough to have invented the thing.

For a moment there, he was so sure the vacation was going well. Now he can barely move—he's sure he's cracked some ribs; his wife is annoyed with him, and his kids are . . . well, largely indifferent as always.

What does it take to make a family happy? Is it even possible? He remembers some famous quote about all happy families being the same and all unhappy ones being unique. Something like that.

But are they unique? The Bakers seem to be a unit made from a perfect mold. The living embodiments of the grinning stick figure families you see on stickers decorating the backs of minivans. A steady marriage, a comfortable home, two perfectly age-spaced kids, one of each gender. A husband who works, a wife who takes care of the house, kids who are addicted to their screens.

All that's missing is a dog and only because Jessie and JJ are too unreliable to take care of one, and Jeff and Jenna are too fastidious for all that fur and slobber.

But otherwise, they are so typical. So straight out of central casting, aren't they? Shouldn't they be happier?

Until this vacation, he might have said they were. Now, he's not so sure.

There's a rift between them that is clearer to see here, at Haven. Some of it is in the things they say, but mostly it's in words left unspoken.

A steadily increasing distance as they drift from each other and from the people they wish themselves to be.

Jeff tries to shake the gloomy thoughts away. It isn't like him. He doesn't like to dwell on the intangibles. He tries to focus on the facts.

Fact: he got something resembling a demotion at work. But it might not affect them too much financially, which is what's really important.

Fact: he crashed the Subaru, which will cost good money to fix. But they can afford it, and hopefully it will be ready by the time they have to leave.

Fact: his wife might be well on her way to never having sex with him again. Or even sleeping in the same bed. But . . . well, he doesn't have a spin on that one. He isn't sure he understands all of it yet. The way she says he acts in their sleep doesn't sound like him at all, nor does he have any recollection of it. What he does remember is the steaming hot movie-like sex they had in the parlor that one time, but even that now feels less like a memory and more like a dream.

There's something about this house that seems to be messing with his sense of reality. What is it?

He looks up at the portrait. "I know you know," he tells his hostess.

She is silent. Her barely-there smile as enigmatic as Mona Lisa's. As elusive as certainty.

Jeff sighs. Contemplates limping over to the bookshelves to find another book to read.

JJ wanders in, startling him.

Brave face goes on like a tie. Like a noose. "Hey, kiddo."

"Sup."

That isn't a question, Jeff knows, but he proceeds like it is.

"Well, you are, a miracle of miracles. And without a phone."

"With a phone." JJ pats his back pocket.

"Well, sure, but you're not looking at it. You're looking right at me. I can see your eyes and everything."

"Are you okay?"

Too much? Jeff thinks. Dial it down?

"I'm fine. I mean, a few bruises, mostly my ego. Nothing like the car. Nothing like the tree either."

"But you hit your head, right?"

"Well, the airbag hit my head, technically."

"Any brain damage?"

"No, the airbag appears to be fine."

JJ pauses for a second, unsure, then laughs.

It's a rare display of pure joy from an otherwise sullen, taciturn kid, and Jeff takes it in fully, enjoying the moment.

"Wanna go for a swim, kiddo?"

"Can you even?"

Jeff contemplates his condition for a beat.

"I mean, I'm not going to Michael Phelps it, but if we take it easy."

JJ scratches his head. Jeff notices dandruff flaking down, like fine dust swirling in the sunlight. Jeff remembers being that age. Kids were cruel then and seem even crueler now. And being ugly is never easy, at any age, but as a teen, it's pure torture.

Jeff had mercifully skipped the worst of puberty. He was always reliably decent-looking. But his son appears to have hit every branch of that particular tree on the way down. His skin is weeping, tiny little volcanos; his hair is a greasy mess; and that weight . . .

It feels wrong to regard his kid—any kid—with such remote objectivity, but Jeff can't help but wonder just how tough it is for JJ in school, in life. His sister is so effortlessly pretty, taking right after her mom. She must have it so much easier. DNA roulette is such a wicked game.

"Yeah, I mean, we can go to the lake," JJ says, rubbing at a particularly angry-looking red spot on his chin.

Jeff was kind of hoping for a no, but he did offer, and he isn't going to pass on a perfectly good bonding experience.

Jessie seems to be pissed at him; he wonders what her mother told her. They both appear to regard Jeff as a man who has effectively trapped them at Haven. But JJ either doesn't know or doesn't care. Either way, it's nice.

Getting up from the couch is a bone-cracking exercise in masochism. The very thought of going upstairs to get his swimming trunks exhausts him.

They ascend slowly, at his pace. The stairs feel endless. Jessie passes them wordlessly, glaring at JJ.

"You guys fighting?"

JJ shrugs.

By the time they finally get to the lake, Jeff is spent. His body feels boneless, muscleless, just a sad, tired bag of meat. He'd kill for a nap, a series of naps, preferably, that flows into a deep steady sleep. But no, here he is, playing the father of the year.

The water does feel good though. The buoyancy takes the weight of his injuries away; he can't swim much, but he floats happily.

JJ zooms by, with an always surprising dolphin-like grace.

He looks like there's something on his mind, weighing heavily.

"Dad, you ever, like, have bad thoughts?"

"Sure. Everybody does."

"But, like, I have a lot of bad thoughts since I came here, to this house?"

Is that a question? Jeff can't tell with the way kids talk these days. Either way, seems like reassurances are in order.

"It's just because there are fewer distractions than we have in the city."

"For real?"

"Sure." Jeff nods his protesting neck. "For real."

"So it's okay to think them?"

"Yeah, it's okay, kiddo. Don't worry."

"But, like, what if you act on them?"

Jeff feels a frisson of something, an alarm, perhaps. Or maybe it's just a gust of sudden wind on his wet skin.

"What'd you do, JJ?"

The kid's face is like a gate slamming shut. Jeff kicks himself mentally. He should have modulated his voice differently. Or phrased the question in another way.

"Nothing," JJ says dismissively. "Nothing. I was just asking."

"It's okay, whatever you did, you know. It's okay to tell me."

"It's fine, Dad. Don't worry about it."

Shit, Jeff thinks, the conversation had such promise but flatlined right before his eyes.

He wonders if sincerity might do the trick of resurrecting it.

"I have bad thoughts too, you know. I mean, I get upset about work and things. Sometimes I sit in the parlor and think about things. It's a lot of time, you know. An entire month to just hang out and do nothing. No school, no work, no schedules. It's nothing to do with the house. It'd be the same anywhere. A month in a hotel, a month in a rental. It's just that people are not meant to sit around idly and just think thoughts. It leads to dark places."

"It does?" JJ says. "Why?"

"I don't know, kiddo. The mind is a strange and mysterious place. It's like the universe. We think we know so much about it because we're always sending out space exploration drones and all that, but in reality, the only thing we can be sure of is that the universe is about 68 percent dark energy and 27 percent dark matter, and we know nothing about those things. The only knowable bit is less than 5 percent. Think about that, it's like living in the dark all the time."

For a moment, Jeff is proud of himself for sounding smart, for remembering those statistics from a book he read. Then, seeing the look on his son's face, he isn't so sure he said the right thing after all.

"Less than 5 percent," JJ repeats as if in awe. "It's like nothing, is it? I mean, if we know nothing, then nothing matters?"

It sounds almost profound, like a riddle or a koan or something. But either way, it shouldn't be how a fourteen-year-old thinks.

"That's not what I mean, JJ. All I meant is that it's okay to have bad thoughts and not know where they come from. And that they have nothing to do with this house."

"Right." JJ nods, but Jeff can see his wheels are spinning in another direction. This is the danger of talking with kids. All those young impressionable minds, you never know how your words might imprint on them.

Not that talking to adults is that much better. It's all frustrating.

Jeff lets go of his float, allowing the water to claim him. For a moment, the weight of it feels soothing, then reflexes take over, and he splashes back up to the surface.

JJ has swum away. Their bonding moment is over. There's nothing but the sun and the water therapeutically lapping at Jeff's wrecked body. For a while, it is enough.

JENNA

LAST NIGHT IN Jeff's absence, her sleep was perfect. Restful, restorative. She woke up feeling like a woman in a mattress commercial.

Jeff slept on one of the chesterfields in the parlor. Jenna doesn't even find them particularly comfortable as couches, let alone beds, but her husband seems to love it down there.

She's putting herself through yoga stretches, enjoying the clarity she feels, mentally and physically, when the dark thoughts descend upon her, like vultures on carrion.

What if it was always like this? they whisper. *What if Jeff was always sleeping elsewhere?*

The thought seems surprisingly tempting, but she shakes it away. Surely, it's only because of their recent tensions that it would cross her mind in the first place.

Jenna doesn't normally like to sleep alone. She needs the comfort of another body next to her, someone to snuggle up to, warm calves to push her perpetually icy toes into. For all his foibles and imperfections,

Jeff has been that body for her for over two decades. She appreciates the sturdiness of him. The way he always seems to run about ten degrees warmer. The way he never steals her blankets. Without him there, she's afraid she would feel somehow untethered.

The few nights he was away over their time together, she slept with a weighted blanket. Most of the time, it lives in a fabric storage box under their bed. Jeff makes fun of it, calls it Albert (as in Fat Albert) and it is objectively funny, the obscene heaviness of it that threatens to pull her arms out of their shoulder sockets each time she has to fold it. But it's better than nothing.

In fact, it's impressive how well she slept last night alone and without Albert. There were dreams, she remembers having them, but morning whisked away the details.

And at any rate, she contemplates while easing her body into Downward Dog, every marriage goes through rough patches, but, essentially, they are happy. Aren't they?

Jenna has never really taken the time to contemplate it, never felt she had the perspective to do so. When you're in it, it's all you see, all you know. It's your entire world.

She has only ever counted herself lucky when compared to other Doyles, who, in feats of staggering hypocrisy, tend to completely disregard their Catholicism when it comes to divorces.

She'd hate to be one of those statistics. To raise their kids separately, to have to start over at her age.

Not that she feels particularly old. Or looks it. Jenna has every confidence she can pull off the hot MILF thing; she hasn't been minding her diet and exercising like a fiend all this time for nothing. It's just that she wouldn't want to.

The thought of trying again, of dating again, exhausts her. Makes her skin crawl.

It's difficult enough to find the right person the first time around when you still have some of that youthful energy and hopefulness.

Before the world beats it out of you. To meet someone who you like and get along with, who doesn't run away as he gets to know you, who shows you kindness and interest, who agrees to build a life with you—that's huge, that's monumental.

By and large, Jeff is still that person for Jenna. He is her rock, her home. They made a choice: to have and to hold, to withstand the hurricanes of life together. That's how it's supposed to be, otherwise it's chaos. Isn't that what marriage is—safeguarding each other? They'll work out whatever is happening between them right now. They'll get their car back, return to the city, to their normal lives, and all will be fine.

That's what she tells herself. It is the sword she wields to banish dark thoughts. That's the power of yoga; it always helps Jenna to realign her brain toward the positive.

She rides that zen wave once she's done as she rolls away the mat, as she takes a luxuriously long shower, as she puts herself together, applying light makeup, slipping into her best vacation silk and linen.

Then, on the way to the kitchen, she espies Jeff's prostrate form on the couch, and the dark thoughts return with such force, they almost knock her down.

Look at him, they scream. A loser. That's your man? Shame on you.

He lied to you. Got drunk on your family vacation. Crashed your family car. And for all you know, he's been trying to get rough with you for days and then gaslighting you about it.

Jenna doesn't want to listen to that. In fact, she's contemplating coming in to say something. She did leave him alone when he was potentially concussed.

"How are you feeling?" she asks, stepping in. The room is never well-lit, no matter what time of day it is. Too many shadows stubbornly clinging to the corners.

"About as good as I look."

"I'm sorry about the other night." The words are out of her mouth before she has time to think them through, and it makes her mad. She didn't come here to apologize and yet here she is, mea culpa-ing out of sheer habit.

"It's fine. I didn't die or anything." His smile is shy and meek and warm and so very much Jeff that it makes her want to go over and hug him. For all his faults, he's never been one to hold grudges.

"Guess you didn't have a concussion after all."

"Maybe it was a very well-behaved one?"

She returns his grin this time.

"Want breakfast?"

"Yes, please. I've been contemplating a trip to the kitchen all morning, but . . ." He shrugs, lifts his arms slightly, and drops them like dead weights.

"Poor baby. Sure you don't want me to take you somewhere to be seen?"

"Nothing they can do for broken ribs. I don't want to pay all that money to be told to rest. I plan on resting anyway."

"Well, okay then. Eggs?"

"At this point, anything. My stomach has been growling like a fiend."

"You can walk, though, right? Or do I have to serve the lord of the manor in his parlor?"

Jeff sighs, then sits up with a groan, and slowly stands up. "I can walk. At least, a zombie shuffle."

"All righty then, shuffle with me toward the kitchen. I'll see if I can rustle you up some brains."

See, this is good, Jenna thinks, walking with exaggerated slowness alongside Jeff. We are good. We banter. Happy people banter.

The kitchen is brighter. The light here is better. Eggs are cracked and whisked. Jenna makes Jeff a proper fatty omelet, with real cheese, opting for a yogurt and fruit parfait for herself. The kids must be still sleeping. Or just not hungry enough to make it downstairs.

Well, Jessie seems never to be hungry, and JJ is always hungry. Between the two of them there must be a happy medium somewhere, but she isn't making extra food on their account. They'll eat when they get here. There's always cereal.

Jeff eats with impressive gusto. Jenna takes his good appetite as a sure sign of speedy recovery.

They tread lightly, skating the surface of their lives, mindful of the treacherous ice. But every so often, something breaks through.

"I'm worried about the car," she says.

"Don't be." Jeff reaches out to cover her hand with his. The sunlight hits the hair on his knuckles. Did he always have that? Jenna could swear he didn't. It makes his hands look strange, brutish. "It'll be okay," he says, and it takes her a moment to realize he's talking about the car.

Good old Jeff always prefers to deal in absolutes.

"Will our insurance cover it?"

"Most of it."

"They should give you a raise. That one percent cost of living bullshit last year was a joke. Maybe once you get that promotion."

Her husband sighs at that and looks away, then down at his plate, as if contemplating the future foretold by the pattern of leftover yolks.

"What?"

"Nothing."

"Jeff. What?"

"I didn't get the promotion."

"What? Why not?" What she really wants to ask is why he didn't tell her sooner.

"Because Richie is better at ass-kissing."

That is true. She met the man at Jeff's work's annual Christmas party. A low-level creep. His nose is so brown, he's like his very own variety of reindeer. She hated Richie; he was one of those men who never actually does or says anything explicitly wrong or offensive, but his words and his eyes make you want to take a long hot shower to wash away the sheer proximity of him.

The scumbag must be doing something right though.

Jenna's been waiting for this promotion. Counting on it. Spending the raise in her mind. She shouldn't have, but she couldn't help herself. It's been so long since they had more than what they needed. Enough to venture into that ever-inviting "want" territory.

Aunt Gussie's money is gone. Jenna meant to hold on to it, but there was a leaky roof, and then she bought her used Honda, and that was it. Ten grand doesn't go as far these days as it might have back in Gussie's.

"Well fuck," she exhales.

What she meant to say was, "I'm sorry." She realizes this hits Jeff harder than it does her. In his ego, not just the wallet.

"Yeah, well." He nods mildly, sipping his coffee.

Suddenly, she feels angry. For Jeff, at Jeff. Doesn't he feel it too? The righteous rage at the injustice of it all. The brunt of the world where trash rises to the top and plays at being the cream.

"Can you fight it?"

"Fight it?" he asks incredulously, putting down his mug. "How would I fight it? The decision is final. He's already been given some of my accounts."

Jenna says nothing. She studies her husband over the rim of her coffee cup, contemplates his slouched dejected form. This is it, she realizes. This is the preview of the future. Of the next however many decades spent observing Jeff languish in mediocrity, placidly accepting every downturn of fate, going along to get along until he runs out of road.

The thought depresses her, turns the delicious brew in her mouth sour.

She tries to come up with something—anything—positive to say. "Maybe it's time to look for a new job?"

"Jenna, no one is hiring people like me."

"Oh yeah?" she wants to say. "Well, where does it leave me? I'm married to a person like you."

What she says instead is, "You can always look?"

Jeff shakes his head, lightly, almost imperceptibly. But she sees it. The "you don't understand" gesture. It fuels her anger further.

"I'm gonna go lie down," he says. "Thanks for breakfast."

"You're welcome," she replies automatically and watches him shuffle away.

Unkind thoughts she seems to have no control over launch themselves like throwing knives at his back.

Did she make the wrong choice tying her life to this man? Jenna hates being wrong. She wants–needs–some outlet for this spite that's burning her insides.

Not that she would ever say anything; it isn't her way. And Jeff will never figure it out on his own, will never know the way he's made her feel. Will never be able to appreciate it or apologize for it.

Maybe she doesn't need words where actions might do. Something subtle, clandestine. A small, delicate, soft revenge, perhaps. Yes, Jenna likes the sound of that.

JJ

ANY OTHER TIME, this progress would have been remarkable. Impossible, even. Back in the city, there are too many distractions. But here, in the middle of nowhere, with nothing but swimming and some forced family evening time to interrupt him, JJ's gaming has been reaching new levels at a most impressive pace.

Now, three weeks in, he's nearly done with it. The end is so near, he can practically taste it. This has been by far the most sophisticated game he's played; one that might even give him something like bragging rights.

And, almost more importantly, it's entirely his own. He bought it, paid for it, played it, succeeded at it. Sure, his family might find gaming meaningless, but to JJ it's a thing of autonomy and thus, a thing of beauty.

For a while there, he was actually enjoying his lake time, but Jeff has been weird lately. Ever since his crash. It's beyond bruises and (potentially) broken bones. It's like his pride has been wounded or something.

JJ can't quite place it, this wind-taken-out-of-one's-sails feeling. For him, Jeff has always been a steady, if not a particularly formidable, force, something like a midsize sedan his family favors. Now he's more like a bicycle with partially deflated tires.

It's upsetting to see his dad like that, but JJ shrugs it off. He isn't really sure who he's pitying more here: Jeff or himself.

Was Jeff drinking when he drove the Subaru into the tree? Is that what happened?

For all their faults, Jeff and Jenna are not big drinkers. Not like some adults he knows. There are the Sandersons down the block who, from time to time, get into epic shouting matches that tend to spill outdoors. JJ has seen them, wasted, swaying like leaves on a boozy breeze, slurring insults at each other. Sometimes the neighbors would call the cops. Sometimes they just observed *The Jerry Springer Show* antics, storing it up for the gossip mill.

Jenna always said the Sandersons were trash. Jeff didn't use that word but did agree the couple were likely bringing their neighbors' housing values down.

For JJ, the drama simply blended in with other city noises like sirens and dogs barking.

Try as he might, he can't imagine Jeff and Jenna ever acting like that. Jeff just doesn't have it in him. Even if he has been drinking lately, all it seems to do is mellow him into furniture.

They almost had a real conversation once, but it died on the vine.

JJ doesn't know how people talk to each other anymore. Exchanging words is easy enough, but exchanging meaning seems to be impossible. Everyone is just too different.

In what world would he and Jeff, for instance, ever talk if they didn't share the same name and DNA? They are, like, thirty years apart and have nothing in common.

Then again, Jessie and he are only two years apart and have even less to say to each other.

Sometimes, JJ comes across people online he suspects might be just like him. He reads their posts or comments and thinks, Ah, there. A kindred spirit. But outside of hitting the like button or typing something inane like, "Yeah, right on," he doesn't know what to do.

He isn't a kid anymore, he can't just say, "Hey, you wanna be friends?"

Fourteen has got to be the dumbest age. No longer a kid, not yet an adult. Just riding out the shitstorm of puberty and hoping for the best. It's worse than dumb, it's so freaking lonely.

At least Jessie, at sixteen, has some freedoms, even if she isn't using them. She can get a driver's license, she can drop out of school.

Sixteen is two impossibly long years away. Eighteen is a stretch further toward an unimaginable horizon. JJ tries picturing himself at eighteen and fails. All he sees is the same fat ugly thing that greets him every time he's near a mirror.

The gaming avatar he's created for himself is strong, his arms have muscles. His hair is buzzed military style, almost right down to the skull. In the game, JJ is a powerful machine. Sometimes, he dreams of it at night, though lately, his sleeping has been odd.

It's almost like something is reaching into his mind and turning his dreams into nightmares. The changes were subtle at first, but lately, they've been getting more intense.

Some nights, JJ runs out of bullets and is left helpless. Some nights, he turns his gun on himself. That last one had him piss the bed, something he hasn't done in ages.

Sneaking his balled-up, wet, stinking sheets to the laundry machine, making sure no one sees him in his shame, it all comes back to him too easily. Like no time has passed at all.

The embarrassment burned his face beet red and raw, the way winter wind tended to abrade it, as he sat on the floor in front of the washing machine, cross-legged, watching the sheets twist themselves, imagining them to be limbs. And then he played some more of his game, because what else was there to do?

Normally, he sleeps soundly enough. At home and even the few times they went away and stayed in hotels. Maybe it's this house. The way it sprawls so much larger than necessary. The way it separates all the spaces like oases in a desert. The way it twists and turns, like some madman-designed labyrinth, like the sheets in a washer.

But no, that's dumb. That's the type of thing his mom might say and his dad would call woo-woo. JJ does not believe in woo-woo crap.

The house is just a house. An ugly old house. The game is just a game. An awesome violent fun game. The nightmares are just nightmares, and they'll disappear the same way urine will from his sheets.

Life is complicated enough without adding to the mix.

There's only one week left until they are back in the city. Until he's back in school. The thought makes him shudder. He scratches at his face until his jagged fingernails come away bloody, then picks his game back up.

The battery signal is blinking angry red at him. Shoot. He was so sure he charged it. Oh well. He plugs the device in and decides to stretch his legs while it builds up the minimum charge.

Normally, he would just pace the house. There's plenty of space, though always a slight risk of getting lost. But today, the ambient tension is thick enough to cut with a knife.

Even for someone who normally doesn't pay attention to that sort of thing, it's palpable.

He wonders if Jeff and Jenna are fighting. He hasn't heard anything, but that doesn't mean much; his noise-canceling headphones are expensive enough to actually work as advertised.

JJ decides to go outside. Nothing crazy, certainly no hiking in the nearby woods, just far enough to get some distance from Haven, which today feels even more oppressive than usual.

There are some outbuildings on the land. JJ figures them to be storage sheds or the like, something the caretaker might utilize. They had never piqued his curiosity before, but today, he decides to poke around.

The sheds are unlocked. Of course they are. An unthinkable thing in the city, but here, no one probably uses locks ever. Who'd come all this way to steal?

JJ explores things slowly, keeping an eye out for Angus in case he's trespassing or treading on the man's territory or something.

The first shed reveals nothing of interest, just an old lawnmower, some rakes, and shovels.

The second one puzzles JJ. It has a sliver of a moon cut out in its door, and inside there's a bench to sit down on, with a covered oval opening. JJ lifts the cover and is assaulted by a musky-sweet stench of dead leaves.

It takes his mind entirely too long to process the purpose of this place, but the moment he does, the lid drops from his hands. Yuck. Gross.

He'd seen and used porta potties before, but never quite like this one. Usually they are perfectly modern-looking contraptions with blue plastic outsides and white plastic insides. This one someone went out of the way to make look vintage-y. The word "outhouse" pops into his head out of nowhere.

He rubs his hands on his shorts, but they don't stop feeling dirty.

Why would there be a freaking outhouse here in a place with perfectly good indoor plumbing?

It's disgusting.

He probably touched some ancient shit particles. He can practically feel them crawling on his fingers.

JJ isn't big on conventional cleanliness, but this is beyond the pale. He rushes home and scrubs his hands under water hot enough to turn them red until he can't stand it anymore.

That's enough outside, he thinks. Outside sucks. Anything other than the lake sucks. It's either gross or itchy or biting or scratching or burning you. It just isn't worth it.

Back to his game he goes. The battery has enough charge, and he boots up the game. The screen that comes up stops him dead. It isn't an exaggeration, for he feels his heart did indeed stop pumping blood and might never resume again.

The screen that greets him is not the one he left behind. It's the one he saw when he first bought and loaded the game. The one with gaming instructions and a blank score.

The game doesn't recognize him, and all of his hard-won progress is gone.

JJ tries to log in. The screen says it isn't recognizing the user. He tries rebooting but nothing changes. He contacts tech support for the game, trying to keep the panic out of his voice, hating how screechy and trembly he sounds, panicky, like a little kid. They say his account has been deleted as of twenty minutes ago.

"Twenty minutes ago," he almost screams at the IT guy, "I was outside, nowhere near the game. I left it charging. How is this even possible? I . . ."

Shit. The thought dawns on him like Monday morning. Shit, of course. Fucking Jessie.

Of course she did.

JJ disconnects the phone call. Tech support can't help him. No one can. This isn't a glitch. This is revenge. Jessie is finally getting him back.

He was wondering if she might, but it was taking her so long, he figured she was waiting until they got back to the city. Or maybe she decided he was invulnerable, having, unlike her, no reputation or social status to lose.

Well, as mad as JJ is—and he is mad, blood-boilingly, wall-punchingly mad—he has to admit it: she got him good.

JJ isn't sure how to come back from this, or how to escalate it further, but he'll think of something. He knows he will.

His sister is going to be so very sorry she ever messed with him.

JESSIE

SHE DREAMS ABOUT Ainsley. And every dream is a nightmare. It starts off nicely enough, like something out of a movie. The other night, Ainsley was here, they were at the lake together, she even managed to talk Jessie into swimming. But then, once they were far enough from the shore, just when she began hoping for another kiss, Ainsley pushed Jessie's head underwater and held it down. It was so vivid that the morning light did nothing to dispel the terrible feeling of it, the suffocating betrayal of it.

Jessie wakes up sputtering, like the mucky lake water is still in her mouth. In the nightmare, Ainsley was so strong, and Jessie couldn't surface, couldn't get to the air. And worst of all was the sound of laughter. Ainsley was laughing at her the entire time. She doesn't know how it traveled down to her underwater—it must have been one of those dream logic things—but she did hear it, and now she can't unhear it.

That laughter—sharp, mocking, cruel—is the soundtrack that plays in Jessie's mind whenever she thinks about her recent humiliation, all those awful photos. Ainsley never posted a single comment, but then again, she never reached out to offer support either. It's like Jessie doesn't even feature in her mind. Unfair, considering how much Ainsley occupies Jessie's.

The only thing potent enough to distract Jessie from wallowing has been planning revenge on her brother. And in the end, it was surprisingly easy. Once she stopped overthinking it, she realized there was really only one thing the little shit cared about, and she took it away.

JJ's password wasn't hard to figure out. The rest was just technicalities. It proved satisfyingly simple. The game looked so pointless, Jessie thought, deleting it. Why would anyone waste their time shooting at fake targets? Shooting at all? Jessie is anti-war and anti-guns, on principle.

Whenever the extended family gets together, and some of the Doyle men get drunk enough to regale the rest of them with their war stories, she rolls her eyes or leaves the room.

The stories all sound the same. It's not like any of them have ever been killed or even seriously injured. She knows for a fact that for all his tough talk, Uncle Donny was stationed down south the entire time and never even saw any action.

The rest yammer on about the never-ending heat and dust and screaming in languages they never learned. The conversations inevitably slip into politics. The politics are inevitably ugly.

Jessie knows the memes and the basics, but not enough to argue her ideas. She's never researched any of the topics in depth. The few times she tried, she found it impenetrably dull. Yawn.

She used to think that if she ever became famous on the internet, she'd have to get some real opinions, but that seems depressingly unlikely now.

And anyway, who cares about that? Who even knows how people like the Kardashians vote? Who even knows what they actually do? They are just famous. Everyone knows who they are, even if no one knows or cares what they think.

It must be nice, Jessie sighs wistfully.

She studies her face in the mirror as she carefully contours it, using the latest online tutorial. Her bruises are almost gone. It's like that terrible time in the woods never happened.

She did contemplate returning, albeit cautiously and only to see if she could find Arlen—no, Angus, ugh, why doesn't she ever remember that name?—again. But she's been too preoccupied with her drama.

Spending more time inside hasn't increased her enjoyment of the house. She still finds it weird and creepy and will be glad to leave it behind in the rearview mirror. If they ever get their car back, that is.

Jessie still can't believe her dad did that. It's so not like him. He's usually so responsible, so careful. What happened makes her feel like now, anything can happen. Like some iron-clad, cast-in-stone rules have shifted.

Her dad gets to the lake less now and doesn't swim as much as he used to. That means JJ's been spending more time in his room, giving Jessie fewer opportunities to mess with him. But she's been patient, and her patience has been rewarded.

The little twerp goes for a walk of all things. That's a first. It gives Jessie, empowered by the research she's done on her phone, the chance to sneak in and exact her revenge.

She is surprised by how good it feels. There is no guilt at all.

Afterward, she takes a victory lap around the house to get rid of leftover nervous energy, and for the first time doesn't get lost. It was almost like Haven itself approves of her actions and is rewarding her in its own way.

She stops in the parlor before Aunt Gussie's portrait and looks at it appraisingly. Did Gussie approve of her too?

"What's up, kiddo?"

Jessie jumps at the sound like some dumb girl in a scary movie. Her father has gotten too good at blending in with the stupid leather sofa.

"Nothing, just walking around."

"There's a beautiful summer day in nature awaiting you outside. You don't wanna take it for a spin?"

"Ugh. No. You and Mom are, like, obsessed with nature, I swear."

"Well, they don't call it the great outdoors for nothing."

"Yeah, real great. It either burns you or stings you or scratches you."

"Ah, a city dweller has spoken."

"Whatever, Dad. I'll see you later."

"You're coming to the lake still, right? After lunch?"

She replies with a noncommittal shrug.

Later, with nothing better to do, Jessie does end up going to the damn lake. There, as if by some cruel trick, her fully awake mind revisits her nightmare in technicolor.

She closes her eyes, trying to rewrite the script. Imagining that Ainsley did kiss her. Out there, away from the shore, away from the prying stares of her family.

She wants to feel that softness, that purity of sensation. Nothing here feels pure. It's like the house poisons everything around it. She doesn't care if she's projecting. Vacations are supposed to be relaxing. This one has been anything but.

None of them are happy here.

And yes, happiness is an abstract concept, and yes, she never really took stock of it before in regard to her family, but she never thought they might be actively unhappy.

Not until coming to Haven.

It's never any one thing, never something solid to put a finger on and label as wrong. It's just around. In the air or something.

She wonders if the caretaker feels it too. Or if he simply got used to it.

He brought her father a basket of muffins this morning for a speedy recovery. From her window, Jessie saw him leaving it outside with a note and rushed downstairs, but by the time she made it to the front door, the man was gone.

The note was kind. The muffins smelled divine. Jessie grabbed and ate one so fast, she barely realized she was doing it until there was nothing but crumbs in her hands. She couldn't remember the last time she ate an entire pastry like that.

She should have thrown it up immediately, but instead, she held on to it like a guilty pleasure, carrying the basket inside, setting it in the kitchen.

There are so few pleasures in life, she mused, eyeing the muffins. The pillowy, doughy goodness of them, the juicy blueberries generously dotting the surface.

Jessie could barely peel herself away from the scrumptious beauty of them. Before she even hit the stairs, she rushed back and grabbed another.

She ate it in her room, losing herself in the sheer somatic happiness of the act.

Now, sitting here by the water in her stupid skimpy bathing suit, she feels fat. Disgustingly, grotesquely fat; her stomach spilling over the sides of her bikini bottoms like a muffin top. Appropriately enough. Ugh.

She reaches for a towel and wraps it around her midriff. Then unfolds and rewraps it around her entire body, grateful for how oversized it is. She wants to melt into it the way her father does with the couch.

Now she's hot. Too hot. Without thinking, she shifts to the rock below the one she's perched on, sits there, and lowers her feet into the water. The instant relief is shocking. The water is brisk, refreshing, nothing like the sluggish humid August air.

Impulsively, she throws off the towel and slides down into the water until it's lapping at her shoulders. It, too, can do a fine job of obscuring her fat.

The bottom of the lake feels strikingly alive in a way Jessie chooses to ignore as she takes a few steps in. It's like grass or fine hair that's catching her feet.

It's creepy, so she pushes off and swims.

Of course, she knows how to. She just doesn't do it in lakes. Not normally.

Jessie hears her parents' encouraging shouts from the shore or the water, she can't tell and doesn't care. This is not about them. She goes under, letting the water mute the sound.

Once below, she opens her eyes. It isn't clear here like in the pool. Not even like in the ocean. This is more like peering through swirling dust. Jessie doesn't like it at all, but at least the water isn't salty. It doesn't sting.

Jessie resurfaces. There goes her hair, her makeup, all ruined now. She's as ugly as she is in all those photos JJ posted. But then she locks eyes with him, floating some distance away. Still not as ugly as you. Never as ugly as you, little brother.

The venom of the thought surprises Jessie, but she leans into it all the same. It's only on stupid TV sitcoms that siblings get along. In real life, it's survival of the fittest, baby.

JJ executes an impressively slick flip and shifts into an upright position so that he's looking directly at her.

This is unusual. The kid more often than not is either studying his feet or hiding his eyes behind the messy fringe of his hair. But now his mop is slicked back, and his gaze is piercing.

It's like they are silently acknowledging what each other did. Laying their cards on the table. Declaring intent.

Their wordless exchange amounts to a single message: "This is war."

Bring it on, little brother, Jessie thinks, as she takes another quick dive and swims away. Bring it on.

AVA

PARIS

The best thing about money is how easy it makes life, how expertly it greases all the complicated wheels and cogs of its inner machinery.

Her first order of business upon cashing in her win was to change her name. She settled on Ava. The most beautiful woman to ever grace the silver screen. Besides, it allowed her to keep the first initial she had become rather used to. The surname was tougher to figure out, but when it finally came to her, the choice seemed obvious. She was never much of a Sullivan, but this way her dear James would forever be with her.

Next thing Ava St. James did was reach out to the Facility to get Max out. Or to be more precise, she hired people to act on her behalf, for she could not, would not, go near the place. The bureaucracy stonewalled her efforts; it would have been faster, she knew, to just go there, grease some palms, and take Max with her, but she couldn't bring herself to ever set foot in those dreaded beige premises again. In fact, she had an irrational fear that if she did, she'd be locked away again and no money in the world would save her. Sometimes, she dreamt about it. Well, nightmared about it at any rate.

The Facility wouldn't allow Max to be contacted. They said Maxine was getting special treatment for some violent outbursts. It sounded like a lie. And Ava could only imagine how much Max would have hated being referred to as a woman. At any rate, by the time her efforts paid off, all she could find out was that Max was gone. Puff. Vanished as if by magic.

It occurred to her that she had never learned his last name and now had no way of tracking him down. How easy it was in those days for someone to just fall off the face of the Earth.

And so, her warlock friend was relegated to a memory, a bright light in a terrible darkness. One who Ava became more and more certain over the years had had a hand in her outrageous fortune. What else could her lottery win have been but magic? With or without the K at the end.

She thought of Max often, wished him well, hoped he was happy wherever he was, that in the end, he got the life he always wanted.

And then she moved on with hers. Pulling a vanishing trick of her own, Ava St. James moved to Paris. A new woman, a new decade. The seventies. Europe. She was ready for all of it.

And Paris . . . It was as far and as glamorous and as beautiful as her dreams had reached at the time. In person, even more so. Her money was being handled and invested wisely by a firm in New York. Within reason, she wanted for nothing.

The romance of Paris was real, she was pleased to discover. The city was just as the books had always described it. Unbelievably beautiful.

Ava surrendered herself to the small pleasures of the sound of the rain on cobblestones, the perfectly flaky baked goods, the musicality of the language.

She went to art museums, galleries, public gardens. Palaces. Restaurants. There was so much to see and no one to see it with.

Ava looked around, and with tactful suggestions from some English-speaking cabbies, was able to find the sort of clubs she and James had frequented in the city so long ago.

How different she looked now–the best hair and clothes money could buy. How different she felt–about a thousand years older and wearier. But on the outside, she was still young enough to attract attention, and being an American, especially one with money, gave her a certain exoticism.

Ava had never been beautiful. She knew that much. But she found herself maturing into her looks nicely. She had always looked older than her years, but now she finally caught up with herself, arresting time with all the steadiness easy living had to offer.

If her face was slightly too long, her features too serious, her gaze too sharp . . . well, she had learned to work it all to her advantage. Taller than average and effortlessly slim, immaculately groomed and tailored, Ava St. James was at long last someone to command admiring looks, even turn an occasional head.

She found company, people to share her bed, to practice her French with. The women were so different here, so free with their bodies, with their affections.

None of it meant anything; the understanding was always mutual, always.

Not that Ava was opposed to more, per se, not that she set off to find exclusively stringless brief connections. She simply didn't feel she had anything left to give. Only some of her time, some of her attention. The rest, she believed, was crushed and buried.

After all, one mustn't be greedy, and she's had more love, more second chances than most. Her ghosts stayed with her, kept her company. For even if they were not dead, loved ones long gone from your life could still haunt you. And Paris was a city perfectly suited for ghosts.

Her tastes had gotten darker here, amid the gothic cathedrals and ancient stones, beneath the steady gaze of gargoyles. She began to read stories that echoed the nightmares keeping her awake. What would James, the staunch classicist, think of her now?

During her first visit to the famous catacombs, Ava almost fainted. Their claustrophobic confines reminded her too closely of the Facility. She rushed outside, gasping for air.

But then, she couldn't stop thinking about it. Found herself coming back to the bones beneath the street time and again.

Strange, she thought. The older she got the more the darkness made sense.

It had always been a part of her life, but only lately had she come to accept it as a norm. The standard from which all happiness, all love, all warmth deviates.

Ava didn't have anyone to share her thoughts with then. Only her body, only her bed, only casual meals, cinema trips, surface conversations.

She hated the idea of turning maudlin, one of those dour women wearing all black she would sometimes encounter in passing, their shoulders stooped by the weight of the world, their faces forever scowling. So Ava sought to distract herself. What more could she do? There was so much culture to enjoy.

Well, she'd never been to the ballet, she thought, studying a bright poster one day. Time to change that.

Watching people dance was about as exciting as watching them cook or draw. Ava preferred the final product, only here there was none, only a story all but obscured by high jumps and endless twirls.

From the opening act, she could tell it wasn't going to be her thing, but stubbornness had made her determined to stay in her seat and watch.

Her mind drifting, she found herself thinking about the latest novel she was reading. Some new American author. A terribly exciting, terribly thrilling story.

And then, a tall blond glided onto the stage, and Ava stopped thinking completely. Just like that, like someone cut the signal. Like someone turned on the light. There was nothing else, there was no one else.

Ava's eyes were drawn to the ballerina as if by magnetism. She had never seen someone move like that, in defiance of all natural laws, of gravity itself. So impossibly elegant, so imperially beautiful.

Ava forgot about leaving, she didn't even get up for intermission. Only in the end, only to give a standing ovation.

She made her way home, thinking of nothing but the ballerina. She had to meet her. Surely she must have known someone who knew someone. Every city is really a small village if you spend time with the right people.

Alas, no one seemed to know the ballerina. She was new to town, or foreign, or both. In the end, Ava found an easier way. One her money afforded her, though she seldom took advantage of it. Ava became a donor to the arts.

And as such, she eventually ended up at the same party as the mysterious ballerina.

ꕥ ꕥ ꕥ

The thought of their first meeting still brought a smile to Ava's lips. After all these years. One of those perfect moments life affords you. A loaded gift, one that makes it all worth it; one that makes nothing else worth it by comparison.

If someone did invent the time machine, would it be able to zero in on those moments? To take you back precisely there, to the precipice of unbelievable, unimaginable happiness?

Ava shrugged, shook her head at herself. How sentimental she'd gotten with old age. How whimsical.

Nina would laugh too. Nina, forever the pragmatic. Nina, who used to say the heaviest thing about her was her Russian soul. She'd float away without it, she joked half-seriously, and Ava believed her.

You couldn't watch that woman dance and not think of flying. Every cabriole, every grand jeté carried with it the possibility of her never returning to the ground.

You had to hold your breath, to watch unblinkingly, to wonder.

A chance in every leap.

How eloquently Ava could speak of it now, but back then, face-to-face at last, she found herself uncharacteristically tongue-tied.

7

JEFF

THESE MUFFINS MUST have healing powers. Jeff could swear by it. The more he eats them the better he feels. Eventually, he gets enough energy to make it down to the lake for a swim.

The atmosphere is different today. It's not the humid summer day, the closed-in feeling in the air; no, it's something else. Something he can't quite put a finger on.

Is it the tenseness between them? The stiltedness of their interactions? Whatever it is, it's the opposite of how they should feel and act on a relaxing family vacation. Even one that has kind of been going to shit lately.

Jeff is still bruised, still uncomfortable, still can't laugh without wincing. Now that there's only a week left, he also can't stop thinking about work. Can't stop dreading returning to it all.

There's not a book in Haven's library good enough to take his mind off of it. Alcohol might have done the trick, but he hasn't been able to find a drop in the house since the magical vanishing library bar.

He should have asked Angus about it when they were discussing the car, but he didn't know how to bring it up and, frankly, didn't want to be yet another one of those people. Jeff imagines the man must be bone-tired of all of the Doyles' drunken shenanigans. Now *there's* a family that never travels without their own booze.

At least the car ought to be ready on time. Allegedly. Jeff has long been skeptical of promises repairmen of any kind make. He's actually afraid to ask what it might cost. Either way, they'll have to pay. No way around it.

Jenna appears to be buried in her latest Second-Wife-of-a-Dangerous-Man-nonsense thrillers. Except that to Jeff, it seems like she's using the book as a shield against him. Their conversation exchanges are brief, perfunctory. The way you might talk to a neighbor you don't particularly like. There's something in how she looks at him. Is it . . . resentment?

Is she really resenting him for one stupid mistake, a single misstep off the path of righteousness that he's been treading so carefully for so long? How dare she.

That makes Jeff angry. Angrier than he normally gets.

After all he's done for this family. While she . . . well, what is it that Jenna does anymore? The kids are practically raising themselves and doing a terrible job of it. Her cooking leaves a lot—Jeff flashes back on those muffins—a lot to be desired. She looks good yes, better than most women her age, better than most wives at the company's holiday parties, but she stonewalls him in bed, so what good is that?

Jeff doesn't like this anger, it feels hot, suffocating. It needs an outlet.

He stares at Jenna until she lowers her book and, with a sigh and an eye roll, inquires, "Yes?"

"Is everything okay?" Jeff says, passive-aggressive to the last.

She shrugs one perfectly shaped, evenly tanned shoulder. "Fine."

"Something we need to talk about?"

"No."

He changes tactics. "Are you having a nice time?"

"Jeff," she says slowly. "Stop it."

"Stop what?"

"Stop this. It feels like you're picking a fight."

"I'm just checking in."

"You're not," she counters. "And it's unlike you. I just want to read."

He says nothing, and she goes back to her book, but the tension is there. It's what's preventing her from turning the pages. After all these years together, Jeff knows her reading speed.

"I'm sorry I disappointed you," he says, aware that there's no apology in his voice. If anything, he clocks in belligerence.

"It's fine."

"Is it?"

She puts the book back down, this time with a bookmark saving her place. "What do you want me to say, Jeff?"

"I want to know how you feel. How you really feel."

"I feel like my husband has made a solid effort of ruining our family vacation."

Hearing it out loud stings no matter how much he thought he was prepared for it.

"I made one mistake, Jenna," he says levelly.

"You lied to me about your job. You lied to me about some secret bar in the library. You crashed our car, incurring expenses we can hardly afford. And you have been acting beastly in bed."

She lists these things with quiet venom, counting them off on her perfectly manicured fingers. The sun reflects off her nails and Jeff thinks it makes them look like talons.

She isn't wrong, but for that last charge. That one throws him completely.

"Beastly?" he repeats. It sounds like something out of her thrillers.

Jenna lowers her voice to an angry whisper even though there's no one within earshot of them. "You've been grabbing at me. Like a fucking caveman. Don't try to deny it. I don't even care if you're somehow doing it in your sleep. I haven't had a good night's rest until your car crash beached you in the parlor like some drunken whale."

"Whoa." Jeff holds up his hands and feels his wrecked shoulders protest. "Whoa."

"Don't 'whoa' me. Don't gaslight me. I'm not stupid. I know what I saw, I know what I felt. And the thing is we don't even need to talk about it. I was going to let it go. But you just had to push and prod. You just can't leave it alone, can you?"

This isn't how Jeff was hoping the conversation would go. He's no longer sure exactly what he was hoping for.

Something reasonable, something where they laid their cards on the table and discussed things calmly and rationally, like adults. The type of conversation you feel better after having.

Nothing like this toxic exchange.

The thought starts playing Britney Spears's "Toxic" in his mind on repeat, adding insult to injury.

"I'm not happy either," he says. It wasn't what he planned to say, it just comes out. And now it's out there, lying between them like a dead body; an ugly truth he can't take back.

"I didn't say I was unhappy," Jenna says, and he can see the very beginning of tears at the far corners of her eyes. There's that telltale watery tinge to her voice.

Jeff may have disappointed his wife, but he cannot abide her tears. Especially being the cause of them.

"Look, this conversation is garbage." He makes a sweeping motion with his hand, though it feels like his arm is being pulled out of its socket. Tabula rasa, he's trying to say. Clean slate. "We're both upset, we're both not at our best. Let's just talk later."

Jenna gives him a look he can't read. He thought he knew all of them.

He glances at the lake, seeking some form of reprieve.

"Oh wow. Behold. Miracle of miracles."

Their daughter, the prissiest of all princesses—and he means that with love—has finally deemed the lake suitable for swimming.

They both smile at that. Whatever else is going on, the happiness of their kids is paramount. That's the deal.

The smiles are tense and fraught, but it's better than before. Jeff will take it.

"I think I'll go in too," he says, slowly, carefully pushing himself upright. "Wanna join me?"

"I gotta finish this." There's no venom there anymore. The book's no longer a shield, just a trite thriller with a cliché cover.

"Have you hydrated?" she asks him, extending a thermos bottle toward him. "I made a smoothie. You need to hydrate."

The concern is touching. That she would care about such a thing even after their exchange warms Jeff's heart. And even though he's not thirsty, he gulps down half a bottle.

"Ah." He makes a show of smacking his lips. "Thank you."

"You're welcome," she says. And there's that look again. What is that?

Oh well, he'll figure it out later. Right now, the water is calling, promising the reprieve from gravity he's been craving.

Jeff slides into the water, feeling all the while like his wife is watching him, but when he turns to look, she appears completely absorbed in her book.

He shrugs and takes a dip under, then pushes his wet hair back and floats.

JENNA

IN HIGH SCHOOL, at the insistence of their guidance counselor, a chubby, cardiganed, well-meaning woman with a buoyant perm and an equally buoyant spirit, they made vision boards.

Jenna remembers it vividly, even as other memories of that so much more innocent era get mowed down by the steamroller of time.

Sometimes, she compares her life to that glued-together cacophony of magazine cutouts and wonders what happened.

Perhaps, she was never cut out to be a career woman, shoulder-padded business suits or not. Perhaps, her Prince Charming is a balding man stuck in middle management without any prospects.

Perhaps, her kids will snap out of their insolence and appreciate her later.

There are so many perhapses. So many ways life can go off track. Even small things. Even this vacation.

Jenna thinks back on all the research she has done, all the activities she's planned. What a waste of time. So far, this vacation has been nothing but increasingly tense and terse game and movie nights, with a smattering of too-quiet family meals. At least there's the lake. Everyone seems to be enjoying the lake. Even after Cousin Frank nearly drowned here two summers ago. He swore up and down at their family gatherings that something grabbed his foot and tried to pull him under, but the man was seldom sober enough to be credible, and the story became yet another Doyle anecdote.

What would Aunt Augusta think of the Doyle clan now? Would she shake her head in disapproval of their loud, tiresome, selfish behavior? Every single one of them living in a glass house of their own, all too eager to cast stones.

After they ostracized her, did she leave? Did she go far? Did she ever look back?

There are only a few ways to love someone, but a million ways to disappoint them.

Did Gussie, heartbroken, ever forgive the Doyles? That's what everyone seems to think; that's how everyone interprets their inheritance. And yet, Jenna is not so sure.

There's something in the air here, something peculiarly closed in. It pushes on her heart and darkens her thoughts.

She watches her husband in the water as he clumsily, effortfully rolls his soft body into a float position.

Calmly assessing her feelings, Jenna struggles to find pity. There's something else instead, something uglier.

How many more years? How many more decades?

The kids will be out of the house soon enough, and then what?

Jeff is too mild, too passive-aggressive to flat-out tell her to go get a job, but would he ever hint at it?

The thought of being judged by strangers gives her terrible, suffocating anxiety. She's already judged all the time by her family.

Sometimes, Doyles' Christmases and Thanksgivings feel like those Comedy Central roasts. She never understood the point of it, never found humor to be an adequate coating for the bitterness of the criticism.

At least she looks good. That's the one undeniable fact she's always been able to take comfort in. Her slim hips need no child-bearing excuses, her butt has the pertness of someone half her age, her calf muscles are perfectly sculpted.

Her appearance is the one unassailable bastion she can hide behind and, if need be, lob insults from, projectile-style and precision-trained.

All the things she can't control may not equal to the one thing she can, but it's still worth the effort. Every single time, she tells herself.

Jenna still remembers the way Jeff used to look at her. Like she was some kind of miracle, a goddess who stepped down to Earth and let him, a mere mortal, worship her. He was so appreciative of her.

He still is, in a way, but it's more like *look at my hot wife*, not the *I can't stop looking at my hot wife*. The difference is subtle, but it's there.

And it's what makes this small, strange revenge of hers feel so worth it.

If it even happens, of course. Taking cues from movies, especially objectively terrible ones, isn't the way to do things, but she was in a mood, following urges that wouldn't wait, and short on ideas and methods. No idea if it'll work, but then again, her effort was minimal.

Only once in her life has Jenna ever done something driven by pure spite. Tracey, a college roommate, who drove her crazy by sneaking sweaty frat boys into their shared dorm and having shameless, loud sex with them, got what she deserved.

Jenna replaced her midterm paper with one she deliberately plagiarized from a book and carefully typed up. There was a scandal. The school had a zero-cheating policy. Tracey was given the boot.

In the years since, Jenna had seldom thought about it, and now, she can no longer tell if what she'd done was just or right. It felt like justice at the time. Afterward, the quiet was delicious. Her next roommate was a mousy Mormon girl from Utah whose greatest character flaw was chewing the ends of her too-long braids.

On a purely intellectual level, Jenna knows that morality doesn't have much to do with the end justifying the means and all that, but she's a realist. This world she lives in creates its own far less rigid morality; rules change, get destroyed and remade.

It's not quite the *do what thou wilt* sort of thing, but it is all about looking out for number one. And yes, sure, that changes once you have kids, and she would have done anything, even perhaps died for them once, but now . . . Is it still true now?

They are already drifting away, already becoming strangers. The tightly knit fabric of family unravels, and what one is left with are individual strands. Is she strong enough of a strand to not blow away in the wind of change?

Sheesh. Jenna shakes her head. What are those thoughts? What is that hideously dark mood she's in?

It's like her nightmares lately; she has no idea where they are coming from. The other night she dreamed of a giant snake coiled at the corner of the bed, watching her sleep. Its slick bifurcated tongue undulated in the night like some evil tuning fork, as if testing the atmosphere.

What was that all about?

Screw all that. Jenna's done one stupid thing that may or may not pay out, and in either case, no one will know she was behind it. At most, she'll be amused, have a secret to chuckle to herself about. That's it.

She reapplies her sunscreen, contemplating the texture of her skin, looking for signs of aging. Then picks up her latest thriller. She thinks it's the husband. Again. But she hopes to be proven wrong.

JJ

THE STARE DOWN WITH his sister unsettles him more than he cares to admit. He has never thought of her as formidable in any way, and now he's not so sure.

JJ thinks he puts up a tough front, but on the inside, he's full of jittery anxiety.

He's glad to find Jeff has made it into the water. Though JJ is much too old to seek parental comforting, there's something subconscious, instinctual about the way he drifts toward his father.

"How you doing, kiddo?"

JJ shrugs. "Are you good to swim?"

"It's the easiest of all evils."

"Bet you can't race though, right?"

"I could if you wanna be an orphan."

They laugh. It's easy enough, these stupid jokes, the floating on the water. But then, the dark thoughts return, crowding JJ's mind, fighting for supremacy.

"Dad?"

"Yes, son of mine."

"You know how the Doyles, like, all booted Aunt Gussie out of the family or whatever?"

"Uh-huh."

"What do you think she did to deserve that?"

Jeff considers it for a moment. "You know, I'm not sure it was a 'deserve it' kind of thing. Doyles can be a bit difficult. A bit sanctimonious. Do you know that word?"

JJ nods, though he doesn't, and makes a mental note to look it up later.

"So, like, maybe she didn't do anything bad at all?"

"Maybe. But we'll never know. That's the beauty and the mystery of family." Jeff rolls his eyes so JJ knows he's kidding.

They are quiet for a while.

All they can hear are the sounds of the water sloshing around. None of the traditional buzzing and chirping one expects in nature.

The silence between them isn't comfortable. Silences, JJ believes, seldom are.

"But do you think, like, there's ever something Jessie or me can do that would be so bad that you'd boot us out?"

"What? No." His father seems disturbed by the question, by the fact that JJ had even asked it. "No, kiddo. Never."

Then, after a while, he follows that up with, "Why? What'd you do?"

"Nothing." JJ raises his eyebrows, his eyes huge with protested innocence. "Nothing. I was just asking."

"Okay, then. That's settled. You know, maybe I do have one quick race in . . ."

Jeff's face contorts into a weird expression, like he wants to cry out but doesn't.

"What's the matter?" JJ asks. "Got a cramp?"

Jeff exhales, mild alarm on his face. "Yeah, maybe."

A moment later, the expression is back, more vivid than before.

"Shit," Jeff mumbles under his breath. JJ's kind of shocked, Jeff never swears. He's too khaki for that.

"Listen, kiddo, I gotta . . ."

A series of bubbles rises behind Jeff, rippling the water. He farted. His dad farted. That's inherently funny, and JJ laughs out loud.

Jeff normally would too, but right now his face looks miles away from levity.

He starts paddling as fast as he can, as fast as his injuries will allow, to the shore. JJ, confused, follows.

His father practically throws himself out of the water onto the shore like some weird seal and backcrawls toward one of the boulders lining the edge of the lake.

"Go away, JJ," he yells.

It sounds mean. It pisses JJ off. Here he was trying to show concern.

He kicks the sand and turns to leave when he hears torturous moans as streams of something disgustingly wet sounding hit the ground. The cussing. Then more flatulence. Then more of those hideous moist eruptions.

JJ gets it, he's had the shits before. But nothing like that. Nothing so mortifyingly humiliating, in front of others.

Jessie has heard the commotion and is swimming toward the shore too.

Jenna is running over, waving Jessie to stay away.

Jenna's got a beach towel in her hands, but the damage, as they say, is done.

JJ peers at his dad, partially covered by the brightly striped fabric, lying slumped over in his own shit, looking pale as a sheet except for the violently red blotches on his face. That's a sight, he knows, he'll never be able to forget.

Jessie has made it ashore, despite Jenna's protestations, and one look at Jeff sends her gagging.

She's gonna hurl, JJ thinks. This is like a scene out of a horror movie, the particularly disgusting kind no one in his family ever wants to watch because, apparently, it has no redeeming values.

Well, lookee here, at art imitating life, or is it the other way around?

Either way, here's his chance to play the hero. Or the villain. The lines have been blurring for a while.

He knows that as frequently as his sister throws up, she's insanely private about it. It's why he let her have the bedroom with the en suite, back before all this when he was still being nice.

"Jessie, come away," he says, pulling his sister by the hand.

He leads them toward the house, but she indicates to him she can't wait that long. So he leads her to the outhouse instead.

"What is that?" Her voice is thick, roiling.

"It's like a porta potty from back in the day. It's got a toilet; look, it's private."

He can tell she hates the idea of it, but there's just no time.

She rushes in and pulls the door shut.

"JJ!"

"Yeah, I know, I know, I'm going away."

And he is. After he latches the door shut from the outside. Because, seriously, who wants to hear someone vomit? It's totally gross.

Once he's far enough that the sound is distant, barely recognizable, he pauses. A thought crosses his mind. A distinctly dark thought.

Why not up the stakes? it whispers wickedly.

The visions of the blank home screen of his game are swimming behind his eyes. The one thing he was going to have to show for this freaking vacation ruined.

He thinks about the way Jessie looked at him when she said he was ugly. She meant it, he knows. It's all she ever sees when she looks at him.

All anyone ever sees. And so, he turns back, takes a solid running start, and rushes at the outhouse. As out of shape as he is, the charge is electric; he doesn't feel winded or side-stitched or anything. It's pure adrenaline or something.

JJ slams into the outhouse, for once grateful for all his extra weight, and the thing goes down like a chopped tree, flat onto its side, with Jessie in it.

He hears sloshing sounds he'd rather never hear again, and then Jessie is screaming, screaming like someone is killing her, like the girls in the horror movies do.

The smell is atrocious. Between Jeff and Jessie, this afternoon is enough to kill someone's appetite for good.

He wonders if all the backed-up old shit stored up from who knows when has spilled over. The thing looked like it could hold a lot, in the bench compartment beneath the seat. But who knows how these things work, exactly?

Jessie is gasping, gulping sobs, banging on the door, the walls. He's surprised the old-fashioned latch holds as nicely as it does through all the commotion.

JJ listens for a moment. His sister doesn't sound particularly injured, just traumatized and upset. He decides to let her stew in there for a while.

Despite the horrible smell, this feels and sounds great—empowerment amid the cries—just like the way righteous revenge ought to.

She'll never mess with him again, JJ thinks. Never.

The kids in school might, but hey, maybe he'll figure out a way to take care of that too.

Lost in his thoughts, he doesn't notice when Jessie goes quiet. But once the realization dawns on him, he knows it's time.

"Jessie," he calls out, pretending to have just returned. "What happened?"

There's no answer.

He feels the tendrils of panic around his heart, as his fingers hurriedly undo the latch.

The door springs open, and Jessie rolls right out of there, covered in a noxious brew too toxic to examine closely.

Her eyes are open; she appears to be conscious, just eerily silent. She gets up on her feet without any help, which JJ is glad about. He'd hate to touch her now.

The expression on Jessie's face is unreadable. Kind of blank, actually, JJ observes. Like her processors have shut down. The lights are on, but no one's home sort of thing.

Shock, the thought strikes him. She's in shock.

"This old thing must have fallen over," he says covering his tracks, unsure she can even hear him. "I came back, and it was like that. Good thing I did come back, though, huh? Are you okay?"

Silence continues. His sister is walking back to Haven as if on autopilot, and he follows her. What else can he do?

When they get back, she heads straight for her bathroom and shuts the door. Not a word to JJ. The sound of the shower turned on to the max is too loud to hear if she's crying. If she's doing anything at all.

JJ walks downstairs to the kitchen and absentmindedly gets a snack. It's one of those good-for-you things Jenna is always buying that tastes like sawdust, but he doesn't care about the flavor, he's only after the soothing repetitive comfort of shoving food in his face.

He isn't given to puns, but it occurs to him that this vacation has turned distinctly shitty over the course of one afternoon. And there are still days until it's over. How will they look at one another? Or will they just sulk in separate corners of this oversized monstrosity of a house until it's time to go home?

JJ can't even think right now about how things will be at home after they come back. School will start soon enough, and that'll take up all his attention, all his brain space.

For now, he's considering the execution of his revenge. Was it rewarding enough? Was the strum of that all-powerful feeling that suffused his veins ever so briefly worth the damage done?

The look on Jessie's face will haunt him, he knows. Possibly long after he's forgotten about his lost game score. But then again, she'll likely never, ever mess with him again; never call him another name.

When they are older, he doesn't ever imagine them hanging out the way all the Doyles always do. Families are useless. There's no reason to love someone you don't like.

In the future, JJ thinks, none of this will matter. If it ever did.

JJ closes his eyes; the food coma is slowly taking over, relaxing his brain into hazy daydreams. In the future, he'll have the power, and no one will mess with him.

He bets the old woman in the portrait would appreciate what he's done. She looks like she didn't take any crap from anybody. Made her own way, made her own money. Left everyone this ugly house probably as a joke. Everyone thinks it's so special, but JJ sees it for what it is: a dark creepy tomb of a home where daylight comes to die, and dreams turn into nightmares.

Nicely done, Aunt Gussie.

JJ looks around for a soda and settles for some low-fat chocolate soy milk instead. He drinks an imaginary toast to an aunt he never met, feeling very much like an adult.

Take that, world, he thinks as he wipes away a milk mustache.

JESSIE

SHE WAS WRONG when she thought before that her experiences had hit rock bottom. It could get worse, and it did. It can always get worse, she now knows.

The rock bottom opened up and she fell, fell into an abyss too disgusting for words. This is the worst she has ever felt. This filth that's making her skin crawl. That feels like it'll never be washed off.

Jessie has taken several scorching hot showers by now and has scoured her skin, and still, she doesn't feel clean. It seems to her she might never feel clean again.

When she replays the events of the afternoon in her mind, there are certain blank spots—things she isn't sure of. There is a jerking time-skipping quality to her recollections.

Jessie remembers the stare down with JJ. Then her dad shitting himself on the beach. Then the weird tiny outdoor bathroom. And then?

She never heard the door actually locking over the sound of her throwing up; can't be sure her brother did it, and he has sworn he hasn't. Whatever lock that was there had to have been old as dirt and likely just as reliable. It might have snapped shut on its own. Maybe. But in her heart of hearts, she holds JJ responsible. She knows, she knows, he's behind it.

It's in the smirk she saw on his lips, a momentary slip, there and gone, when he didn't think she was paying attention. The same smirk she could swear she saw on her mom's face when she was covering Dad with a beach towel. A secret hint of pleasure taken at another person's misery. There is a word for it she saw on social media. She digs around in her memory. Ah, yes. *Schadenfreude*. That's what it is.

Her family is officially kind of evil. She'd like to think it's this house, this vacation that's turning them into monsters, but she isn't sure. Maybe it's merely amplifying what was always there.

Short of flat-out killing JJ—and she can all too easily see herself strangling the little shit—Jessie has no idea how to get back at him for this. Her imagination fails her.

She locks herself in her room, sneaking to the kitchen only once the coast clears, to stock up on food, then sits on her bed, eats, and lets the internet obliterate her mind. It's usually so good at it, but right now, it's no help.

The food helps though. Calorie after delicious calorie. For the first time, she gets how JJ must feel. She hates him but, at last, she understands him.

There are only a few days left. She'll soon be home, in the city, where things make sense. Has she put on weight? Will she be judged?

Jessie tiptoes her way back on social media, horrified she is still remembered, equally horrified she may have been completely forgotten.

She hasn't been on or posted anything in a while, and the absence of likes, comments, and instant feedback makes her feel invisible.

If a tree falls in the woods and no one's there to hear it . . . How appropriate, she thinks.

Jessie has fallen, fallen, fallen, right here, amid all these woods.

She never even had a proper talk with Angus. Never found him again. Never uncovered Aunt Augusta's secrets. They never did go shopping. Or did any activities her mom had planned.

What happened? Where did the time go?

This is by far the longest vacation they've ever gone on as a family, and it's an abject failure. Is that how long vacations are with other families?

And then do they just lie to cover it up, to not let their dysfunction show when they say they had fun?

She wouldn't put it past the Doyles. Her aunts and uncles always struck her as liars. They talk too much not to be. It's the gift of gab, as old great-uncle Conor says. Some gift, Jessie thinks.

When she's older, when she has a family of her own, they will be nothing like this. Then again, whenever Jessie imagines the future, her ideal family is too perfect, too curated, like Barbie World people. Nothing is ever quite real.

Her image of a future is cobbled from parts of other people's lives; things she saw on TV or read about on social media.

It reminds her of an old art project of her mom's she once found in the attic. Her mom said it was a vision board. It looked silly, unrealistic. Just cutouts from old magazines with ugly clothes and dated hairstyles. It looked nothing like their family, and it made Jessie feel like maybe no one gets the family they want, the life they dreamed of.

The thought depresses her and makes her reach for another cookie. They are delicate little things, almost insubstantial, but Jessie thinks about what's in them, the fat, the butter.

Then she eats it anyway.

When one of them tastes salty, she realizes she has been crying.

It's been so long since she has cried over something intangible. Small irritations have given way to quick hot angry tears, sure, but nothing like this. The oppressive sadness feels like a crushing weight on her shoulders.

Jessie goes to the window and looks out. The woods are dark and deep, though not at all lovely as the poem they read in school described.

The more she looks, the more her eyes get accustomed to the dark, the more she thinks she sees a figure lurking there.

It must be Angus, she decides, who else would be here, at the end of the world?

The figure stops and, Jessie swears, looks up, so she waves an uncertain hand. Then a gust of wind blows the tree branches all around it, and when it's over, the figure is gone.

Jessie feels more alone than before. She goes to the bed and lies down. She feels bloated from all the food, but the thought of regurgitation is too much. Eventually, she falls asleep, and then the nightmares come.

AVA

FLYING

"Ah, perfect, come, come," the ballet director boomed, his voice shockingly resonant for such a slender man. "Nina Mars, our rising star, meet Ava St. James, our newest and most generous of donors."

"Pleasure." Nina smiled, extending her hand. Offstage her gestures were just as graceful but far more economical. Even her smile.

Ava took her hand, long elegant fingers, pleasantly icy despite the hot ballroom.

"Chat among yourselves, my darlings, I've got to say a million hellos." The director flitted away, his long blue scarf flowing behind him like a contrail.

"Okay, then, we chat." Nina lit a cigarette. "I would offer you one, but you do not strike me as a smoker."

"I'm not."

"What do you do for fun then?"

Ava gestured around. "More fun than this?"

"Ah, imagine the possibilities." Nina's laugh was deeper than her speaking voice and completely, utterly seductive. Ava resolved there and then to become funnier if only to hear that laugh again.

But this was work. A conversation under pressure. Even small talk became weighted. And her still-not-quite-sturdy French became the leaf in the wind.

"Mars is an unusual last name."

"Do you like it?"

"I do."

"Well, then, I chose well."

"Ah, it is your nom de plume."

Nina blew a perfect smoke circle into the air. "No one here can pronounce my real last name."

"Is Nina your real first name?"

"Yes. Is Ava yours?"

"Define real." Ava shrugged as casually as she could. She shouldn't have worn heels. She was tall enough as is. Though with Nina's hair up, she couldn't tell if they were the same height.

"A woman of mystery. I like this."

"I'm a big fan," Ava blurted. "I've seen you dance so many times."

Nina squinted and blew smoke out of the corner of her mouth.

"What do you like about it?"

Ava took a moment to consider this. Parisians were seldom this direct.

"I like the way you make it seem like you're not bound to Earth. Like gravity doesn't matter."

"That, Ava St. James, is precisely how it feels when I dance."

"All this," Ava said, nodding at the crowd, "must be terribly disappointing then by comparison."

"You have no idea." Nina grinned conspiratorially. "Why don't you steal me away from it all?"

Ava did just that, for by then she was already in love. A gravity of her own had found her falling, falling . . .

That first evening all they did was walk and talk. There was no better place to do that than Paris at night.

Nina had told her of her Russian family. "Intelligentsia through and through. And how they pay for it."

Of all the years she had spent dancing. "It goes by like a strange dream."

Of being discovered. "Jean-Luke is a doll, but he could not abide Russian winters. I think he chose me just to end his search and return to Paris." All the effort leading her to this, the pinnacle of her career.

And now here she was, alone in a strange city, a star with bloody toes, freer than ever before but bound to strict schedules, rehearsals, diets.

"They won't let me drink," she drolled, rolling her eyes dramatically. "Imagine."

"Torturous," Ava agreed. "Unusually cruel."

"They are only afraid for their pride. I can drink them all over the table."

"Under."

"What?"

"Under the table. It's how the expression goes."

"Ah, yes, that does make more sense. Thank you."

Ava found herself distracted by Nina's lips. The way they moved, the inviting softness of them. Would they be as icy as her fingers? She longed to find out, but how to tell the right moment?

In the bars and clubs she frequented, things were easier, with everyone being on the same page.

In real life, it was all but a guessing game. And a risky one at that.

"No one ever corrects me, you know. I speak and speak and probably blunder and everyone just smiles and nods."

"It's because you're beautiful. People, I find, are disarmed by extreme beauty."

"And you?" For a moment Ava mistook the question, almost answered that yes, she was, completely, utterly disarmed. "Do you get corrected on your French?"

"Sometimes," Ava admitted. "Though I practice like a fiend not to."

Nina dropped her cigarette into the river below; they both watched its brief comet-like descent.

Then Nina exhaled the last cloud of smoke into the night air and turned back to Ava.

"I would not correct you," she said, smiling. "I would be too . . . disarmed."

That, Ava decided, was as perfect of a moment as she could have ever hoped for. She took a step forward, which felt like a balletic leap, and kissed Nina. She found her lips surprisingly warm. Time stopped.

❧❧❧

Afterward, they were just bodies in motion, just people in love. For Ava, all else fell by the wayside. Nina continued to dance, but what free time she had, they spent together.

The memories came back in flashes, in bright fleeting explosions of color and flavor, and then they were chased away. There was nothing like it to sweep her world clean and restart it, nothing like being in love.

Whatever connections she had shared in the past had been training wheels, preparing, conditioning her heart for this, its ultimate performance.

She had loved before–loved, left, found a way to move on–but this, Ava knew with startling clarity, this there would be no moving on from. Nina was lodged in her heart like shrapnel. Removing it would kill.

On her nights alone, doubt would creep in, slithering into her bed, into her head like a serpent. Was she too old for Nina? Was Nina only using her? Ballerinas' careers were notoriously short, and a donor's backing could go a long way to provide security. Was this a mere fleeting fancy for Nina?

But then, she'd see her, those clear blue eyes, that sly half smile, and she'd forget it all, forget herself. Surely this was love. No two people could fit together better, more perfectly.

In bed, Nina was insatiable, indulgent, indefatigable. She'd switch languages, exclaiming passionately in Russian; all the strange words that over time Ava had learned to recognize phonetically.

"You are going to have a very dirty vocabulary at this rate," Nina would comment come morning. "I had a parrot like this once. All he spoke was dirty words."

"So teach me other, cleaner ones."

"Oh no, too difficult. It'll take all of your time and patience, and those are better spent on me."

Instead, Ava taught Nina English, which they both agreed was the easiest of all languages. They laughed at each other's accents and pronunciation but persevered.

"Will you want to go back to America someday?" Nina asked her once.

Ava didn't pause to think. "No, never."

"No family to visit?"

"No family worth visiting."

"Ah, that is sad."

Ava shrugged. Kissed Nina and pulled her down onto the bed. "Do I seem sad?"

If Nina was ever after her money, she certainly didn't show it. In fact, she appeared to relish her independence, continuing to keep her tiny attic apartment in Montmartre.

"All the famous artists have lived here," she'd say proudly. The place was but a small, overheated room atop too many narrow stairways, too many creaky stairs. A giant old bed took up most of the floor space. Large windows above it were perpetually swung open, even in the dead of winter.

"I miss proper winters," Nina liked to say, blowing smoke into the streets, ashing her cigarettes out of the windows. "Russian winters. There is nothing like it. Everything is still." She searched for a word. "Crystallized."

"Like the inside of an iceberg," Ava joked.

"Joke all you like, but it is how we win wars."

"There is that."

They looked out into the night for a while. It was dark but never quiet, always someone somewhere having a later, louder night than them.

"Would you ever want to go back?"

"I had thought of it, but"–Nina paused to exhale a perfect smoke ring–"it would be . . . complicated."

"How so?"

"Well, how would I explain you?"

How would she? How did they? They never really did explain one another, not to each other, not to others. What they had was larger than words, no language sufficed in defining it.

And though Russia held no appeal to Ava, she knew even then that if Nina asked her, she would follow. She'd follow her anywhere.

The time for serious questions was still years away. For now, they simply enjoyed each other.

"When I'm on stage, when I dance, I think of you," Nina would whisper to her in bed, their bodies entangled, vibrating on the same frequency of pleasure.

She tended to say things like that, things that stuck in Ava's mind, things that came back in the light of day and flooded her with happiness.

"When we kiss, it's like fireworks."

Fireworks, indeed.

Ava came to every performance she could. Never got tired of it. To know that the beautiful woman up there in the lights thought of her as her feet left the stage, as she spun and leaped and stretched and wove herself into an impossible, implausible arrangement of limbs–it boggled the mind, took one's breath away.

"Why me?" Ava asked once, though she hated the inherently simpering, whiny nature of the question. "Why me?"

There was no shortage of fans. Clamoring to meet the star after the shows, clutching in their sweaty hands the programs to sign, waiting to take a picture.

"Because you did not sing that song to me."

"What song?"

"You know, that new song all over the radio, 'Nina, Pretty Ballerina.'"[1]

Ava gave her a blank look.

Nina began to sing a pop tune, off-key. By now Ava was laughing hysterically.

"Oh poop. You were just faking to make me sing."

For someone who could dance so beautifully, Nina couldn't sing to save her life. Though to her credit, she was perfectly good-humored about it.

"Are you kidding me? ABBA doesn't know what they are missing."

"I hate you."

"You don't."

"I don't," Nina conceded with a quick kiss. "Anyway, everyone would always say that to me. Ever since that song came out."

"What'd you do?"

"I told people it was written about me. Naturally."

"Oh, that's perfect."

"Thank you." Nina took a bow and toppled into bed.

"You are, though, you know."

"What?"

"A very pretty ballerina."

"Well, you're not so bad yourself."

Ava rolled her eyes, never one to take a compliment smoothly.

"No, seriously. Listen." Nina grabbed her hand, pulled her near, until they were as close as two people could get, their noses touching, their lips nearly brushing each other, their breaths entwined.

"I think you are magnificent, Ava St. James," Nina whispered.

This is what people mean when they say they are so happy they could die, Ava thought.

This time their kiss lasted much, much longer.

The following fall, there was a new ballet taking up all of Nina's time. A challenging, complicated piece with a new male lead: a brash Belgian hotshot named Aric whom Nina detested.

"He's young and fresh and pretty, but he does not have the right mindset, the right stamina," she'd complain. "I want this, I need this to be perfect," she fretted. "He'll ruin it."

Why the urgency? Ava wondered. It hadn't occurred to her until much later into the rehearsal process that Nina was pushing herself like it was her last performance. She asked her about it, later, when it was just the two of them.

"At my age, every performance could be the last one," Nina said somberly.

"But you are still so young," Ava protested.

"Not in ballet years. They are like dog years, yes? We age like dogs in this business."

"You'd make a very lovely dog. What do you think? A poodle?"

"A poodle?" Nina threw a pillow at Ava in mock outrage. "A poodle?"

"Well, what do you think?"

"A borzoi, for sure," Nina declared proudly.

"What on earth is that?"

"That, my love, is a Russian Wolfhound. Named from a word for swift. The royals would use them for their hunts before the Revolution."

"What do they even look like?"

"Lean, blond fur, shaggy. Graceful. Fast."

"Yes, okay, that does sound about right."

Another pillow toss.

"Are we having a pillow fight right now?"

"Looks like it." Nina grinned.

"Oh, you're on."

And afterward, all the work-related fretting was forgotten for a time.

Sometimes, Ava came to the rehearsals. Her donor status allowed her certain privileges.

She could see what Nina meant about Aric. There was a certain unpleasantness about him, a preening way, a poorly hidden hunger for the spotlight. But surely, the director would tame all that before opening night, she reasoned.

And meanwhile, she rubbed Nina's feet, listened to her complaints, and did her best to distract her.

Opening night came so soon, it seemed.

"You are the star. A prima ballerina. They came here to see you," Ava told Nina backstage. "Don't let anyone–anyone–take that away."

She left her love with a kiss and took her seat in the audience, front and center. The crowd was alive with excitement, barely simmering down before the curtains went up. Ava loved to watch the ballet goers, imagine what brought them there, what they were thinking.

Then, Nina came on stage, and there was nothing and no one else.

Even Aric, she could ignore. No more than a prop, a stage setting.

Ava held her breath for the grand jeté she knew was coming, when the unimaginable happened. And so fast too, you could hardly tell one limb from another except that you knew they were tangled the wrong way. There was a cracking sound that Ava heard over the ascending violins, a sound she would never forget. And then, the prima ballerina fell to the stage floor, crumpled, broken, her foot at an impossible angle.

There was a collective pause of uncertain gasps and confused murmurs.

The orchestra caught on, at last. The music slowly, unevenly ended. The instruments screeched themselves to a halt, all symmetry lost.

The only noise was now from the crowd, and it was a cacophony.

In ordinary circumstances, the understudy would be ushered on stage, the performance would go on. But here, now, it seemed impossible, like carrying on in the darkness. The show was over. Nina looked up. She wasn't crying, Ava noted with pride; she wouldn't cry in front of all these people. She tried standing up, and collapsed immediately, her ankle refusing any pressure.

Their eyes met. She mouthed something at Ava, and Ava understood.

In the ensuing commotion, she made her way to the stage and wrapped her arms around Nina.

"It's okay," she whispered, "it's okay. I'm here. I'm here to steal you away from it all."

And Nina held on, as the curtains fell, as the audience left, as help arrived.

Only once she was in a private room, her ankle saved and put in a cast, and well-meaning, slightly starstruck people had told her she might eventually get rid of a limp, but she'd never dance again—only then, when it was just her and Ava alone at last, did the tears come.

⁂

Ava stopped writing for the night. Her hands, she noticed, were shaking. The memories of that terrible night came flooding back with a force that time should have mitigated by now. If only it worked that way. She closed her eyes, but there were no tears. All dried up by now, all cried out. Live long enough and find out the limits of all things. Tears, for instance, were not a renewable material. You were only entitled to an allotment of it in life. Like youth. Like love.

Should she write of that terrible time? Is she strong enough to relive it?

Nina would, Ava thought. Nina was fierce. A force of nature. It was what made it all that much harder to see her cut down like that. So swiftly, so brutally brought back down to earth after floating above it for so long. Gravity claiming its prize, after all. And Ava was there, bearing witness to every moment, her heart breaking over and over again.

She'd try to write about it, for Nina's sake. But tomorrow.

JEFF

THE MAJORITY OF adult life is a steady, soul-crushing procession of small humiliations. Jeff has been aware of that lamentable fact for a long time now. Nevertheless, it doesn't always prepare one for an embarrassment of truly epic proportions.

If there is a way to live down shitting himself in front of his entire family, it is yet to materialize for him. Right now, his beaten-down psyche is running high on mortified shame, and he can't see his way past it.

Jeff has barricaded himself in the parlor with only Augusta's portrait for company. He's shut the doors that have remained open for the duration of their stay, and despite their screeching protestations, they complied. The screeching protestations of his family would be another thing, but they never come. Everyone, it seems, is glad of some space. And space is one thing Haven has in abundance.

Was it the car crash that has somehow upset his innards, he wonders? Was it the muffins that he had, admittedly, been overindulging in? Was it something in the lake's water?

The latter gets ruled out almost immediately. After all, they've been swimming in it for weeks. And the caretaker doesn't strike him as someone of malicious intent. Jeff hopes it isn't some deep-seated trauma to his insides.

He reads. He drinks.

This couch really is deceptively comfortable. Real leather, too, by the feel of it. He'd like to own one just like it, but with the way things have been going, it doesn't seem like a possibility. The near-future budget looks as tight as Jenna's yoga pants.

"They are not even pants," he used to argue when they first came into vogue. Then he stopped caring.

Jeff shifts his body gently and groans. He's hungry and needs the bathroom, but he's dreading going out there and facing the family. How'd it come to this? This was meant to be their perfect family vacation. What happened to all the plans Jenna made for them? Did all those good intentions go and prove the proverb right by paving the road to hell?

Time just gets away from you, doesn't it? When you're not paying attention.

When you think you have plenty of it.

Jeff once read a thing about time being a mere illusion and didn't quite buy it. But it is an illusionist. Just look at its bag of tricks.

One moment they are arriving at a free lakeside mansion for a month of relaxation, next, he is battered and bruised and humiliated, counting down the few days until they can leave.

He wonders if the rest of the family feels the same way. They certainly don't seem happy.

Is he projecting?

Jeff can't quite force himself to move, so he's waiting for his bodily needs to overwhelm him into action.

The world outside is quiet. Eerily silent, now that he thinks about it. Where are the birds? The squirrels? Something? Anything?

To his city noise-proof ears, it feels like sudden deafness. Yet another slight from the universe, which has been using him for a punching bag lately.

"Were you ever happy here?" he asks the portrait.

Augusta Doyle smiles back enigmatically.

Groaning, he shifts upward and nearly pisses himself with the effort. Okay, it's time to tend to the bare necessities.

Jeff makes his way to the doors and cracks one open just enough to peer out. The coast, as they say, is clear.

In socked feet, he pads upstairs, slides into the bathroom he's been sharing with Jenna and JJ, and shuts the door.

Light flicks on, and the stranger in the mirror greets him wearily. Frankly, his appearance is a shock. Bruised sallow skin, bristly whiskers speckled with gray, bloodshot eyes.

Not much he can do about the former, and there's no energy to shave, but at least he can address the horror-movie dead stare.

Jeff ruffles through the first aid kit they, as responsible parents, always have on hand, looking for a small bottle of Visine. It isn't there.

He could swear he'd seen it earlier.

Surprising himself, he does the thing that, until now, he had only ever associated with movies and goes through the small metal trash bin. Gross, gross, ah, there it is. Right next to an empty white bottle without a label, probably Jenna's, and a folded pantyliner. He squints at the Visine container—there's nothing in it.

Why is it empty? he wonders. Jenna doesn't use it; they bring it for him. Started carrying it since his allergies accelerated in his thirties. He could have sworn this one had at least a few drops left.

Oh well. It's perfectly in keeping with the way things have been going lately. He shrugs and tosses it back in. Sighing, he washes his hands thoroughly with water hot enough to burn.

Then he turns the faucet knob all the way in the other direction, presses the stopper down, and lets the water accumulate in the sink's basin. Satisfied, he shuts it off and plunges his face down, welcoming the arctic shock of it.

Something, anything, to feel differently, feel alive, if only for a moment.

One can drown in mere inches of water. But in a sink? How strange would that be? Call the *Guinness Book of World Records* strange, that's how. Why is he thinking of it?

Jeff tries to resurface and feels a strange resistance, like an insistent hand upon his head, pushing him down. He panics, splutters, and comes up splashing. Water goes everywhere.

There is, of course, no one there. Never was. Just a broken-down man and his nightmares reaching for him, hungrily heedless of daylight.

He finishes up, without taking the time to clean up the splashes, and leaves.

The kitchen is empty too. His timing is impeccable.

Unwilling to push his luck, Jeff loads his arms with portable food: a half-finished loaf of bread, a jar of peanut butter, some weird-looking organic chocolate, bananas, individually wrapped cheese triangles, a bag of chips that somehow made its way through Jenna's rigorous policing of their groceries. Water, too.

He carries his feast into the parlor and shuts himself in once more.

The food soothes him into a contemplative stupor. He'd be perfectly happy to remain in it until Angus or whoever brings back their Subaru, and they can go home and put Haven behind them. *If* they can put Haven behind them.

But something is nagging at him. Some niggling detail is plucking at his brain strings.

It's not until the long August day surrenders to the night that Jeff remembers a scene from some truly, repulsively inane movie about a young hotshot running down the lobby, crapping his pants after some woman takes revenge on him by slipping a few drops of Visine into his drink.

No, surely Jenna would never do that. Right? None of them would ever do that to each other. They may argue, they may fight, but they are not vengeful people. Are they?

And anyway, that was just a movie. What happened to him has to be one of those random things, a mere coincidence. As spoonful after spoonful of peanut butter disappears into his mouth, Jeff tries to convince himself of it. But as surely as the darkness takes over the parlor, the thought invades every corner of his mind and refuses to leave.

JENNA

IT ONLY FELT good for a moment. That sharp pleasant jolt of justice served. The guilt and remorse set in too soon after. Yet Jenna remembers the sensation, goes to sleep drunk with the feeling.

In a practical sense, it was hardly worth it. She didn't envision the effects to arrive with such immediacy. Thought there would be more time. Thought her revenge would be a much more private matter. It was such a small thing, really. An idea dredged up from a truly disgusting movie they once watched, chased down with some laxative, just in case the Visine thing was one of those made-up facts. All she did was make a smoothie. But if that was all she did, a small voice whispers in her mind, then why did she claw away the label from the laxative bottle before throwing it away? Covering up one's tracks screams of guilt.

The kids should not have seen that. Whatever issues Jenna might have with Jeff, she firmly believes in keeping the kids out of it. She saw some abysmal parental examples set by the Doyles, from neglect to outright abuse. The majority of them are firm believers in corporal punishment, and that brutish mentality seems to travel down the DNA pipelines to younger generations as sure as light hair, broad cheekbones, and alcoholism.

One of Jenna's cousins, Jody, is permanently on disability as a result of a condition stemming directly from years of being beaten as a kid.

Jenna and Jeff pride themselves on being a different—superior—breed of parents. Loving and supportive, they'd never raise a hand to their kids. Never deliberately expose them to something ugly.

Until now, she sighs to herself. Seeing their father slopped over in a puddle of his own excrement is certainly ugly. Unforgettably so.

They should talk about it, together. But how?

It isn't the sort of thing to bring up over a family meal. She doesn't even know if there is a family meal in their near future. Everyone has been so distant since it happened, sulking in their own corners the house is all too happy to provide.

At least there are only a few days left. Soon enough, they'll drive away and put it all behind them.

One good thing about this young generation is that their screen-addled brains don't seem to hold on to information, resentments, etc. No one wants to overload their delicate processors.

The older generation of Doyles knows how to hold a grudge. They practically wrote a book on it. For people as naturally gabby as they are to practically never mention their only sister in all these years—now that's something. That's the blood in my veins, Jenna thinks. In my kids' veins.

The more she thinks about her husband, the guiltier she feels. A new day dawns and everyone is still doing that living-separately-together thing, and Jenna knows it's her fault.

Plus, she can't quite get the image of Jeff, all wrecked and shivering on the ground, out of her mind. She loves him. Or at least she can still access the part of her that does. It makes what she's done so much worse.

Jenna sighs. Goes to make breakfast. The fridge looks raided. She wonders if everyone has been sneaking into the kitchen and taking things for themselves. Surely not everyone; not Jessie, at least. Jeff and JJ she wouldn't put it past.

Poor Angus, he'll have his job cut out for him, she thinks, having seen what her son's room looks like at home when he starts hoarding food in there. Having dealt with the smells and the garbage and the ants. And even maggots, once.

Boys are objectively disgusting creatures. Though it is difficult to imagine her neat, fastidious husband had ever been a teenager like that.

Jessie's room has always been like something out of a magazine. Jessie seems to take pleasure in modeling herself and her surroundings on inspirational images she finds on the internet. Her personal version of a vision board.

Jenna is still thinking about Jessie when the girl walks into the kitchen.

"Good morning," she sing-songs at her.

"Mooooom." Ah, there's that eye roll.

At some point in her life, Jenna seems to have traded in her personhood for "Mooooom." Not even "Mommy" as it had been originally, when affection could still be inferred.

"Want some breakfast?"

"Sure."

Jessie takes a seat at the breakfast bar.

Jenna whisks the egg whites and chops the bell pepper, regarding her daughter out of the corner of her eye.

There's something different about her. What is it?

She looks less . . . gaunt? Is that right? Maybe she's just wearing less makeup.

Jenna is aware enough of her own glass house to avoid casting stones at her teenager for tending, however obsessively, to her appearance. Still, there's something else. Something almost haunted in her expression.

"You okay?" Jenna asks, imbuing the question with all the maternal warmth she can muster.

A shrug. "Fine."

"Didn't sleep well?"

"Do you? I mean, do you sleep well here? I've been, like, having weird dreams."

Jenna contemplates sharing her nightmares, decides against it. "It's always difficult to get good rest in new environments," she prevaricates.

"S'more than that," Jessie mumbles, picking at her cuticles.

Jenna thought she broke that nasty habit years ago.

"Well, we'll be home before you know it." She beams false cheer. "Are you looking forward to the school year? Seeing all your friends again?"

Something shifts in Jessie's face, sweeps over her tired features like a dark cloud.

"You know what, I'm not really hungry after all," the girl says, sliding off her seat.

"Oh, come on, it's almost done. Stay and keep me company, at least."

"Maybe later," Jessie tosses over her shoulder as she walks away.

So young and she's already mastered the art of saying no without saying "no."

Jenna shakes her head. What did she do? What did she say? Teenagers are so freaking moody.

She eats her omelet alone, the family-size breakfast bar dwarfing her.

The house is eerily quiet. Should there be birds happily trilling outside—isn't nature's soundtrack as persistent as sirens in the city?

If only Angus would come by, there'd be at least some company, but the housekeeper only appears when he is needed, and even then, briefly. It's almost like magic, in a way, how he takes care of things. So seamlessly.

She's watched enough *Downton Abbey* to have the impossible ideal of a perfect servant ingrained in her mind. Trying to imagine Angus in livery makes her smile. There's something so vague about him. When he's out of sight, he's difficult to recollect. His features, his stature all too average, too easily rendered invisible by their natural blandness. She'll likely forget him after this trip. No wonder the Doyles seldom talk about him directly, only mentioning the things he does for them.

The take-take-take approach.

Well, they can have this stupid house. Jenna doesn't ever wish to come back here. They'll go back to their normal vacations: overcrowding in budget motel rooms, burning themselves by the ocean for a few days at a time.

That's all they need. That's plenty of togetherness.

Any more would be overdoing it. If their stay at Haven has taught her anything, it's that there absolutely can be too much of a good thing.

Jenna finishes her meal, chases away the vague hunger that always lingers after she's done, like a stubborn stray dog, asking for more.

The day stretches ahead like an unwelcome challenge.

As she washes up, Jenna thinks of ways to pass the time. She's got one more thriller left. There's always yoga.

Going back to the lake seems unlikely.

She passes the parlor and notes that the doors are shut. Sigh. It's difficult to blame Jeff for wanting to lick his wounds in private.

There's a strong sudden desire to call Angus, to have him reassure her that their car will be ready on time, that they will still be leaving as scheduled, but when she dials his number, the call fails.

The reception and Wi-Fi have been spotty the entire time, but just then it feels like a personal slight. She dials again. Same.

All that unfathomable technology, and the phone feels like nothing but a useless plastic block in her hand. She feels the urge to hurl it into the wall but suppresses it. Eventually, the reception will resume. It always has before. There's nothing to do but wait. Jenna can wait, a skill honed over the years.

She chooses to read outside, in daylight, hoping for a visit from the caretaker, for the return of their Subaru, for something, anything to break up the monotony of the day.

Whenever she thinks she hears a car approach, it turns out to be nothing more than an auditory mirage.

The book is flying by. The terrible things its characters are doing to each other entertain Jenna. Fiction, she shakes her head bemusedly. In real life, what sort of family would do that?

JJ

THE INTERNET CUTS out suddenly, and it feels like someone turned off the world. In the city, even when the internet freaks or the power cuts out, it still feels okay, like its temporary, like you just gotta wait a bit and it'll be back.

But here, in the middle of nowhere, it's like JJ had one small window out and someone boarded it up.

There's no hotspot to use, and whatever data they had is now long gone, with the month being nearly over. Shit. JJ throws his phone on the bed, where it bounces once and settles into a messy pile of sheets.

What else is there to do?

His snack stash is gone. It's not even Jessie's fault anymore. He doesn't think she's been back to stealing, not since he padded his treasure trove with dirty socks, and certainly not after recent events.

JJ shakes his head; he doesn't want to dwell on that. Doesn't want to examine the tendrils of guilt around his heart. She's fine, isn't she? Everyone's fine. Well, maybe not Jeff.

What was that all about? JJ imagines having a superpower that can inflict diarrhea on others. All the things he would do with that in school.

His father he just feels vaguely sorry for, but it seldom crosses his mind.

The silence from Jessie's room is much more worrisome. A girl in her class killed herself last year. JJ is surprised he can't remember her name; at the time, it was everywhere.

Counseling sessions offered, assemblies, compassionate looks, suicide hotline prevention posters everywhere. All that garbage.

Like it matters.

JJ figures that once someone gets to that point (or is, likely, pushed to it), there's nothing anyone can say to change their mind. It's almost admirable in a way. The strength, the dedication, the determination to take and exercise control.

Does Jessie ever think about that? Would she ever do that?

JJ vaguely remembers the girl, from one of Jessie's birthday parties—large eyes beneath designer bangs—or maybe not. Surely someone popular enough to be invited to parties wouldn't just go and kill themselves.

If JJ was pressed to offer an opinion, he'd say he doesn't believe in suicide. To him, the problem has always been with others. Take care of that, and you're good.

It's always the others, isn't it? Anyone with even a hint of power is always looking to lord it over you in the worst possible way.

He idly wonders if being seen covered in his own shit will change the way Jeff acts. Normally, he isn't particularly strict, leaving the disciplinarian chair to Jenna. But maybe now . . .

Once, years ago, a kid at the playground slipped on the banana peel JJ tossed. It was comical, laughable, really, like something out of a slapstick comedy, only the kid didn't find it funny and didn't like the others laughing at him, seeing him like that. And so, for that entire summer he made it his mission to torment JJ. Stupid childish things, but still.

There was a lesson to be learned there, and JJ thought he did: never let them see who threw the banana peel. And never laugh in their face.

Revenge is a dish best served unseen.

There's nothing to do here, nothing in the room to entertain him, to distract him from his own head. But there is still enough daylight to go exploring.

Reluctantly, JJ hefts himself off the bed and finds his shoes amid the debris on the floor. Frankly, he's surprised Jenna hasn't asked him to clean it up yet. Maybe she doesn't care. Maybe it's Angus's job.

Either way, JJ's pleased to be left alone.

The house is quiet, too quiet. His footsteps echo in the hallways, creak the old stairs. He thought old buildings were supposed to be built better, more solid. Their home in the city is all updated modernity in a century-old shell. Not that JJ particularly cares about things like that, but he knows the rest of his family does, sees how proud they are of it, how they preen showing it off to guests.

On YouTube, he has seen videos of people living in their vans. At first, he thought it was sad, but then he came to appreciate it. After all, what does he ever need but his games, some food, an internet connection, a toilet? And being on wheels seems so freeing.

Maybe once he's old enough to drive. He should look into it, see how much it costs.

Jeff and Jenna would flip, which only increases the idea's appeal.

The parlor doors are closed. Weird. Perversely, it makes him want to open them, if only to spite whoever's in there, but he resists the urge.

Soon, he knows, it'll all be over. They'll pile into their Subaru and drive back. Haven will become a mere memory and, eventually, nothing at all. None of this matters. None of this will matter. There's a certain freedom in that too.

The world, when he steps into it, shocks him with warmth and brightness. The house seems to have a microclimate of its own, making it easy to forget about the dead of summer outside.

JJ sets off to explore the grounds and finds himself headed back to the outhouse, even though he would have rather avoided the place.

He once heard somewhere that criminals like to return to the site of their crimes. Which makes no sense. Because then all the police would have to do is set up a trap there and wait.

Besides, he's no criminal. It was just a joke. A practical joke. A prank.

They've made entire TV shows about things like that. It's supposed to be funny. Harmless.

Still, his guilty feet seem to have a mind of their own.

The outhouse is gone. Like it was never there to begin with. There isn't even an imprint on the ground where it used to be. If JJ didn't know any better, he'd never guess there was anything there but earth and grass.

The caretaker must have hauled it away, but when? How? Did he do it by himself? The man looks kind of small for the job. JJ likely outweighs him.

Did someone say something, or did Angus just stumble upon it and take care of it like his job title says?

When would he have had the time? How come no one noticed it or heard it? In a place as quiet as Haven, you'd think someone would.

It suffuses JJ with a dizzying buzz of irreality. Like maybe he imagined the entire thing to begin with. Like maybe he dreamed it.

Not impossible with the nightmares he's been having.

Not like he can go ask anyone either. He shudders to imagine Jessie's reaction if he did.

JJ approaches the exact spot slowly, as if he doesn't quite trust the nothingness in front of him. Once he saw a kid walk straight into a glass door. Just didn't see it there. It was simply too clean, a precision-Windexed deception.

JJ thinks about it as he extends his hand. His fingers meet nothing but air. He kicks the ground, his old sneakers turning up nothing but soil.

So freaking bizarre.

He paces, deep in thought. After a while, it occurs to him that, really, this is for the best.

Now even if Jessie decides to tell on him, she'll have no proof at all. No evidence, no crime.

Not that it was ever a crime, of course.

He walks away, jauntier, a spring in his step. There are several other outbuildings to explore. They look like shacks, but who knows what treasures they may hold.

Further examination finds no treasures. Just thick layers of dust, old, rusted tools, ladders with missing rungs.

His skin feels itchy, like the cobwebs he's been walking into are still clinging to him. When he was younger, he was terrified of spiders. Then he killed one. It happened by mistake, he simply tried to brush it off and crushed it instead, misjudging his strength. That tiny dead body in his hand looked like nothing. Certainly like nothing to fear. And he hasn't been afraid of spiders since.

They are gross though. And their webs.

JJ still thinks that as he brushes them off an old stainless-steel box he found in the last shed. The lock on it has nearly rusted away. The U-shape part crumbles beneath his fingers, and the thing opens with a metallic screech.

What lies within takes JJ's breath away. Only in his wildest dreams . . .

He sets the box on the ground, gently, carefully, then lowers himself in front of it, legs crisscrossed.

"Wow," he whispers to himself.

His dirty fingers trace the metal, admiringly, reverently. The weight of the thing when he finally picks it up feels so much heavier than he thought it might. It feels so . . . right.

JESSIE

FINALLY, FINALLY, *FINALLY*. It's the last day. The thought gets her out of bed. Jessie feels like she's been cocooned in it forever, burritoed in a blanket much too warm for the weather. In reality, she knows, it hasn't been that long.

Automatically, she checks her phone. To her surprise, there's no signal. She doesn't know why she is surprised, this has happened before. Haven's connection to the world is tentative at best. But each time, it's an unpleasant shock, a reduction of her universe.

Oh well, it's the last day. She can practically throw her windows open and sing it like some clueless Disney heroine. Only twenty-four hours left. Or maybe even less than that now.

First thing tomorrow—provided Angus brings the car back on time, the alternative is too grim to consider—they'll drive out of this horrible place never to return.

The idea of reentering her life in the city suffuses her with reluctant joy, but the dark thoughts of her social status degradation linger in the background, tinting everything a hideous shit-brown. Jessie takes a shower. She's been taking so many showers lately, and yet she never feels quite clean.

In her dreams, she falls down in an upright claustrophobic wooden coffin over and over again. Always trapped. Always screaming screams no one can hear.

Sometimes her brother is there, laughing at her.

Sometimes he turns into a large snake. She doesn't know what to make of that.

The one time she looked it up, the meanings overwhelmed her. Way too many interpretations. Ugh. She focused on words like powerlessness, resentment, helplessness. But really, they are just stupid dreams.

Back home, in her perfectly arranged boho chic bedroom, she sleeps like a baby.

Jessie pinches the skin above her hip. Is that fat beneath it? Is she really putting on weight?

All that careful rationing and managing of calories, and her body betrays her like that after only a few binges. Ugh.

She pinches herself harder, hard enough to leave a bruise.

Just as her other ones have begun fading into almost nothing.

She feels so disgusted by it all. By food. By life. So tired of it.

Now she can understand what Claire must have been going through before she killed herself. Poor pretty little Claire, forever overcompensating for her weak chin, for her not quite upper-middle-class family, her not quite city upbringing. Poor Claire, with her doll-huge eyes and perfectly ironed hair. Always just a bit too eager to please, a bit too quick to laugh at a joke.

Jessie didn't mind her, even invited her to her birthday parties. Might have even gone to one of hers.

Claire never seemed particularly unhappy, and what happened gave Jessie a bleak vertiginous feeling, like you never really know another person.

Afterward, in all the well-meaning sanctimonious hoopla, glimpses of another Claire emerged. One who struggled with depression and volunteered at the animal shelter. There was even talk of her being a victim of rape, but the tones were too hushed to pay attention to, the details too murky and uncertain. After all, one didn't just throw accusations like that around, certainly not against the football team stars.

Jessie remembers the way her parents watched her after it happened, as if sizing her up, trying to figure her out. Carefully, considerately, they tiptoed around her, starting and dropping awkward soul-searching conversations.

Ugh, as if she would ever.

Back then, she couldn't even fathom the depth of despair a decision like that must take. Now, she believes, she can. She isn't quite there, but Jessie can see the place from where she's standing.

It's an ugly, ugly place. But then, it's an ugly, ugly world.

All she ever tried to do was bring some beauty into it. All she ever wanted was to be beautiful. Popular. Happy. Was that so wrong? Too much to ask?

The shower pummels her skin, the nozzle all the way into the red zone. It's like she's on fire. Like she is fire. There is nothing but this, she tells herself, leaning against the tiled wall. Nothing that matters.

When the water turns tepid, she turns off the shower and steps out, wrapping herself in an oversized towel. She likes how small it makes her feel.

Perhaps, she'll pull herself together, go downstairs, be social. Soon, they'll be back to their much smaller home, forced to relearn all the basics of cohabitation.

Strange to think that this month will be nothing but a memory. When considered individually, there's been no great tragedies, more like a steady procession of smaller ones, increasing in magnitude.

Her dad must feel even worse. At least her latest humiliation had been private.

JJ saw her though.

She hasn't stopped thinking about her brother since it happened. Tried to, but it's always there, in the back of her mind. It feels like if she stops, it means he gets away with it, and he can't. He just can't.

The little shit may never admit his guilt, but she can see it on his face as clearly as the wretched pizza-skin that covers it. He did it to her, did it on purpose.

If only there were more things he cared about, more friends he had. If only there was something she could take away from him. But no, his loserdom is like his ultimate protective shield.

Jessie feels like she's going to have to get really creative with her revenge.

She wishes she could give him diarrhea like what happened with their dad, but that had to be a freak thing. Probably something in that dirty lake water. She's so glad she never has to set foot in it again.

Dad must be pissed though, she thinks. After it happened, she almost wanted to go to him, to comfort him, to tell him it didn't matter because no one but them saw it. Whatever shame he might have felt could be negated by the absence of a larger audience. "Not like it was on the internet," she'd say, and he'd laugh, and that would be that.

But of course, that sort of thing only happens on stupid TV sitcoms. In real life, there are awkward looks, unfinished sentences, shrugs, closed doors, silence.

A thought occurs to her as she is putting on makeup, a notion so dark it disturbs her to even contemplate it.

What if she just killed JJ? And made it look like he killed himself? No one would be surprised if he did. The kid's an ugly friendless loser, a punching bag for his classmates, not even that good of a gamer, and fat enough to die of an early heart attack anyway.

How would she do it? Wait for him to fall asleep and slice his wrists? From TV and the internet, she knows one must do it vertically not horizontally. Or maybe push him down the stairs and let gravity do the rest?

She can see so clearly the image of JJ lying at the bottom of the stairs, his neck twisted at an unnatural angle. Too clearly. What? No. Wow. No. She slaps her hand to her mouth and shakes her head as if to physically dislodge the horrific thought. Where did that come from?

Sure, what he did to her was terrible, but no, she would never kill him. He's her little brother. In their house, the wall by the staircase is lined with family photos. There are pictures of Jessie and JJ, she an unsteady toddler and he a chubby-cheeked baby. And later, snaps of them mugging for the camera.

Before he gained all his weight, before she lost so much of hers, when their resemblance was stronger, easier to see.

Aren't they going to eventually age out of all this teenage animosity? People in the movies always do. Who knows, maybe down the line they'll even learn to like each other again, to become friends.

No, Jessie shakes her head in front of the mirror, her resolve effectively doubled. She doesn't think they'll ever be friends. She doesn't think she'll ever forgive him to that extent.

But still, she would never kill him. She isn't that kind of person.

What kind of a person she *is* remains to be seen. When she gets back to school, to her life, will she bear the brunt of the sharp digs and thoughtlessly cruel comments? Will she surf the waves of sweeping insults or let them pull her under?

And worse yet, if she has been forgotten altogether, what then? How will she cope with being a nonentity?

Jessie reaches for her phone as if on autopilot, but there's still no signal. She desperately wants the screen back, the feed back, her old life back. What she wouldn't give now for her not-quite-popular-enough status, her not-quite-enough followers.

The blankness that greets her instead makes her sad beyond the relief of tears. She stares at it for a while, then puts it down, and finishes her face. Selects a cute cropped T-shirt, a pair of strategically destroyed denim cutoffs.

She can be sad and still look good. No one needs to know her secret sorrows. No one really cares anyway.

The house feels a bit livelier today. Maybe everyone's getting into the "last day" spirit of things. Maybe it's the house itself, glad to be rid of them at last.

Her parents are in the kitchen. JJ is slouched over the breakfast bar, spilling over the counter stool.

"Want some lunch?"

Lunch? Just how late in the day is it? All the time staring at her phone screen, and she has no idea what time it is.

"Sure." She shrugs, feeling vaguely disoriented. "Thanks."

She sits at the breakfast bar, as far away from JJ as she can. He looks up at her with one eye, as baleful as a beached whale, and says nothing.

"Last day. Anyone wants to do anything special?" her father's joviality feels forced and unnatural, his cheerful tone at odds with his tired expression.

"Ugh. Let's just get it over with and go home."

"Oh, come on, daughter of mine. Didn't you have any fun this past month?"

For a moment, Jessie seriously considers telling him just how little fun the past thirty days have brought her. Telling him the entire ugly truth of it, play by play.

Then she pushes it down, into that same lightless, airless cellar she's been pushing all her dark thoughts.

Instead, she shrugs again. A surprisingly effective method of communication, all things considered.

"Anyone got Wi-Fi?"

A round of nos replies to JJ's whine.

"Shoot," he mumbles.

"Look, it may or may not come back, but Angus left a message earlier, before all this, saying the car will be ready on time. We got one afternoon and one evening left of this vacation. Let's make it count."

And one night, Jessie thinks, one more night of nightmares.

She can't help but notice how her father doesn't mention the lake when he lists their recreational options.

"I dug up an old game of Sorry. Remember? You kids used to love that game."

Jessie remembers no such thing.

But after their late lunch consisting basically of everything in the fridge so they don't have to throw it out or drag it back with them, they settle in the parlor around the board game.

The room smells sour and stale, like all of her father's sadness has permeated it. Jessie goes to open the window only to find it stuck fast in the frame. Tries another one to the same effect.

She doesn't like how trapped it makes her feel.

The game is stupid, childish. But they take their turns diligently moving along the primary-colored lines, issuing meaningless apologies.

Now that they're playing, Jessie seems to vaguely recall it from her childhood, though this board is older, practically retro.

Were they happy back then, playing it? Were they ever happy or always just faking it the way they are now?

When JJ says sorry, she thinks she hears his voice slip a notch, the way it did for the entirety of last year before puberty eased up on him.

Jessie says sorry in a barely audible whisper. Any louder and it will really sound like a lie.

Her dad booms a jolly sorry each time, her mom decidedly less so.

For the first time, Jessie feels like she is surrounded by strangers. Trapped in a charade.

But they play on. And then once more until the sun goes away.

It's almost like if they stop, then there will be nothing holding them there, holding them together.

At some point, someone gets up and puts the lights on. The chandelier above them casts an unevenly spaced illumination, draws sharp reliefs on their faces, throws entire corners of their vision into shadows.

The night descends slowly, then all at once. And so, it is really dark, middle-of-nowhere dark, pitch-black dark, when the power cuts out. The darkness rushes in like a surging river bursting through the floodgates and envelops them. Holds them as tight as lost children, warmly exhaling its recognition. Its gratitude.

AVA

CH-CH-CH-CHANGES

Nina's ankle broke in the worst possible way.

"Two hundred and six bones in the human body, and that's the one that decides to go," she joked grimly.

The rehab process was long and slow. It gave Nina every reason to complain, and yet she persevered with a calm, steady, almost maddening determination.

"We Russians are stoics," she'd say, stretching and stretching the damaged ankle, gradually putting more and more pressure on it. Lips pressed tight into a tense thin, colorless line, the only indication of what it cost her every time.

On the other hand, Ava was glad for the rehab, grateful for Nina to have something to do, to apply her razor-sharp focus to. She dreaded to think what would come after, when the ankle was officially good enough to walk on but never to dance on.

Ava had never had such an abiding passion. She liked a great many things, books, art. Even investing had been getting more and more of her attention lately. She had become fascinated by all the emerging new technology, enough to persuade her rather conservative-minded wealth managers to invest in it. The concepts seemed abstract to her, the details incomprehensible, but the ideas behind it—the sheer beauty of global connection on the level that only Esperanto-speaking dreamers might have envisioned before—beguiled her, enticed her, excited her.

But she had never loved anything the way Nina loved dancing. Never had so much of her life caught up in and defined by a single pursuit.

Then again, of course, that wasn't exactly true. She had Nina. Nina was the one who occupied such a place in her heart, her mind, her life.

And Nina, she feared, was drifting away. The sturdier her walk became, the less pronounced her limp was, the further she seemed. Not less loving, per se, but more distant, too ensconced in a cloud of her own sadness. The sadness she was reluctant to talk about, because, of course, of that damn stoic thing.

Ava wished she'd scream, go tilting at the windmills of life's senseless cruelties, lash out at the unfairness of it all, but Nina remained calm, reserved, remote.

She had to give up her beloved apartment in Montmartre. The expense of it and all those endless stairs—one had to be practical.

They came together to collect Nina's few possessions, for by then most of them were at Ava's, to say goodbye, to return the keys to the landlady, a wizened gnome of a woman who occupied the first floor.

Afterward, Nina was quiet, too quiet. She wore her giant movie-star sunglasses despite the gloomy cloudiness of the day.

"Are you crying?" Ava asked. It was something that happened so seldomly that it took Ava by surprise every single time.

Nina shrugged, reached into her purse, and produced a cigarette. Lit it, took a long drag, and exhaled thoughtfully.

"No," she said at last, "not crying. Just . . . letting go."

At Ava's place, Nina only smoked outside, on the balcony, or in the small overgrown backyard that only a generous soul or an overeager estate agent might refer to as a garden. She'd pace restlessly, like a caged tiger. And Ava watched and fretted about what such restlessness might bring.

"What would you like to do next?" she tried asking casually.

"What else is there? What is that expression?" Nina narrowed her eyes, searching for it. "Those who can, do; those who can't, teach."

"Do you want to teach?"

"I think it'll break up the monotony of being a kept woman rather nicely," Nina replied. And then, noticing the grave expression on her lover's face, laughed to indicate it was a joke.

"Oh darling, you are far too serious."

"I'm just worried."

"Don't worry. Nothing to worry about. We. Have. Everything." She kissed Ava deeply. Then pulled back to look into her eyes. "I love you, Ava St. James. Do you hear me? Your broken ballerina adores you."

And Ava adored her broken ballerina right back.

But those were the good days. And then there were the other days.

When Nina didn't want to get out of bed, when she sat on the balcony's chair chain-smoking into the night, when she found herself being pulled in by the quicksand of self-pity, suffocated by the bitter waves of regret.

Every day, it seemed, Nina fought a valiant battle against the darkness, and every day the outcome was uncertain.

Ava had tried distracting her in every way imaginable, but she felt the resistance. Some days, it was almost as if Nina was pushing her away.

"You didn't sign up to be with a cripple," she'd say.

"You're hardly a cripple."

"It's false advertising."

"How so?"

"You fell in love with a ballerina. I am no longer that."

"Of course, you are. You will always be the ballerina I fell in love with."

"I can't . . . dance." Nina's voice broke. Ava's heart echoed it.

"I don't care."

They were getting louder, more heated, and Ava brought the volume down.

"I don't care," she repeated quietly. "I stole you away. You're mine. I'm yours."

"You're hopeless," Nina proclaimed dramatically. But she smiled too, a genuinely happy smile.

"Here, listen." Ava took a deep breath and recited.

"But do thy worst to steal thyself away,
For term of life thou art assured mine;
And life no longer than thy love will stay,
For it depends upon that love of thine.
Then need I not to fear the worst of wrongs,
When in the least of them my life hath end.
I see a better state to me belongs
Than that which on thy humour doth depend:
Thou canst not vex me with inconstant mind,
Since that my life on thy revolt doth lie.
O what a happy title do I find,
Happy to have thy love, happy to die!
But what's so blessed-fair that fears no blot?
Thou mayst be false, and yet I know it not." [2]

"Is that Shakespeare? Did you memorize that entire sonnet just for me?"

"Yes, and it took forever, so you better appreciate it."

"I do. I love it. Thank you." Nina reached for her lover's hand and led her into their bedroom. "It's no Pushkin but it'll do." She laughed, pushing Ava into bed.

"You're a terrible snob about poetry, you know," Ava said afterward, their sweat cooling in the breeze from the large open windows. It was a perfect Parisian evening. The city was seemingly designed for steamy nights and airy refreshments that followed.

"Not just poetry," Nina pointed out, laughing. "I'm a multifaceted snob."

Nina was convinced no one did poetry better than dead Russians. "Nor drama," she would add, "but they go overboard there. No book should weigh enough to pass for a murder weapon."

Shakespeare was the only English-language poet she ever approved of. Ava didn't much care for poetry at all, and the sonnet took ages to stick in her memory.

It appeared to have been worth the effort, for that evening served as a turning point for Nina. Perhaps it gave her the reassurance she needed; one she could put in her arsenal for the next time darkness challenged her to one of their duels.

She even suggested something she never had before. "Why don't we go visit my parents?"

"Are you sure?" Ava couldn't help the question. She was surprised. Thrown. The visit had never come up before, even casually.

Nina wrote letters and occasionally phoned home, but that seemed to be the extent of it, which alone spoke volumes about the strength of her familial connections. Besides, Ava had always found Russia to be a distinctly unwelcoming destination, and things Nina had told her over the years had only served to reinforce that impression.

"I'm sure," Nina said. "It'll be fun. Or at the very least, you know . . . educational."

And so, they went.

And so, it was.

∞ ∞ ∞

Irina and Igor were just as Ava had imagined them: tall, thin, tired-looking people. Too smart for their home country, too proud to leave. Both of them teachers, both of them dramatically underpaid in keeping with Russian economics. They lived in a hideous monolith of an apartment building, in a drab and drafty apartment that they had done their best with but at some point had obviously given up on, surrounded by too many books.

They both smoked and talked with the same desultory elegance.

It was impossible not to see the family resemblance, and impossible not to feel the gratitude for life's generosity in getting Nina out of this place early enough, before the pervasive bitterness and sadness took a permanent hold on her soul.

Ava could see the ghosts of Nina's beauty in her mother's exhausted face, worn thin with worry.

The more they talked, the more Ava found them to be intelligent, dryly funny, even charming in their own way.

This is what a bad life did to good people, she thought. This is how it wrung them out.

Nina had introduced her as a friend, and no one seemed to question it. Either they were too happy to see their daughter or too broad-minded to care.

Or maybe just indifferent.

Ava had sensed something of that. There was love in this family, she was sure of it, but it was, like everything else around, tired, worn, reluctant to shine. Their separation had gone on for too long, and they had become all too accustomed to it.

They loved Nina; it was obvious. They were proud of their daughter, grateful for her help over the years, worried about her future. But all of these feelings had a distinct underscore of remoteness, like the light of distant stars. These people—and Nina was right, Ava could not pronounce their last name properly—were just too reserved.

So unlike the Doyles. So completely unlike the Doyles.

As they lay together in a too-narrow bed in Nina's childhood room, shivering under an old wool blanket too thin for Russian winters, Ava was overcome with memories she had for so long struggled to avoid, thoughts she had long fought to never think again.

"I like them," she whispered. "Your parents."

"I believe they like you too. The exotic American," Nina teased.

"Were you happy here?" Ava gestured around, to the small room with an old wind-rattled single pane window and too many books lining the walls, but she meant a larger world with her question.

"One doesn't think much of those things as a child," Nina prevaricated.

"I bet you did though."

A long, slow sigh. "I did. I wasn't. I don't think I'd given happiness a lot of thought until much later in life."

"When you came to Paris?"

"No, stupid." She kissed Ava. "When I met you."

They kissed again. Anything more was unimaginable on a bed that small, with walls that thin.

"I am happy now," Nina said. "I want you to know that. Not about everything, obviously." She rolled her eyes and kicked Ava with her bad foot under the blanket. "But mostly. You make me happy."

"Ditto," Ava whispered back.

After a while, the north wind howled them to sleep as sure as a lullaby would.

Irina and Igor spoke enough French and English between them to make their conversations clunky but functional. They were even kind enough not to make fun of Ava's atrocious Russian. They asked her cautious, reserved questions about her life, her family, her business. She answered honestly but elusively; the best she could, avoiding outright lying, but understating things whenever possible.

They didn't, she reasoned, need to know the exact extent of her wealth or any of the true hideousness of her family, or the precise tragic nature of her past vicissitudes.

She had only told those things to Nina, and even then, circumspection was practiced. Though Nina had surprised her at every turn with her acceptance, her understanding.

"I'm surprised you don't go back there and set them all on fire," Nina had said, eyes flickering with sparks of rage, after Ava told her about James's fate.

"Is that what you would do?"

Nina thought it over. "I don't know. I had always thought revenge was a dish best served slow."

"Slow? You mean . . .?"

"I mean, slow. You know, like in The Count of Monte Cristo.*"*

"Or Sweeney Todd."

"Yes, yes, your beloved demonic barber." Nina was forever making fun of Ava for her love of musicals.

"So maybe I'm just biding my time."

Nina squinted at her. "Are you?"

Ava shook her head. "No. I thought I would just do my best to forget."

"I had this friend once who told me that people can be smothered with kindness just as sure as with a pillow."

"Nice friend." Ava guffawed.

"The nicest. She also told me that sometimes it is best to give someone enough rope to hang themselves with."

"Um, is this person still in your life?"

"No, we have"–Nina searched for the right expression–"drifted apart. A long time ago. But I have a feeling she never takes any crap from anyone wherever she is."

"Or she does, and then turns around and comes back with pillows and ropes."

They laughed about it, but the conversation stuck. One of those things the mind revisits from time to time, teasing out meaning, reconsidering.

∞ ∞ ∞

Igor and Irina suggested places to see. Nina and Ava diligently did the touristy things. The country was gray, bleak, tense, and seemingly on the brink of great upheaval. A new leader had recently come to power, speaking of openness and change.

Beneath a large birthmark, his face seemed sincere, but who knew how far that went in politics? The country seemed vast and set in its ways. Ava found it distinctly uncomfortable and unwelcoming. She was glad to leave, and upon their departure, had a curious feeling they were never coming back.

"You didn't like Mother Russia," Nina said, mock-pouting on the way back.

"Well, you know me and families," Ava joked back. "Though I did like yours."

"They are nice," Nina agreed. "I have disappointed them, you know, though they'll never say it. They wanted me to excel academically, to get places by the power of my brain, not my feet."

"Nonsense," Ava protested, "you are the best of both worlds."

"Oh yes, the smartest ballerina. Well, former ballerina, a decommissioned one."

"The prettiest, too." Ava winked.

❧❧❧

They were glad to be back in Paris. A perfect ballet studio location was found, a lease secured, and Nina began teaching. Her stoicism made it impossible for Ava to gauge whether she was truly happy doing so, but all outward signs pointed to yes.

Life went on.

❧❧❧

If it wasn't for the posters, Ava would have let it go. She was sure of it. But they were everywhere. Gaudy oversized promotional sheets, impossible to avoid. How quickly the public forgets their darlings. How quickly they forgive their villains. Aric Arnault was back in the spotlight and advertised widely, bombastically.

In the immediate aftermath of the tragic performance that ended Nina's career, it seemed that everyone believed Aric to be at fault. Ava still remembered the arrogant look on his face when it happened, with nothing like remorse in his smug features. But then, somehow, nothing ever came of it. And now he was back in the spotlight. All these horrid posters. They glared like garish taunts.

Nina said nothing. That damned stoicism again. Only her mouth tightened each time they passed one, only her cheeks paled. You had to really know her to notice these minute changes.

And so, in accord, Ava stayed quiet too, but her mind churned. Kept her awake at night. Ava knew Aric was at fault for what had happened to Nina, it was one of the tragic unspoken facts of their life. The bastard showboated too much to mind his partner's safety, got cocky and careless.

If Nina wanted some form of justice she never said, but the conversations they had about revenge replayed themselves in Ava's mind, coming unbidden and lingering.

Serving it slow wouldn't do in this case, she realized. Aric was happy now, dancing now, while her beloved could not. The unfairness of it all kept Ava awake at night; her mind formed a plan before her heart had even set on it, turning it over and over in her head like a jeweler might a diamond, looking for flaws.

It was a poisonous thorn in her side, a splinter that wouldn't come out. She had to act if only to get rid of this feeling.

Ava brought along one of Nina's old canes. Nina abhorred them, resented having ever needed such things, and told Ava to throw them all away the moment she could walk unaided, but somehow, they never made it out of the storage closet. Ava chose the one she liked best, the one that fit her hand the easiest, the one that could inflict the most damage.

She still knew all the haunts ballet people frequented. Leaving her car parked nearby, Ava waited in the shadows, outside of a club she remembered mentioned as Aric's favorite one night, dressed in an oversized men's trench coat, a knit hat pulled low on her brow, a scarf wrapped high around her face, feeling ridiculous but purposeful.

When Aric finally stepped outside, his white pocket square and a glowing cigarette tip marking him in the dark alley, she tried to move and couldn't. Her leaden feet betrayed her. He was walking away from her, from her vengeance.

She had to summon the memory of Nina cradling her shattered ankle on stage to the tune of a dying orchestra to fortify her will. Only then did she start after him.

Aric turned around. Her footsteps must have been loud. Ava couldn't hear them over her pounding heart.

She tried dodging back into the shadows, got tangled up in herself, somehow loosening her scarf.

"Ava," Aric said, surprise and alcohol in his voice. "Is that you? What on earth are you doing here?"

She couldn't find her voice.

"Is that . . . a cane? Do you now require one too? You simply must be more careful."

That insufferable arrogant tone fueled her rage, but she felt paralyzed. It was nothing like she imagined, nothing at all.

"How's Nina?" Aric continued, oblivious. "I sent her a bouquet, you know. Such a tragedy."

Ava turned around and walked away, shaking like a leaf. At some point, before she reached her car, the cane must have fallen out of her hand. She hadn't noticed.

Too busy tying and retying the stupid scarf around her neck and face until it felt like a noose.

The tears blurred her vision, burning hot trails down her cheeks. She had failed. Failed.

She started the engine and drove, barely seeing the street in front of her.

The thud of something hitting the front of the car jarred her. She hit the brakes. Got out. Walked back.

Everything felt surreal. Perhaps, I'm just having a terrible nightmare, Ava thought. Perhaps, I'm in bed right now with Nina next to me, and the morning light will make a joke of it all.

The night air was brisk. A light mist was falling. It was all just a dream, just a dream.

There was no one around, only a streetlight as a witness, a silent sentinel.

The prostrate shape on the street was merely a part of a dream.

The shape moaned.

Ava had to look.

And when the shape turned face up and revealed itself to be Aric, she thought, Well, at least there's justice in dreams.

The mechanics of it all eluded her. Did they take the same street or stay on the same street? Was he that drunk? Was she driving that fast? It seemed an almost impossible coincidence. Something one might find in fiction.

"Help," Aric groaned. The arrogance had gone out of his voice. He sounded so small now.

Ava wiped her tears and looked at him. His elegant form was crumpled like a discarded paper doll, right leg sticking out at an obscene angle, face bloodied.

"Help," he rasped again, with a wretched gurgle in his voice.

That's blood, Ava thought numbly. I caused it. My vengeance.

"Help." Quieter this time.

"No," Ava said just as quietly. Then she walked away. Back to her car. Back to the real world.

ꟹ ꟹ ꟹ

He lived. Though not well. The damage was too extensive. The trauma to his head too severe. The oxygen-starved brain leading to amnesia. Something like that. It was in all the news. A tragedy once more striking the Parisian ballet world. It sold some newspapers and then was forgotten. Aric Arnault never danced again. The posters were gone.

The streets no longer felt like minefields.

And in the end, the kindest thing to do was to say nothing at all. Confessions were meant for unloading the sin's weight onto the shoulders of others. She couldn't do that to Nina, and so she carried the weight alone. It felt fair.

But lying awake at night, Ava turned the events of that night over and over in her head, realizing that vengeance comes at too high of a cost. Her own method of coping with life's various injustices–boxing them up, storing them in a cellar, the deepest darkest recesses of her being, and doing her darndest to forget and move on–was best. It was right for her.

It wasn't guilt that kept her awake, rather its absence, and a startling realization of the presence of the darker side within her. An eye-opening firsthand experience of one's own terrifying potential. The abyss-gazing venture left her breathless with fear.

It felt wrong.

It felt unclean.

There are some curtains that should never be pulled back, some windows that should never be opened, some vistas that should never be beheld if one is to enjoy their house.

Better to avoid the darker sun-forgotten side, better to stick to the light.

Revenge, it seemed, was made for sterner hearts and tougher souls.

Ava would choose to listen to her better angels from now on.

And eventually, like all nightmares, Aric faded into the darkness.

Slowly, steadily, life reset, realigned itself, and restarted.

"Are you reading the news?"

"Same as you, same paper and everything." Nina smiled over her tea.

"It's horrible," Ava declared, dramatically tossing the paper into the trash. "I'm going to stop. Just stick to finance. And arts."

"Then you'll be tragically uninformed, and I'll have no one to complain to about all the horrible news."

"Uh-huh."

"You just don't like change," Nina pointed out.

"No one really likes change," Ava grumbled.

"Ch-ch-ch-changes, turn and face the strange . . ." [3]

"No, no, please don't sing. I promise, I'll continue reading the news. Just don't sing."

"I think you secretly love my singing," Nina said.

"I can neither confirm nor deny that." Ava reached for the last of the baguette. "No, wait, I can. I can categorically deny that."

"You're ridiculous," Nina said, but with a kiss and a laugh that made it seem like another way to say I love you.

ॐ ॐ ॐ

Still, the news was getting to them. There was restlessness all around. One suffusing the entire continent, it seemed. The walls were crumbling, the iron curtains were being torn down. It didn't affect them directly, but it created a certain unsteadiness of atmosphere neither of them, having been through too many changes, appreciated.

They began talking about moving, first idly, then more seriously.

Where would they go? Not Russia, of course. And Ava vetoed America.

They went traveling, extensively, staying long enough in each country to really get a feel for it. The more places they'd seen, the more their hearts seemed to settle on Scandinavia. Their compasses appeared to have firmly set themselves to the true north.

A perfect combination of all they wanted and needed: the calm stability, neutrality, polite reserve, surprisingly lively art scene, great natural beauty. The toughest decision was choosing between Sweden and Norway, but then, they both fell in love with Bergen and that was that.

The rest was easy enough. Or rather it comprised a myriad of complexities: closing up the dance studio, packing, relocation logistics, house selling and buying, all of which having money easily took care of.

That, Ava had learned over the years, was the best thing about having money: how easy it made the tedious things in life, how smoothly it enabled the cogs of the everyday to operate.

"I'll never learn the language," Ava groaned. She'd been trying, memorizing sentences from a phrase book, reading the dictionary.

"Of course you will, there are so many similarities to English."

"It's the similarities that trip me up. Sometimes the meaning is similar, sometimes it's something else completely. Look at this . . ." She pointed to a word on paper. "Hevn. What do you think it means? You'd think it means Heaven, right? Or at least, Haven?"

Nina laughed.

"Hevn," Ava repeated, feigning outrage.

Nina corrected her pronunciation, smoothing out the consonant transition. She had always been better at things like that, despite the fact that for years now, she had a distinguishable though unplaceable accent in every language she spoke.

"It means revenge," she said.

"Exactly, see. It doesn't make any sense. I'm going to have to hire a translator."

"Don't be silly. They all seem to speak English here. I'm going to be the one at a disadvantage."

Nina's English, unlike her French, was still curiously unsteady and, Ava thought, charmingly creative in its use of idioms.

"I can't learn any more new languages. I'm too old for this."

"Well, you're right about that." Nina winked. "You are rather old."

"Come here," Ava said. And then, books were abandoned, and tongues were given greater pursuits than linguistics.

Norway it was, then Bergen it was. Their new home. Another fresh start. Would life ever run out of those?

Ava had always been a fast reader; even old age and glasses never slowed her down. So it surprised her how long writing took. Every time. She seemed to start in broad daylight and write her story well into the dark.

Perhaps, it wasn't the writing process itself, but the weight of the words, perhaps it was what this chronicle of her life had signified.

She gave herself a deadline, the word amusing her. How morbidly appropriate. Write until you run out of life to write about.

Gustav was on his way. Steady, faithfully devoted Gustav, after all these years. They were the only two people in the world now rendered bereft by Nina's absence.

Only ones to recognize that the sun shone a bit duller now, offered less warmth.

How impossible it was to foresee sometimes what role people come to play in our lives. She knew from the moment she laid eyes on her that Nina would forever change her world, but with Gustav, she had never guessed, never imagined. Thought he was but a passing ship at best, but no, Gustav had become a citadel, a castle.

Ava picked up her pen and let her mind travel back to when they first met.

CODA

IN THE MORNING, the power is restored. The sun is shining brightly, and their car is ready and waiting to take them home. It even appears freshly washed. Not that it matters.

The Baker family leaves Haven quietly, heads down, like chastised children. There is more there, feelings unnamed and simmering, resentments unshaped and unspoken, but for now, it seems they have nothing to say. Not to the house, not to each other.

They drive away, and their car ride is a tense, silent continuation of their morning. There are no conversations, no music. The eyes so accustomed to screen-provided entertainment are staring out into the world through the windows, though it seems what they are seeing is not the endless procession of trees, road, and other cars outside. Instead, they are seeing the scenes from the night before. When the darkness came for them. When the darkness ate them up, spat them out, and set them free.

Free to be their worst selves.

It's not the sort of thing any of them can unsee, no matter how hard they try.

It's not the sort of imagery nature, in all its magnificence, can unseat.

Words were said. Words that cannot be taken back. Words that come alive and prey on those who speak and hear them. Words nightmares are made of.

In the dark, all knives were out.

Now the Bakers are bleeding from a thousand cuts. They don't know if they are going to make it.

But they drive on. Until the road is done with them. Until it takes them home. That's as far into the future as any of them can imagine, for their past is too vivid, too recent, and its stranglehold on them is too tight.

Haven recedes in the background, looking as satiated as a house can. Though none of them dare to look back.

AVA

BERGEN

"A godson?"

"A godson," Nina said. "Don't be so dramatic. People have godsons."

"People mention they have godsons."

"I'm mentioning it now. Come to think of it, I'm positive I have mentioned it before."

Ava tried to remember a single instance. Nothing came to mind.

Over the years, they had accumulated and cultivated a steady group of acquaintances. Their associations variedly casual. Some might even call such individuals friends.

Both of them being intensely private people, they didn't particularly seek closeness in their associations, often comfortably settling for pleasant company, shared meals, shared interests.

Their collective aura of mystery, internationally flavored no less, and their freedom of resources left them with no shortage of people to spend time with, but they had no illusions. These were no friendships of early years, with their desperate intensity and hearts thrown wide open.

They were both too old, too experienced, too jaded for such things.

They were each other's best friends, and that was all that mattered. Everyone else was just . . . decorative.

Adding an extra person into their tightly knit, precision-crafted world seemed precarious. Dangerous, even.

"Look," Nina said, handing Ava a drink, "it was one of those stupid things. At the time, I never gave it much thought. I told you about this friend of mine. She danced once, too, but got tired of it. Wanted a 'normal' life, whatever that means. Children, apparently." Nina rolled her eyes. "I sent the kid Christmas and birthday gifts. When I remembered. That was all. Now his mother has died, and he wants to 'connect.' His word, not mine. He seems perfectly nice on the phone. What harm could a visit do?"

Ava could think of many ways to answer that question, but she caught herself, realizing she could be projecting.

It did all sound perfectly innocent.

Neither of them had particularly liked children. They certainly never wanted any of their own. They couldn't even agree on a dog. For the longest time, they had been comfortably, perfectly wrapped up in each other.

Ava sipped her drink, biding the time.

Nina wagged her eyebrow in that funny way that never failed to make Ava laugh. "I know what you're thinking."

"What am I thinking?"

"You're thinking: kids, we hate kids. But he is not a kid. He's seventeen. Practically a man."

"Right, yes. So, no diapers. Whew."

"It's a real relief. The only person I'm ever changing diapers for is you, and only if you're really old and really helpless and really nice."

"That's a lot of conditions for the supposed love of your life."

Nina shrugged nonchalantly, then whispered with comic exaggeration, "It's poop."

And just like that, Ava caved in. Just like they both knew she would.

"Oh, all right," she said. "Let's meet this Gustav."

The kid turned out to be perfectly nice. None of the teenage angst, none of the surly attitude, none of the monosyllabic answers one might have expected from only knowing teenagers from popular media and friends' complaints.

He was peculiar but in a difficult-to-pin-down way. Slightly built, shorter than either of them, with plain nice features, the kid had a strangely unspecific quality to him, as if he was destined to become the sort of person who could easily disappear into any crowd, adapt to any environment.

He certainly took to their life like a fish to water.

It was Nina's understanding that since Gustav's mother's passing, he had been living with his aunt and uncle whom he didn't particularly like.

To the boy's credit, he never bad-mouthed them either, only alluded to their strictness, their rigorous religiosity, their heavy-handedness. They never approved of his mother's ways and sought in their own harsh manner to reeducate their nephew out of them.

Going from a suffocating small family in a suffocating landlocked municipality to the bohemian luxury of their seaside paradise must have felt like a new world. Like a fresh start.

Ava could understand that, could see it in the boy's eyes; the eyes she could swear shifted from blue to green to hazel depending on the light.

Gustav was polite, clever, respectful, impressively helpful. He never got in the way, never overstepped boundaries. Too serious to make jokes, but he always laughed at theirs.

There was simply nothing objectionable about the boy. Gustav was so easy to like. He slipped into their life seamlessly, like a slender brochure into a busy bookshelf, demanding almost no time, taking up almost no space.

They decided he could stay.

There were three of them now. A cobbled-together happy little family.

"I will not call you Gus," Ava said when he first offered his family's chosen diminutive. She didn't explain why just then, and he didn't press.

"You can call me whatever you like," he said plainly. "It's just names."

Over time, Nina and Ava found the kid almost too easygoing, but how could you fault someone for that?

He turned eighteen, and they wanted to know his plans for the future. Did he wish to go to a university? There were so many good ones, and he was so smart. His linguistic skills had already outpaced both of them.

He didn't know. Wasn't sure what to study.

"Well, study anything," Ava declared. "It's good for the mind. You can figure out the specifics later."

They paid for his schooling; it was easy enough. His gratitude seemed to know no bounds.

"You don't need to thank us for every single thing," they told him.

"I feel like I do. I feel like I ought to. You've done so much for me."

"You're family," Nina said, and the kid positively beamed at that.

He was fascinated by both of them, by their lives.

Too polite, too reserved to ask, but you could see the questions glimmering in his eyes.

Sometimes they told him stories, and he hung onto every word.

"There's something positively Dickensian about the entire situation," Ava told Nina after Gustav enrolled at the University of Bergen. He had a choice of schools but opted to stay close to home.

They were discussing the possibility of formal adoption. Legally, it worked, Ava had her lawyers check–his father had died at sea years ago–but did it make sense?

"He's too old for a street urchin," Nina pointed out, smiling.

"But can one ever age out of being an orphan?"

"What would it change?"

"It would make him our heir, I suppose."

"Ah." Nina thought it over. "But do you want to?"

Ava shrugged one shoulder. "I suppose, he is family."

They decided to discuss the matter with Gustav, who by then shared an apartment with some college friends and had a part-time job to assert some independence, but still came home to visit them every Sunday.

"I always thought we would end up adopting something like a cause or"—Nina waved her hand ephemerally—"an elephant. Not a teenager."

"He's twenty in a week."

"Exactly. Practically an adult. It's so strange."

They made a decision, had the paperwork prepared—all they were waiting for was the right moment to bring it up. It felt strange, Ava thought, for them to have an heir. Strange but nice.

Gustav did well in school, academically and socially. But he never lost that peculiar outsider/observer quality. He always appeared so much older than his classmates, so much more mature. The typical shenanigans of youth seemed to have no appeal to him.

On the other hand, he was curiously unmoored, uncommitted, never dating for long, never quite settling on a major.

When he finally told them what he decided on, they were surprised. Stunned, even.

"Acting?" said Nina, regaining her composure. "Why on earth acting?"

"I think I could be really good at it," he replied in that calm, even tone of his.

And curiously enough, he was.

Gustav never gained the height, the presence, or the looks of a leading man, but he shined in character roles, disappearing into the skins of others with mesmerizing ease.

It seemed so effortless for him to change his appearance, his voice, his mannerisms.

At last, all that peculiar undefined manner of his found a proper outlet.

"It's like he was born to it," Nina would say, smiling after seeing him onstage, on-screen. "But will it be enough?"

It was for years, it seemed. Gustav traveled all over, and they steadily and proudly accumulated a collection of cut-out reviews and postcards.

Nina combined it all into an album. They'd browse it, shaking their heads at the impossible, unexpected fortune of having a son they never asked for and had little to do with raising but whom they were now so very proud of.

The years passed pleasantly. It took some getting used to, some tempering of their caution caused by a lifetime of great upheavals, but they were finally able to truly relax into the flow of things. To enjoy themselves unreservedly. It was like easing into a wondrously comfortable sofa. A sigh of great relief that followed lasted for years and years.

They traveled, went to museums and restaurants, socialized, read, swam. Nina was winding down her teaching, finally claiming she was ready to retire.

∞ ∞ ∞

"I heard the most beautiful song the other day. This British singer, I can't remember his name at all, but the lyrics were absolutely haunting."

Nina abhorred people who didn't pay attention to song lyrics. Claimed it was a lazy, inferior, half-assed way of enjoying music. Ava would laugh and call her a snob, but she agreed.

"If I asked you what it was about, would you promise not to sing?"

Nina rolled her eyes. "I'll play it for you. I bought the recording. Here."

Ava sat and listened. Then listened again. Nina couldn't sing, but she knew how to pick a song. This one was beautiful. Sad. It broke Ava's heart. She felt tears building and couldn't recall ever having that reaction to a song.

The lyrics were about the end of the world. Ava thought she would remember them forever; they'd etch into her mind the way Nina's performances did once upon a time.

A thing of beauty forever preserved by the amber of memory.

In the song, the performer asked his beloved if they'd stay by his side in the last five minutes as the world around them ended. How poignant, Ava thought. What a way to sum up a lifetime of love. And of course, the reverse was true too. She would stay by Nina's side always. There'd be no life, no world without her. [4]

"So?" Nina said.

"I love it. And yes."

"Yes?"

"I'd stand there and spend them with you, the five minutes. Happy."

Nina kissed her. It was like fireworks, still.

❧❧❧

Gustav surprised them once again, announcing he was retiring from acting, having found a new passion. They wondered what it might be. Perhaps a who? Was there, at last, a woman or a man to steal his mercurial heart?

But no, he told them on his long-awaited visit, it was architecture. "Ah," Ava exclaimed. It wasn't quite what they expected but seemed like a perfectly respectable pursuit.

"And . . ." Gustav hesitated. "Magic."

Ava choked on her drink.

"Magic?" Nina said, arching her beautiful eyebrow in a motion she had perfected over the decades into sublime.

He smiled shyly but, Ava noticed, proudly. So, then, she thought, his mind is made up.

"With a K or without?" she asked.

He was surprised by the question, delighted too. A long, excited explanation was provided.

"You know how some houses have this feeling? An atmosphere of their own?"

"Yes," Nina said pointedly, "haunted houses. We tend to avoid those."

Gustav laughed, undeterred. "Well, sure, but not all of the feelings are negative. Yours, for instance, is a perfectly happy house."

"Because we have made it so."

"Yes, certainly, but not everyone has what you guys have. But everyone wants a happy house. I was thinking, doing all this research–what if there was a way to build that?"

"You mean, have happiness as a built-in feature? Like central plumbing?"

"Sure, something like that."

They laughed. Ava tentatively, Nina incredulously, but laughing was good. Gustav smiled, encouraged.

"So, you propose to do this by magical means?"

"Something like that. I joined a society of like-minded individuals when I was living in England. I've been learning things."

"Things like magic?" Nina asked.

"Occult too."

"Doesn't it make you, what, a witch?"

"A warlock," Ava corrected automatically. "A witch is a female practitioner."

Gustav raised his eyebrow and his drink in appreciation. "Not quite," he answered enigmatically, a shy smile playing on his lips.

"Ah." Nina sighed. "Pity. Always wanted a witch in the family. Ever since I was a little girl, and my parents read me all those fairy tales."

Ava found her mind spinning, had to make a conscious effort of pushing memories down. She considered Gustav's idea instead, seriously, from every angle.

"Is it just happiness you're thinking of putting into those houses?"

"Oh no." His lips quirked upward enigmatically into a curiously unrecognizable expression. He didn't use to smile like that, did he? "It can be anything. Any emotion at all."

That night Ava couldn't sleep. Max was on her mind. Her tall, wild warlock. What had become of him? Why didn't she try harder to find him? Over the years, she had gotten so good at leaving, at saying goodbye, at never looking back. Was she too good at it?

Should she look for him now? What would she find? A wealthy old magician steeped in luxury? A broken-down old fogy? A dead man?

It seemed so much kinder not to know, to let someone perpetuate forever, stuck in time, in a beautiful scenario her hopes and well wishes created for them, than to look and find the often-unpalatable truth.

She never looked in on her family either, but for different reasons. Them she didn't wish happiness; them she had only ever wanted to erase from existence by scrubbing them from her mind.

"Can't sleep?" Nina asked quietly, warm breath on Ava's cheek.

"I'm sorry. Did I wake you?"

"It was the absence of snoring that I found particularly jarring."

"I do not snore."

"You do too." Nina laughed lightly and reached to take her hand in the dark.

Ava sighed.

"You're thinking about your friend, aren't you?"

Ava could no longer remember exactly when she told Nina about Max. After all these years, it seemed that the books of their lives became spliced into one, their stories collected, shared, read, and known.

Another sigh, heavier this time.

Nina began massaging Ava's hand with her own. It never failed to have a calming effect.

"What do you think of Gustav's ideas?"

"I think if anyone can make it work, he can. And besides, wouldn't it be wild if he succeeded?"

"Do you believe it's possible?"

"Stranger things, my love," Nina whispered, leaned over, and kissed Ava on the nose. "Stranger things."

Gustav left to pursue his new passions, always staying in touch, calling, visiting.

They had people in their life, social obligations. They had each other to comfortably, crankily get old with.

With the impossible arrogance of two people happy and in love, they never gave thought to what came next. Their todays were too pleasant to contemplate the darkly looming tomorrows.

Death featured in their life but as a distant player. Nina's parents died, and they traveled to bury them in a bleak Russian cemetery. The country, it seemed, never really improved, never got closer to sunlight.

Some of their friends and acquaintances passed away. They sent wreaths, choosing not to attend, both of them hating funerals.

If Ava was to pause the pleasant small-tasked business of their days to allow the dark thoughts to rush in, she supposed she would have imagined she'd go first, just for being older. Or maybe it was simply because she couldn't imagine life without Nina.

She had been wrong before. Wrong to not leave her family sooner. Wrong to take James back to that nest of vipers. Perhaps wrong to leave Max behind. But this one last wrongness took her breath away with its cruelty as surely as Russian winter.

Nina, her pretty ballerina . . .

Ava was done. She told herself she was done. Enough. She had already written down more than she thought she would, already dug deeper, bared her soul more than she had ever expected. But this . . . she wouldn't. She couldn't. How would she ever find the words for the terrible emptiness that followed Nina's absence? A great vast chasm of darkness, of nothingness?

The last couple of years they were given were so full of love, so full of sadness. Ava had tried to stay strong, to avoid the clutches of self-pity, but it was always there, waiting for her hungrily, greedily.

But then, she had always been a completist. Even going as far as finishing books she didn't like. Nina was forever making fun of her, saying life was too short for that, and now the irony of it all . . .

But Ava decided she'd finish. After all, she was so close. It was so close to the end now.

THE END OF THE WORLD

Nina didn't suffer. She couldn't abide that. She'd exit on her own time, she said. They helped. Gustav came back, and whatever magick he brought with him, Ava didn't question it. She was only grateful; they both were.

In the end, Nina whispered to her, "Last five minutes," and Ava, who promised herself she wouldn't cry, shook with the effort of holding back the tears.

In the end, Ava held her hand as Nina slipped away quietly, peacefully. It was like falling asleep, just like Gustav said it would be. Only for longer.

In the end, there were no words; the love flowed unspoken between them. In the end . . .

It was the end of the world.

ꕥ ꕥ ꕥ

The world restarted once again. Only this time, it wasn't welcome. Did it miss the Do Not Resuscitate sign on Ava's heart? Didn't it know she was done?

She'd had a great long life. If it were a book, it would have been a magnum opus. With some dark chapters, sure, but still, a good, happy life full of love, and beauty, and art.

You couldn't ask for more. You'd have to be greedy to.

And there she was, continuing on a journey long after she'd run out of fuel, sticking around long after the movie ended, and the credits rolled. Who did that? What was the purpose?

She wasn't depressed, she told Gustav, who came for an extended stay. Not in the way she understood depression. She was merely tired. Merely done.

They talked a lot in those days. All her truths came spilling out. It shocked her how easy it was to tell in the end.

Once nothing really mattered anymore.

Or maybe just not to her. To Gustav, it seemed to matter a great deal. The small shriveled-up thing that over the years she had made out of her hatred for the Doyles got revived and now burned brightly within Gustav. A terrifying inferno, his outrage.

"They have never paid for what they've done to you," he said, his voice thick with feeling. "Never."

"It's all right," she told him. "It doesn't matter anymore."

"It matters always," he countered. "Great injustice is like great love. It perpetuates."

"What are we going to do?" She smiled. "Go seek revenge?"

He returned her smile, but she noticed it didn't reach his eyes.

She tried to distract him by asking about his projects, the houses he'd been working on.

He told her he had never managed to build one as happy as hers and Nina's.

"I'd like you to have it after, you know . . ."

"Ava." He caught and kissed her hand.

"Oh, come on, we have to talk about these things. It's the mature thing to do."

He said nothing.

"I miss her."

"I miss her too," he whispered. "I miss her every single day. Even her singing."

Ava couldn't help herself; she laughed out loud.

"Are you . . . Oh, I know it isn't the sort of thing that people go around asking, but we're family, right?"

"The best kind," Gustav replied firmly. "The kind you choose."

"Are you happy? Have you been happy?"

Gustav considered his answer slowly, thoughtfully.

"I don't know if I'm quite built for happiness, to tell you the truth. I have my work, my hobbies, my pursuits, and I'm happy enough. Sometimes, I find it difficult . . . to be me. Sometimes, I think I was the happiest when I acted, when I could be anybody."

"You can still do that, you know. You'll be able to afford to."

"Ava," he chastised quietly. "Don't. Please."

"Whoever you choose to be, whatever you choose to do, I wish you happiness. Love, too, if you want it."

He nodded his thanks.

"I wasn't sure about you, you know. At first." She smiled, ruffling his light hair. "But you turned out all right. Nina said we'd be gaining an heir, but we gained quite a bit more than that."

"You're being uncharacteristically sentimental. Should I worry?"

"Not for a moment. But I do have a favor to ask of you."

"Anything," Gustav said. "Anything at all."

"I was hoping you'd say that." Ava smiled again.

Then she told him her plan.

∞ ∞ ∞

And in the end, because he loved her, he agreed.

He only asked for time. It seemed fair.

And with nothing but time, Ava wrote. Until her life was but a book. And she was but a protagonist in it. Making things smaller and smaller and easier to make disappear.

❧❧❧

Gustav was working on some impossible project he didn't want to discuss. Something that kept him in America, though they spoke frequently, and he seemed pleased enough with his progress.

"What are you putting into this house of yours?" she asked. "Happiness?"

"I thought I'd try something different this time."

"Like what?"

"Revenge."

"Hevn," Ava exhaled. The memory hit her like a gust of wind so strong, she had to sit down.

"Did you say Haven?"

"Not quite," she replied.

"Well, I like it anyway. I think that's what I'll name it."

"When are you coming back?"

"Soon, I promise."

"We had a deal."

"I know, I remember."

It occurred to her that he'd been working on this project of his on purpose, dragging things out, forcibly prolonging her existence. She knew it was coming from a place of love, but she was tired of waiting.

"October 1," she said.

"Why then?"

"It was the first time I saw Nina dance. Our anniversary of sorts."

Gustav sighed. "I'll be there," he promised.

❧❧❧

It wasn't long now. The leaves had already begun to turn. Ava never appreciated autumn the way Nina did. For Nina it was a prelude to her beloved winter, for Ava it was a season of dying. How could one appreciate a season named after a fall? It was such an inherently tragic action.

She'd finish her writing now and wait. Time had such a funny way of passing these days. The new century had dawned a decade ago, barely noticed. And yet her seven decades upon this Earth felt heavy, so heavy. She'd welcome some rest. Before she knew it, Gustav would come. He'd help her fall asleep. The world would end once more.

And if there was any justice, any fairness in this storybook of life she'd been writing, she'd find Nina and they would be together once again.

Ava closed her writing, set it aside, put on her favorite song, and let it break her heart once more. She fell asleep dreaming of Nina, dancing, dancing—as light as love.

EPILOGUE

"NOT A BAD place, huh?" Chuck says, looking around.

"It's kind of odd, but hey, it's free, I'll take it," Lynda replies. They haven't been on a vacation in two years, and she's been looking forward to this for ages. Her husband's side of the family is generally a bunch of lazy drunken brutes, but at least they come with a free vacation house.

Could be worse.

The kids are upstairs, figuring out who gets which room. They let them be. They've only got a week here, which Lynda thinks is terribly unfair, though she isn't quite sure how the Doyle vacation share works.

"How is it again that Jeff and Jenna got the entire month of August?" she asks Chuck.

"Come on, hon, it's not like I could even take that much time off if I wanted to."

Chuck is all about the "happy wife is a happy life" scenario; he's busy looking for enough booze to hurry up the happiness.

Lynda sighs. "I still can't get over what happened to them, you know."

"It's a tragedy," Chuck says, checking the top kitchen cabinets.

At first, it was all the family could talk about, but then, like most news, it faded into the background.

Lynda's side of the family has their own crap to deal with, but nothing like the Doyles. There's something about that sprawling Irish clan that seems to attract misery in disproportional amounts.

They must have really screwed the pooch in the past life or something.

Lynda doesn't say these things out loud, because Chuck is touchy about his family.

And she is glad to be here. Even if the house is ugly as sin, albeit less welcoming. No matter how much that small man tried. What was his name? Arthur? Albert? There's something so slippery and forgettable about him. But it's nice that the house comes with a caretaker. Fancy. Now all they need is a butler.

She snickers to herself, then shares the thought with her husband.

"That's right," Chuck says. "The butler would know where the booze is."

"Maybe they hid it?"

"Doubt it."

"Well, who was here last? Maybe they drank it all."

"I think it was Jeff and Jenna."

"Shit."

"Yeah."

"Just keeps coming back up, doesn't it?"

"Yeah, like cheap Chinese food."

Lynda hits Chuck on the arm playfully. But her mind is on the Bakers. She liked Jenna and Jeff, they were some of the nicer cousins, and their kids were almost the same age.

"I keep thinking about it, you know. What if it was Drew?"

"Drew would never," Chuck says dismissively.

"I bet Jeff and Jenna didn't think JJ would either."

"Oh, I don't know. That kid was always sort of weird."

"Not that weird. Not shoot-up-his-family-and-his-classmates weird."

She pauses in horror of having just blurted that out. Too casual of a mention for such an unspeakable tragedy.

Chuck pauses his search and looks at his wife. Puts his meaty paw on her shoulder. "Don't think about it too much, hon, it was just one of those freaky things. Nothing to do with us, really."

"They were family," Lynda says. She finds herself tearing up.

"I wonder where he even got a gun," Chuck wonders. "Jeff and Jenna were forever riding me about mine. They were always so against it."

"Not the thing to be bringing up now," Lynda chastised him, wiping her tears away.

"I know, I know. I'm just curious."

"I'm curious as to why. Didn't they seem happy?"

"Guess you never know." Chuck shrugs and resumes his search, moving on to the parlor.

"Doesn't it bother you? They were just here in August, and now they'll never be here, be anywhere, again?"

"It sucks, sure. But that's life. Plus, Jessie's okay, isn't she? That's something."

They saw the girl at the funeral. She seemed so different, like a stranger. Older than her years. The bullet got her shoulder, but she survived. Poor thing had put on weight too, Lynda couldn't help but notice. But then again, who could blame her? Lynda isn't sure which of the Doyles she went to live with. She asks, but Chuck doesn't seem to know either.

"Do you think we should get rid of your guns?" she says.

"I don't think the guns were the problem there, hon." Chuck sighs patiently. They've had this conversation before, in the aftermath of the Bakers' thing. It's always the same.

"Do you think we should talk to our kids more?"

"Ha. Good luck with that. They are teens. Be grateful they say hi and bye to you."

"But we're happy, right?" Lynda looks at Chuck hopefully.

"Sure we are," he says, shooting her what he considers to be a reassuring smile. He had just found a bottle of scotch in a desk drawer, so his response is quite genuine.

Lynda looks at the portrait on the wall; it seems to dominate the parlor.

"What was her story, anyway?" she asks. "Your aunt?"

"Who knows," Chuck replies, locating the glass. "Dad never talks about her. No one did. Or does."

"A mystery," Lynda says.

"Yeah, a mystery." Chuck glug-glug-glugs some scotch into a glass and toasts the portrait.

"To Aunt Gussie," he says.

I bet she preferred Augusta, Lynda thinks, it's a much prettier name. It suits her more. She studies the not-quite-beautiful but oh so interesting face in the portrait, the knowing smirk playing on its lips. Aunt Augusta looks like a woman of secrets. More interesting than most of the Doyle family, that's for sure.

But then, she feels her curiosity fade. Why dwell? They are here to have a good time.

A proper happy family vacation.

THE END

---

1 "Nina, Pretty Ballerina" is a song by ABBA.

2 Sonnet XCII by William Shakespeare.

3 "Changes" is a song by David Bowie.

4 "The End Of The World" is a song by British singer/songwriter Rob Dickinson.

ACKNOWLEDGMENTS

HAVEN IS QUITE likely the strangest (also the longest) novel I've written to date. It is difficult to explain or even to place within a particular genre. In other words, it's a weirdo, much like its author.

I love it, but then, I'm biased. The main thing is that you, dear reader, love it too. It is, after all, a novel first and foremost about love and its failures. Or it's a novel about revenge and its blind and vast reach. Or it's a novel about a psychologically manipulative house. Or it's a literary dismantling of the myth of a happy family. Or . . .

Read it any way you like. I believe in giving readers the freedom to choose their own adventure, so to speak. All I do is set up the parameters, give you a map, maybe light the way. After all, a good story should be a treasure hunt. I hope you have found some treasures on your visit to Haven.

And now, gratitude outpour:

To CamCat Books for turning *Haven* from a file on my computer into the beautiful book you hold in your hands. My heartfelt gratitude goes to the extraordinary team of Sue Arroyo, Bill Lehto, Helga Schier for terrific edits, Maryann Appel for the amazing cover, and the rest of the CamCat crew for general excellence.

To all my beta readers, Sally Feliz, Leigh Kenny, Emily Haynes, and more, for your time and input. Special thank you to Jordan Triplett for her invaluable editorial assistance in preparing this manuscript.

To my superfan, Atticus Morton. Thank you for your faith in me. The wait is over!

To my dear friends Gary Sarno and Jethro Wegener, for steadfast friendship and support.

To Cherry Hill Public Library for being so proud of their local author.

To all the wonderful friends and fans I've met at signings and through social media—thank you so much for your kindness, support, and everything else.

To my readers everywhere, thank you so much for taking a chance on my work. I will always strive to entertain (and occasionally unsettle) you. There is a term "beholder's share": the realization that art is incomplete without the perceptual and emotional involvement of the viewer. I believe it is very much the same for books. Without your readership, I am merely a scribbler of tales. With it, I am a storyteller. Thank you.

And last but not least, thank you to my beautiful wife, Chelsea, who makes me a better person and a better writer every day. Every word I write is for her. Until the end of the world.

ABOUT THE AUTHOR

MIA DALIA IS an internationally published author, a lifelong reader, and a longtime reviewer of all things fantastic, thrilling, scary, and strange. Her short fiction has been published online by *Night Terror Novels, 50-word stories, Flash Fiction Magazine, Pyre Magazine, Tales from the Moonlit Path,* and in print anthologies by Sunbury Press, HellBound Press, Black Ink Fiction, Dragon Roost Press, Unsettling Reads, Moon, Anthology of Lunar Horror, Phobica Books, PsychoToxin Press, Wandering Wave Press, Bullet Points Vol. 3, Critical Blast, Exploding Head Press, Sinister Smile Press, and *Dracula Beyond Stoker Magazine.*

Her fiction will be featured in upcoming anthologies by Nightshade Press, Off-Topic Publishing, RebellionLIT, Unsettling Reads, and Crystal Lake Publishing.

Mia's noir tales have been published by *Mystery Magazine* and *Bang! Noir Anthology* from Headshot Press.

Her short fiction has been featured by narrative podcasts such as Zoetic Press's *Alphanumeric* and *Tales to Terrify.*

Mia's novelettes, *Smile So Red*, *Spindel*, and *The Trunk* are available on Amazon.

She has released two novellas with PsychoToxin Press: *Tell Me a Story* and *Discordant.*

Her debut novel, *Estate Sale*, was published in April of 2023 to rave reviews.

She makes her science fiction debut with *Arrakoth*, due out in the summer of 2024 from Spaceboy Books.

Her collection of dark psychological fiction, *Smile So Red and Other Tales of Madness*, has been published by Anuci Press in January 2024.

Find her at:

Official website: https://daliaverse.wixsite.com/author

Twitter: @Dalia_Verse

Instagram: daliaverse

FB: DaliaVerse

https://linktr.ee/daliaverse

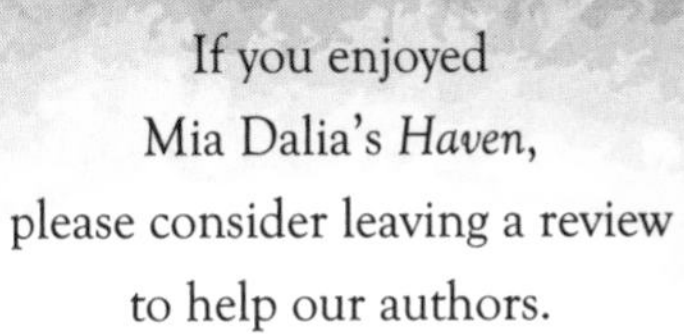

If you enjoyed
Mia Dalia's *Haven*,
please consider leaving a review
to help our authors.

And check out another horrific tale from CamCat,
Jennifer Sadera's
I Know She Was There.

CHAPTER ONE

Friday, August 11

JANE BROCKTON WAS GOING TO GET CAUGHT.

My heart raced when Jane emerged from the side door of her home; what she and I were *both* doing was risky, but it was too late for regrets. I wondered if she thought so, too. Probably. Her behavior was becoming alarmingly brazen. I pulled Emmy's stroller closer and pushed aside boxwood branches, widening the portal I peered through. Although Jane's across-the-street neighbors' hedge was directly in front of her farmhouse-style McMansion, it was too dark this late at night for me to be seen.

Go back inside if you know what's good for you. I pressed my fingers to my lips as the man emerged from the house next to hers. Even if I'd yelled a warning, Jane Brockton wouldn't heed it. Who the hell was I? Certainly not someone her neighbors on Woodmint Lane knew. If Jane observed my late-night excursions through the streets of her stylish suburban New York neighborhood, her first instinct wouldn't be to worry about *her* behavior.

I was prepared. If confronted by any resident of the exclusive enclave, I'd explain I walked the streets late at night to lull my colicky baby to sleep.

I couldn't admit my ulterior motive—worming my way back onto Primrose Way and into my former best friend's good graces. And there was no need to share how lately the lives of this neighborhood's inhabitants lured me like a potent drug—or how Jane Brockton was fast becoming the kingpin of my needy addiction. Jane stood out, even in this community of excess: gourmet dinner deliveries, drive-up dog grooming, same-day laundry service, and weekly Botox parties.

Her meetings with the mystery man were far from innocent. The first tryst I'd witnessed was late last Friday night—exactly a week ago. I'd strolled around the corner of Woodmint Lane just as the pair had emerged from their side-by-side houses and taken to the dark street like prowlers casing the block. I followed their skulking forms up Woodmint, being careful to stay a few dozen yards behind, until all I could discern was their silhouettes, too close to each other for friendly companionship. They'd eventually crossed Primrose Way and veered into the woods where the bike trails and picnic areas offered secluded spaces. When they didn't emerge from the wooded area, I backed Emmy's stroller silently and reversed my route, heading away, my pulse still throbbing, echoing in my temples.

It was impossible to deny what was going on as I watched similar scenes unfold three nights this week: Jane slipping soundlessly from her mudroom door like a specter, the flash of the screen door in the faint moonlight an apparent signal.

Tonight, as they hooked hands in the driveway between the houses, I slicked my tongue over my dry lips. She risked losing everything. I knew how that felt. Tim had left me before I'd even changed out his worn bachelor pad sofa for the sectional I'd been eyeing at Ethan Allen. I watched them cross through the shadows, barely able to see them step inside the shed at the far end of Jane's yard.

And all under the nose of her poor devoted husband, Rod. He couldn't be as gullible as he appeared, could he?

A voice called out, shattering the stillness of the night. I flinched, convinced I'd been discovered. I looked around the immediate shadows, placing a hand over my chest to still my galloping heart.

"Jane?" It was Rod's voice. I recognized the timbre by now.

Settle down, Caroline.

My eyes darted to the custom home's open front door. Rod had noticed his wife's abandonment earlier than usual. Warm interior light spilled across the porch floorboards and outlined Rod's robed form in the doorframe.

"Are you out here? Jane?"

The worry in his voice made me hate Jane Brockton. I flirted with the idea of stepping away from the hedge and announcing I'd witnessed her heading to the shed with the neighbor. Of course, that would be ridiculous. I was a stranger. My name, Caroline Case, would mean nothing to him.

Rod closed the door and my gaze traveled to the glowing upstairs window on the far left of his house. The light had blinked off half an hour ago, like a giant eyelid closing over the dormered master bedroom casement. I knew exactly where their bedroom was because I'd studied the Deer Crossing home models on the builder's website. I knew the layout of all three house styles so well I could escort potential buyers through them. I'd briefly considered it. Becoming a real-estate agent would give me access inside, where I could discover what life behind the movie-set facades was really like. Pristine marble floors, granite countertops, and crystal vases on every conceivable surface? Or gravy-laden dishes in sinks and mud-caked shoes arrayed haphazardly just inside the eye-catching front doors?

I suspected the latter was true for almost every house except for my former best friend Muzzy Owen's place on Primrose Way. Muzzy could put Martha Stewart to shame.

I wedged myself and Emmy's stroller further into the hedge. Becoming a real-estate agent wouldn't connect me as intimately to Jane and Rod Brockton (information gleaned by rifling through the contents of their mailbox) as I was at this moment. Trepidation—and yes, anticipation—laced my bloodstream and turned my breathing shallow as I waited for Rod to come outside and start his nightly search for his wife. Some may consider my interest, my excitement, twisted but I didn't plan to *use* my stealthily gathered information against anyone. It was enough to reassure myself that nobody's life was perfect, no matter how it appeared to an outsider. A faint click echoed through the still night. I squinted through the hedge leaves, my eyes laser pointers on the side door Jane had emerged from only moments before. Rod appeared.

As he stepped into the dusky side yard, I thought about the people unknown to me until a week ago: the latest neighborhood couple to pique my interest. Even though they were *technically* still strangers, I'd had an entire week to learn about the Brocktons. A few passes in my car last Saturday morning revealed a tracksuit-clad GenX-er, her wavy hair the reddish-brown color of autumn oak leaves, and a gray-haired, bespectacled Boomer in crisp dark jeans and golf shirt standing on the sage-and-cream farmhouse's front porch. Steaming mugs in hand, their calls drifted through my open car window, cautioning their little golden designer dog when it strayed too close to the street, their voices overly indulgent, as if correcting a beloved but errant child. The very picture of domestic bliss.

I studied the Colonial to the Brockton's right. On the front porch steps, two tremendous Boston ferns in oversized urns stretched outward like dozens of welcoming arms. The only testament to human activity. Someone obviously cared for the vigorous plants, but a midnight peek inside that house's mailbox revealed only empty space. It made me uncomfortable not knowing who Jane's mystery man was. And did Rod usually wake when his wife slipped between the silk sheets (they had to be silk) after her extracurriculars? He obviously questioned her increasingly regular late-night abandonment. He wouldn't be roaming the dark in his nightwear if he hadn't noticed.

Perhaps Jane said she couldn't sleep. She needed to move—walk the neighborhood—to tire herself. Hearing that, he'd frown, warning her not to wander around in the middle of the night. Rod was the type—I was sure just by the way he coddled his dog—to worry about his lovely wife walking the dark streets, even the magical byways of Deer Crossing. Hence, the need for new places to rendezvous each night. But the shed on their very own property! Even though tonight's tryst was later than usual, it was dangerously daring to stay on site. Maybe Jane wanted to get caught.

A scratching sound echoed through the quiet night. I looked at the side door Rod had just emerged from, saw his silhouette turn back and open it. The little dog circled him, barking sharply. The urgent yipping cut clearly through the still air, skittering my pulse. I quickly glanced at Emmy soundly sleeping in her stroller. If the dog didn't stop barking, I'd have to get away—fast. Emmy could wake and start her colicky wailing, which would rouse the Brockton's neighbors whose hedge I'd appropriated. One flick of their front porch light would reveal me in all my lurking glory.

As if to answer my concerns, the dog ceased barking and scampered toward the shed. I rubbed at the sudden chill sliding across my upper arms. That little canine nose was sniffing out Jane's trail.

Rod stepped tentatively forward. It was too dark to see what he was wearing beneath the robe, but I pictured him in L.L. Bean slippers with those heavy rubberized soles and cotton print pajamas, like Daddy used to wear. Daddy's had line drawings of old-fashioned cars dotted across the white cotton background. Model T's and Roadsters. I felt angry with Jane all over again. *How dare she . . .*